Praise for The Keeper of the Key

Nicole Willson's *The Keeper of the Key* is a tense and twisty contemporary Gothic that kept me reading late into the night. Supernatural and domestic terrors combine to propel this story, focused on themes of trust and control. I found the imagery and situations truly frightening!"

— Christi Nogle, author of the Bram Stoker Award-winning novel *Beulah*

"Nicole Willson has crafted a riveting story with a fierce protagonist. Brave and honest, Rachel stands strong in the face of terror and is unafraid to speak truth to power. An inspiring YA heroine.*The Keeper of the Key* is gripping gothic horror you won't want to put down."

— Meghan Arcuri, Bram Stoker Award-nominated author

"*The Keeper of the Key* is a suspenseful YA horror that subverts familiar horror tropes in ways that will surely keep readers turning pages in a rush to uncover the terrifying secret of Morgan House. I loved every moment of this unexpected story!"

— Katya de Becerra, Aurealis-winning author of *When Ghosts Call Us Home*

First published in November 2024

E-book ISBN: 978-1-956136-78-4

Paperback ISBN: 978-1-956136-85-2

Parliament House Press

www.parliamenthousepress.com

Cover illustration by: Cho-hyun Kim

Edited by: Alexandra Buchanan and Malorie Nilson

The Keeper of the Key

Nicole Willson

For everyone I lost in 2023. I miss you all and really wish you were here to read this.

"Her curiosity increased to such a degree that, without reflecting how rude it was to leave her company, she ran down a back staircase in such haste that twice or thrice she narrowly escaped breaking her neck. Arrived at the door of the closet, she paused for a moment, bethinking herself of her husband's prohibition, and that some misfortune might befall her for her disobedience; but the temptation was so strong that she could not conquer it. She therefore took the little key and opened, tremblingly, the door of the closet."

— BLUEBEARD, CHARLES PERRAULT.

Chapter One

RACHEL

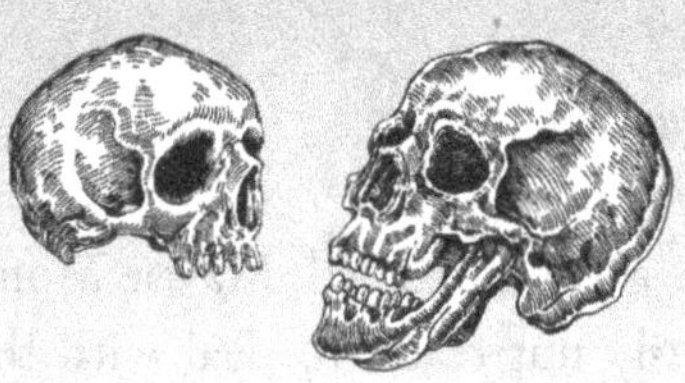

My mother is wound so, so tightly that if someone even drops a napkin, she's going to shoot right through the ceiling. Whenever she's nervous about something, she picks at her cuticles, and now the skin around her fingernails is raw and pink.

Something big is happening. She's way too tense for this to be an ordinary dinner out.

I don't know why I didn't see this coming. Mom's boyfriend Geoff, who hates any food that strays too far from burgers and fries, is eating at Thai Kitchen with us tonight. His short dark hair is newly trimmed, and the beer he's having with dinner makes him pinker and louder than usual. He even tries using chopsticks. The piece of beef he picks up while holding one chopstick in each fist flies across the table, and I wish we still had our menus so I could hide behind mine.

"Just don't understand how people can eat without a *fork*," Geoff says, and Mom's laugh swivels heads at nearby tables. Geoff's beef chunk sits in a far corner of our table, foiled in its escape attempt, and I know how it feels. I want to fly across the room, out the door, out of here.

I usually love Thai Kitchen with its purple and aqua décor and the sweet and spicy smells in the air, but right now I can't wait to go home. I focus on scraping my leftover food into a plastic to-go container so I don't have to watch their faces anymore.

Mom and Geoff clear their throats and trade looks as he drains the last few drops of his beer. I try to guess what those looks mean.

You want to tell her?

No, you.

When do you want to tell her?

How about now?

Maybe they're getting married. Maybe Mom's *pregnant*, God forbid. I'm seriously not ready to deal with the possibility of a miniature Geoff who's related to me. Mom's dated a few guys since Dad died, but for some reason I can't figure out, Geoff of the polo shirts, khakis, and burgers is the one sticking around. And I liked it better when it was just Mom and me.

They wait until the check's been dropped off before Mom clears her throat again. A lock of her carroty-orange hair has fallen loose from where she's piled it on top of her head, and she twists it around a finger.

"So," she says. "We wanted to talk to you about something."

Crap. Here it comes. The basil fried rice I've eaten churns inside me.

Geoff's round face is even pinker than usual as he grins at me. "I've got a big house, and I'm all alone in there. And I know you and your mom are always on top of each other in that tiny apartment, Rach."

I *hate* being called Rach even more than I hate being called Wednesday Addams, which Geoff did until Mom told him to stop it.

"It's not that tiny," is all I can think to say.

"Sweetie, Geoff's asked us to move in with him." Mom's smile is a taut rubber band stretching her face, and my stomach does another flip. The server comes to pick up the check, giving me a few extra seconds to decide what to do about this.

I could start crying. I could run out of the restaurant. I could tell them *Hell, no*. Mom and Geoff haven't even been together all that long, and I could ask them why they're in such a big hurry. My heart pounds. My mom can be impulsive, but it's usually a "Hey, let's both take a sick day, and I'll drive us to the beach" kind of impulsive. Not "Let's uproot our lives and move in with my boyfriend, who you barely know."

"It's okay if you're a little conflicted." Geoff hasn't lost that big doofus grin since Mom dropped the bomb, and there's a speck of something red in his front teeth. "I know it'll be a major change, and you've had one of those in your life pretty recently, but I think you'll love it there. Tara sure does. It's a big old house. It's even kinda... well, spooky. You like spooky, right?"

"Oh, it isn't *that* spooky." Mom shakes her head. "You'll have a nice big bedroom. And I'll have a room for painting and sculpting."

"But ... school," I say.

"We *do* have schools out where I am, you know." Geoff smirks. "St. Mary High is one of the best in the state."

But my best friend Elena Garcia won't be there. Nobody I know will be there.

And I already know it doesn't matter, any of it. It's cute that Mom and Geoff are acting like I actually have a choice.

"In fact," Mom continues, "we were thinking we could all stay over there tonight so you could start getting to know the place."

"Tonight?" No, no, no. This is happening way too fast. "But I don't have any overnight stuff."

"Oh, Rachel. We'll stop at our place so you can pack a bag."

Our apartment is claustrophobically small, but I've gotten used to it over the past few years. I like sitting out on the deck with a cup of tea or hot chocolate on chilly autumn evenings. I like playing on the swings in the apartment's playground, even if I'm sixteen.

Geoff and Mom are giving each other stupid, simpering looks as if everything's already settled and it's all going to be great.

And I don't get a say at all.

We stop by our apartment long enough for me to gather a toothbrush, my phone charger, and some clothes for Saturday. I pass the small, cluttered kitchen where Mom first taught me how to cook and the corner where Mom stashes her easel and her art supplies. Faint whiffs of nag champa incense and linseed oil scent the air, smells I think of as home.

My bedroom window overlooks a grove of oak trees. When their leaves turn in the fall and the morning sun hits them just right, they light up my room with a beautiful soft golden hue. My heart sinks when I think that next autumn, I won't be here to see it.

Mom comes in as I'm packing my stuff and trying to think of some way to get out of doing this.

"Hi, sweetie. Need any help?"

"No thanks." I toss a pair of black socks into my overnight bag.

"You okay with this?"

Now she cares? The tops of my ears start to burn.

"Does it matter if I'm okay with it? Sounds like everything's already been decided." My hairbrush makes a satisfying *thunk* as I drop it into the bag.

Mom licks her lips before speaking. "I know this is sudden, but I think it'll be a good thing. We'll have so much more space there—way more than I could afford on my own. And the town is so cute! Lots of funky little boutiques and restaurants. Geoff's excited too."

"Geoff barely knows me. And I barely know him." And I don't really like what I do know.

"Well, this will be a great chance to change that. I'd love for the two of you to start spending more time together."

"What's the rush, Mom? You two haven't even been dating that long."

Mom puts a hand on my shoulder. "Rachel, look. Can we just give this a try? If you're unhappy there after you've given it a shot, I'll figure out something else."

She didn't answer my question, and I'm just about to point that out when Geoff pokes his head in my door with one of those huge fake grins.

"Tara? Rachel? Everything okay?"

Mom turns away from me. "We're fine. She's almost done. Aren't you?"

"I'll be out in a minute."

She leaves with Geoff, and I stare around my bedroom wishing I could will myself to stay here permanently.

I start running through what I know about Geoff: He's in marketing. He and Mom met when she did some freelance work for his company. He's nice enough, I guess, but he often talks to me like I'm six instead of sixteen. It's not natural to be as constantly cheerful as he tries to sound. The idea of being around him day in and day out makes my skin crawl.

Maybe this won't work out, and Mom will come to her senses and move us out.

Or maybe there's more for me to find out about Geoff. Something that could help put an end to this.

Maybe Mom's right, and this *is* a great opportunity—just not the way she's thinking.

I zip up my black duffle bag and leave my room at last.

MOM DRIVES to Geoff's house, which is a little over an hour away from our apartment. She keeps up a steady stream of chatter the entire way. That greedy landlord is going to raise the rent sky high because of the Metro stop going in close by, so we're going to have to move anyhow, and won't it be wonderful to live in a house again, Rachel? Geoff keeps chiming in with "You bet!" and "Sure will!" as if Mom's trying to convince him instead of me.

We cross over the Maryland/Virginia state line as Mom babbles. I've only been to Virginia to tour Arlington Cemetery and go to performances at Wolf Trap, so it surprises me a little when the tall clusters of concrete and glass buildings I'm used to seeing give way to trees and rolling farmland. Horse barns and signs for wineries pop up along the road.

We travel steadily downhill past lots of big brick houses that look like clones of each other, complete with SUVs in the driveways and magazine-perfect manicured lawns. Mom takes a turn leading away from McMansionville and navigates a narrow, twisty road. The hair on the back of my neck stands up as we wind through endless barren trees that look grayish-white and lifeless, like skeletal hands reaching up from the ground in the night. Occasional house lights flash by in the distance, but even those are few and far between.

I'm used to our apartment complex, to being surrounded by neighbors and cars rolling in and out. How am I supposed to get used to living in the middle of nowhere?

A sign painted in black letters on faded wood appears in the headlights: MORGAN HOUSE. Mom turns at the sign and onto a narrow gravel driveway that crunches under the car tires.

"This place has an actual name?" I ask.

"Pretty neat, huh?" says Geoff.

The gravel drive seems longer than the road we took to get here, and my dinner reminds me of its presence with the bumpiness, but Mom reaches the house at last. A steady hum of crickets greets us as we climb out of the car. There's precious little light way the hell back here in the woods at night, so I can't see much.

But Morgan House is big, way bigger than all the McMansions we passed. It's two stories tall. Lighting illuminates the front walk, the doorway, and the porch that wraps around the front and sides of the house. But the lights are fighting the darkness back here in the woods, and the darkness is winning. What little I can see of the brick looks dingy with age. The arched dormer windows on the second floor make me think of cold, pitiless eyes staring down at me.

"Here it is, ladies," Geoff says, beaming. "Morgan House is part of local history, and soon it'll be part of yours too. Welcome home!"

Sparse shrubs and flower beds surround the house, but they're not enough to make this towering place feel homey or welcoming. I shiver, and not only from the chill in the evening air. Something like an electric current passes through me as I stare up at those eerie windows. My legs start shaking.

"It's pretty amazing, isn't it, sweetie?" Mom squeezes my shoulder.

Amazing is not the word I'd use. "Is someone else in there?"

Geoff laughs. "I'm out here by myself, Rach. You know that."

Then why does it feel like someone's in there watching me? I know Geoff would come up with some stupid reply, but I can't shake the creeps I've had ever since I got out of the car. I take a deep breath, trying to calm myself down. It's just a house.

Clouds in the evening sky part and reveal the moon. As we walk to the front door, the shadows the trees cast on the ground look like long fingers stretching out to grab us and drag us into the woods. A breeze rushes over us and I wrap my arms tightly around myself.

Morgan House looms over all of us, cold and empty, looking like it's waiting to swallow us whole.

Chapter Two

WELCOME HOME

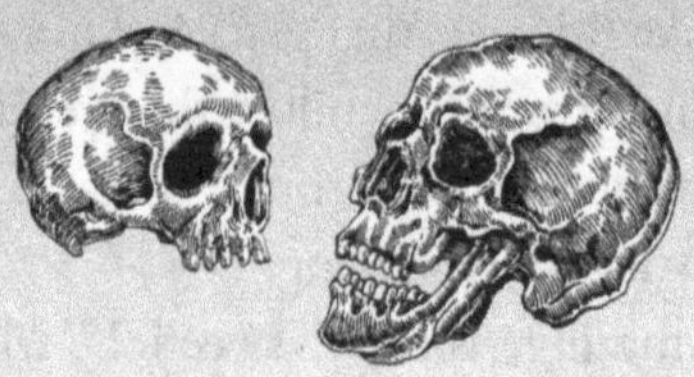

Inside Morgan House, Geoff switches on a chandelier in the foyer. It's pretty, but the dim light reveals cobwebs laced between its crystals. A mahogany newel post with sunburst patterns carved into the wood sits at the foot of a wooden staircase that winds up the right wall, leading to a large stained-glass window that dominates the upstairs hallway. The walls are paneled in dark wood, and the chandelier does little to brighten the gloom. I think again about being swallowed up as I peer down the hallway, wondering what the rest of this house holds.

Geoff leads us through the foyer and clicks on a light to reveal a kitchen that's much larger than the one at my apartment but also much emptier. The yellow paint is faded, and the chipped tile backsplash behind the stove might have been white once but looks dingy gray now. The only items I see on the counter are a skillet, a coffee pot, a toaster oven, a microwave, and a dishtowel.

"Your mom told me you like to cook."

"I do."

"Well, you should have fun in here. Lots of room to spread out. That kitchen in your old place was so tiny."

How many more times will Geoff remind me that his house is so much bigger than our apartment? I take a deep breath and hold it for a minute before letting it out in a slow exhale, trying to release my annoyance.

Mom's wearing one of her flowing purple hippie skirts with tiny bells around the waist ties, and she jingles as we follow her into a living room furnished with a TV, a bookshelf, a couple of wooden end tables, and a black leather sectional with a matching armchair. She lights a white pillar candle in a glass holder and places it on an end table, and soon, the powdery smell of jasmine fills the air.

Even though the house looks huge from the outside, the rooms strike me as strangely small and claustrophobic, with low ceilings and narrow passages. Faded yellow and green floral wallpaper lines the walls. The lemony scent of furniture polish lingers in the air and fights the jasmine from Mom's candle, but there's a musty odor lurking underneath. The wooden floors look scuffed and grimy. We're headed out of the living room when I catch my toe on a warped floorboard and almost fall flat on my face.

"Whoops! You found the trick board." Geoff cracks up laughing like that's the funniest thing he's ever seen.

"We're going to get that fixed." Mom sounds a little anxious now.

"Look at that fireplace, Rach. It's a beaut, huh?" He's still giving me that look like he's offering me some amazing gift while Mom lurks behind him, picking her cuticles as she studies my face. She really, really wants me to like this house. I can see it in the way she tilts her head and widens her eyes as she looks at me. And I wish I could do that for her, but it's so soon, and this place is so weird.

The fireplace looks like little more than a big hole in the wall lined with smudged, ashy bricks and an equally dirty grate. I have no idea why Geoff acts so proud of it. One of Mom's blue art glass vases sits filled with flowers on the mantel, and the reds, yellows, and purples are by far the brightest colors in the room.

"If it was a little colder out, I'd fire that thing up for you right now. In a few months, it'll be chilly enough again," Geoff says.

"That'll sure be nice in the winter. Won't it, sweetie?" Mom moves close and squeezes my shoulder.

"Who's Morgan?" I ask Geoff.

"Sorry?"

"The house is called Morgan House, right? So, who's Morgan?"

He shrugs. "A family that practically ran this city, from what I've heard. But they lived here a long time ago."

A parlor on the ground floor features a bare wooden coffee table, a crimson velvet sofa with thick, curved wooden legs, and another wide stained-glass window. An easel and some blank canvases are propped up against a wall, and a candle has been placed on the table beside a chunk of fiery red carnelian. Mom has obviously claimed this as her new studio space. Carnelian helps her with creativity, so she says.

Geoff leads both of us up the stairs, which creak as if the house is groaning in protest, and points to a room two doors down the hall that's going to be mine. He also shows me a bathroom in the hallway and tells me we're going to be sharing it, so we'll all have to be *considerate*.

"Older houses didn't always have master baths in the bedrooms," he says when he sees the look on my face. "I've wanted to have one put in, but it's not that easy in an old place like this. And when it was just me, it didn't matter."

Is he serious? All three of us and just one bathroom? "There's the one downstairs, right?"

"Well, that's a powder room. I mean, I'm sure you could use it in a *pinch*, but I'd rather keep it tidy for when company comes over."

He shrugs, and I have to bite back a sarcastic remark. Even in the little apartment back in Maryland, we had our own bathrooms. Now we're moving to a big house and have to share? What the hell kind of sense does that make?

"So? What's the verdict?" He raises an eyebrow. Behind him, Mom presses her lips together.

"Well. It's pretty nice here. Not bad."

And Geoff smiles big, for real this time. "All *right!* Attagirl!"

Mom exhales, and her shoulders relax. "I know it's going to be an adjustment, Rachel. But I think you'll really like this place and the town once we've settled in." I wish I could be as sure as she sounds.

"Well, let's give her a chance to put her bag down and get to know her room. Just call down if you need anything, Rach." Geoff and Mom head downstairs.

My new bedroom sits empty except for a four-poster bed covered in a blue quilt, an old nightstand with an alarm clock, and a battered dresser. Aged wallpaper with pale blue daisies and green leaves peels away from the tops of the walls, revealing worn plaster. A musty smell—that stuffy odor rooms develop when they've been closed for ages—lingers inside. Geoff must have opened the door and windows and aired everything out in the last day or so. I try to imagine living in a house so big that I don't ever go into some of the rooms.

Guess I'm going to find out what that's like.

I open a window and check out the view, but there's not much to see in the night. Trees surround the house, winter-barren and slate gray in the darkness, entirely unlike the lush, pretty oaks outside my window at home. Anybody—any*thing*—could be moving around out there. The woods are so dense and black that I'd never see them coming.

That's not an idea I want to dwell on right now, and I kick my shoes and socks off and flop on the bed, drained even though it's only about a quarter after ten. The mattress is hard under my back, and I have to shift around to settle into a comfortable spot. Downstairs, Mom giggles. No doubt, she's pleased with how well I'm taking all this. What a trooper. What a *good sport*.

There's dust high up in the corners of the room. My room, now. Other than the voices downstairs, it's depressingly quiet. On a Friday night at our apartment, there'd be a steady stream of people coming in and out and chatting in the parking lot.

In this room, there's silence. Too much silence. I'm thinking about grabbing my headphones and listening to music when I hear footsteps in the hallway. They're light and tentative as they move past my door and then back again. Back and forth. Back and forth. The floor creaks at the same spot with every pass. Someone's pacing out in the hallway.

I didn't hear anyone on the stairs or the tinkling bells on Mom's skirt, but this has to be her. Geoff has a much heavier tread. Maybe she came upstairs to change clothes, and while she's up here, she wants to ask me what I really think about this place.

"I can hear you, Mom," I call after her footsteps pass the door for the fourth time. "Just come in already. I'm not asleep or anything."

The footsteps pause for a moment before starting the back-and-forth-and-*creak* again. The pace is a little faster now, like Mom is getting anxious.

"Mom? I said come in."

No response.

"For God's sake." I walk to the door and fling it open.

A rush of warm air sweeps into the room, and a smoky smell lingers in the hall as if Geoff had lit up the fireplace after all.

No one is outside my room. Mom and Geoff are talking, but their voices are definitely coming from the living room. Downstairs. My fingers tighten on the doorknob, and I take a deep breath, trying to make sense of this.

Maybe one of them came up to grab a few things and hurried downstairs before I could catch them. I can't think of any other way to explain those footsteps.

When I close the door and head back to my bed, something sharp jabs the sole of my bare foot.

"Ow!" I hop on one leg, shaking my injured foot. Whatever I stepped on clatters to the floor. At first, I think it's a stray pebble we dragged inside, but something about the sharpness bothers me, so I bend over to pick it up.

It's a dingy gray molar, its roots broken off and jagged. And it's human-sized.

My stomach lurches, and I shriek and fling the thing away. How the hell did a tooth get up here? What else might be lurking in this old and withering place? My knees shake, and I grab the nearest bedpost to steady myself.

"Rachel? What's going on?" My mom's voice sounds at the foot of the stairs.

"I stepped on a tooth!"

"What on earth?" Footsteps hurry up the stairs, and Mom appears in the doorway, Geoff right behind her.

I look around, but the tooth is nowhere to be found. Wherever I threw it, it's gone.

"You sure it was a tooth?" Geoff asks. "Gravel from the outside gets in here all the time. Could have just been one of those little pebbles."

"I *know* what pebbles look like. It was a tooth, Geoff."

"Well, I suppose I could have tracked that in from a critter outside. You do come across dead things in the woods out here sometimes. It's pretty gross." He's talking to me like I'm a little kid.

"Ugh." Mom shudders.

I know damn well it was a human tooth. But without being able to find it, I can't show them I'm right. Mom checks my foot and doesn't find any bleeding, and Geoff apologizes for not running the vacuum up here a little more thoroughly. They look at me and then at each other. Mom bites her lower lip, and Geoff shakes his head.

"Your foot looks all right. Is everything else okay?" Mom asks.

"Sure," I lie. What does it matter? It's not as if I can just up and leave.

"Sorry about that. I'll run the sweeper in here again tomorrow," Geoff says.

And with that, they head back downstairs.

I look under my bed and the dresser, but the thing is gone. I want to find it because I saw the way they looked at each other. They think I was overreacting, maybe even making the whole thing up. I want nothing more than to march downstairs and shove that tooth right in Geoff's patronizing face.

After another minute of useless searching, I lie back down on the bed and grab my phone. I want to text Elena and tell her about all the stuff that's happened tonight.

I send her a text—or try to. The phone stubbornly shows "NO SERVICE" up in the left-hand corner. Of course.

I give up and head down the creaking staircase to the living room, where Mom and Geoff sit together on the sectional holding glasses of red wine. His arm is slung around her and she's resting her head on his shoulder. The black leather looks way too modern for this old house.

"So?" Geoff says. "What do you think?"

I rub the back of my neck. "What's the WiFi like out here?"

Geoff snorts. "It can get slower than molasses in January sometimes. Sorry, kiddo, but you might have to come up with some ways to entertain yourself that don't involve the internet. We used to have to do that all the time back in the olden days. Books and board games and stuff. Think you can manage?"

Why does he have to answer me like I'm a little kid and he's a hundred years old? He could have just said, "It's not great."

There's a TV in the living room, but I know by now that Geoff and Mom won't want it on while they're all cuddled together and drinking their wine. I've been through that with them enough back at the apartment.

"What's up, honey?" Mom studies my face.

"I dunno. I thought I heard someone upstairs."

"That's one of the joys of living in an old house," Geoff says. "They settle. Everything creaks and thumps until you'll swear there must be fifty people living in here. Or maybe it's just haunted." Mom gives a shrill, loud laugh as if Geoff is the funniest guy in the world.

I've had enough of them both. "Well, whatever. I'm turning in. I'm kind of tired."

"Are you okay, honey?" Mom asks for the third time, though I doubt she wants an honest answer.

"Perfect." I hope my answer sounds as unenthused as I feel.

ONCE I'M SETTLED in the bed, it's oddly comfortable. Or maybe I'm just too tired to care. I don't know how long I've been asleep when a light knocking at the door jars me awake. Mom probably wants to have a Girl Talk, to tell me she knows how hard all this must be on me. Not that that'll stop Mom from going through with the move, of course.

The knocks continue and grow louder, and I edge out of bed with great reluctance. It's strangely warm in the room as I open the door a crack.

Nobody's out there.

"Hello?" The hall is empty, unlit, and sweltering like I just opened an oven door. And as I glance around, a faint thrumming sounds inside my head and my chest, as if a creature trapped beneath my bones is trying to break out. And for a moment, a metallic odor fills my nose as the thrumming gets stronger.

I slam the door, my pulse pounding. Sweat beads on my forehead, but the vibrations and the metallic smell disappear.

Maybe I dreamed the knock. Maybe I've dreamed this whole night, and everything will be back to normal when I wake up in the morning in my own bed in our apartment.

But first, I need to sleep, which doesn't seem to be happening. The moonlight makes shadows of tree branches on my walls, and I think of long fingers reaching down, wrapping around me, and holding me hostage in this place. The red numbers on the bedside clock count off the hours and minutes relentlessly, and I remain awake.

Listening.

Chapter Three

LETTING GO

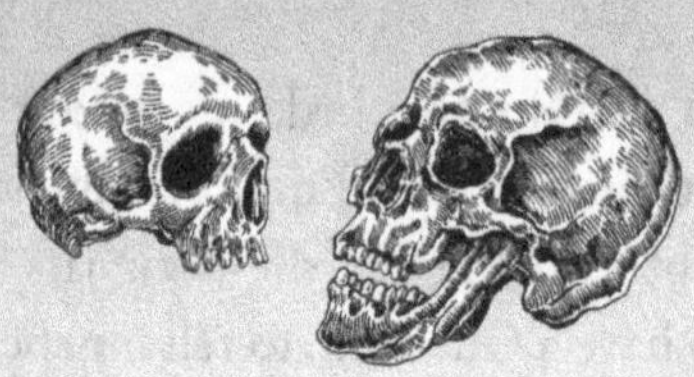

"THIS IS ALL BULLSHIT," I tell my grandmother. We're having Sunday afternoon coffee out on her deck, which overlooks a man-made lake. Mom and Geoff are off at Home Depot picking up stuff for the house, and right now, I don't care if they never come back to get me.

Gram decorated the outdoor space with hanging plants and wicker furniture. Everything here is sunny, welcoming, and warm —as unlike Morgan House as possible. The wind chimes by the sliding door ring softly in the light breeze. She recently dyed her hair a deep burgundy color that reminds me of an eggplant as it shines purple in the sunlight.

She shakes her head. "If I were a decent grandmother, I'd tell you to watch your mouth." But I know better. Gram doesn't get upset by curse words. Everything about Gram is blunt: Her bangs. Her bob haircut. The odd angles of the clothes she likes. The sharp edges of her eyebrows and her brick-red lipstick. And, most of all, her personality. There is no soft-peddled phoniness anywhere in her, and that's why I love her. There's no better grandmother anywhere, and that's a fact.

"Well, what else can I call it? They haven't even been dating all that long, and now we have to go live with him?"

Gram takes a sip of the black coffee in front of her before responding. "I know this is all happening pretty fast."

"I don't get why, though."

A small line forms between Gram's eyebrows, like she's considering what to say next.

"Your mother's someone who's always been happier when she's in a relationship," she says at last. "She's been like that since she was your age."

I wrinkle my nose. "But why is she so into *him*? She wasn't like that about the last couple of guys she dated, and they seemed pretty okay. He's...a lot."

She chuckles. "She says he's always treated her with respect. Didn't play games like the others did."

"Do you like him?"

Gram frowns. "I don't *dislike* him."

"Gee, Gram. Don't get too carried away there."

"Well, I've only met him once when he took your mother and me out to dinner. He was a little overbearing, yes. But I think he was maybe trying too hard because he was nervous. Sometimes people are like that. Maybe he'll settle down after you've moved in."

Gram doesn't like Geoff either. She hasn't actually said the words, but I can tell. A little surge of triumph rises in my chest.

"Believe me, he tries too hard all the time. It's just not natural for someone to be so constantly *perky*."

Gram raises an eyebrow. "Be that as it may, you're going to have to learn sooner or later that some things are beyond your control. Tara's a grown woman. She knows her own mind, and she's been taken with Geoff since their first date. And he makes my daughter happy. That counts for something."

I roll my eyes. "I'm glad she's happy. I just wish it didn't have to be with him."

"He's not my cup of coffee, to be sure. I never did go for that preppy, clean-cut type. But he could be the right person for her. Sometimes you know these things, even if others don't see it."

I'm obviously not going to get much else from Gram on the subject of Geoff, so I switch gears. "How's Margaret these days?"

"On a European cruise. Poor thing." Margaret is Gram's ex, and well before I was born, Gram left my grandfather for her. Margaret shares Gram's blunt toughness, and I was a little sad when they split up a few years ago, even though they're still friends.

"Anyhow, what do you think of the house, Rachel?"

I bite my lip, thinking of how to answer that. I'm not sure I'm ready to tell Gram I keep hearing people who aren't there or that I found a human molar lurking on my bedroom floor.

"I hate it. It's big and creepy, and it's in the middle of nowhere. And the WiFi sucks. It's so hard to get a signal. I can't even text anyone without trying a thousand times."

"I'm sorry you aren't happier there." Gram pats my hand. "You know you can come stay with me whenever you like."

Can I stay here for good? I want to ask. But I know that would really hurt Mom, and I can't bring myself to do that.

Not after what happened to Dad.

BEFORE THE MOVE, Elena and I spend a Saturday afternoon making pet toys at the local animal shelter. We started volunteering there for a school project, but we both liked it so much that we still go. Elena can't have a pet because her little sister is allergic to every creature on earth other than actual humans, and my apartment doesn't allow pets. It's our way of getting animal time. The place always has too many animals and never enough volunteers, so they're happy for the help.

On some days, we have to mop dog pee off the blue tile floors or scoop litterboxes, but today, we get to do something more fun. Elena's curly brown hair is piled loosely on top of her head and looks in danger of tumbling into her face as we cut strips from old faded T-shirts to make catnip pillows and chew toys. The sweetish herbal smell of the catnip almost blocks out the odors of litter-boxes and wet dogs.

"You're not going to forget me when you start running with all the spoiled rich brats, right?" she asks like her doctor-father and lawyer-mother are destitute or something.

"Spoiled rich brats?"

She nods. "Mama said there's lots of money in that area."

"Well, don't worry. I mean, the stupid house barely gets internet, so you might have to wait forever to hear from me, but I won't forget."

"So, do you hate the house because it's Geoff's house, or do you just hate it in general?"

I roll my eyes. "Can't it be both?"

Elena laughs, making her dimples stand out. "What's so bad about it?"

I glance around before telling Elena about the footsteps and the knocks. And the tooth. It's not like anyone's listening to us, and they probably wouldn't be able to hear us over all the barking dogs anyhow, but this feels private.

Elena gets all wide-eyed over the thought of ghosts and quickly touches the gold Our Lady of Guadalupe pendant around her neck, which she does whenever something makes her tense. "God, that's so creepy. How old is the house?"

"I don't know. Definitely old, though."

"And it's way out in the woods? Man. Who knows what might be out there?"

The idea makes me shudder. I like horror novels and scary movies, and I style myself in a way that Gram once described as "Winona Ryder in *Beetlejuice*." I wear black clothes and dye my red hair black to match. People tend to blame my look on what happened with my dad, but they're full of it. I've always been drawn to Shirley Jackson, Edgar Allan Poe, and Stephen King.

But with horror movies and books, I can hit the stop button or close the cover when they get to be too much. The idea of horror and darkness lurking around the corners in a place where I have to live? That's another thing entirely. And definitely not good.

"I don't know, Laney. I probably imagined it all or something. I mean, we were having dinner, and then Mom was like, 'Oh, by the way, we're moving in with Geoff and too bad if you don't like it.' I was kind of on edge that night."

"Does your mom know about all the stuff that happened to you?"

I yank a strip off a faded cotton T-shirt more roughly than I meant to, and the scrap of fabric is jagged. "She knows about the tooth. I didn't tell her about the other stuff. I don't know if she'd even believe me."

"Seriously?" Elena's brown eyes widen. "But she's always talking about spirit energies and stuff."

"It's not that. I think she just really wants me and her and Geoff to be a big happy family out there in the woods. Every time I criticize the house, she says, 'Just give it a chance, okay?'"

"Man. That's rough."

"Yeah. She used to listen to me a lot more. Before Geoff."

I don't want to talk about the house anymore, and we change the subject. But as Elena chatters on about the day camp where she will be a counselor with a few other girls from my school this summer, a heavy feeling spreads inside me. She's got plans, plans that actually sound exciting. I have Morgan House.

When we're done, an employee takes a couple of animals out of their steel cages so we can give them some exercise with our finished toys. Oz, an adorable orange tabby kitten, tears into one of my catnip pillows, and Elena laughs as a German shepherd tries to pull a chew rope from her, *grrrrr*ing and jerking its head as it tugs the braided cloth out of her hand. I have an idea while scratching the kitten between his enormous ears. His purrs almost drown out my words, and I pick him up and hug him close.

"Maybe now we can get a dog or a cat. Maybe even both. The house is more than big enough. I wish I could hide this little guy in my purse." Oz purrs some more, like he's agreeing with me. His warm, vibrating little body wriggles against mine, and I decide he's too tiny and sweet for Morgan House. I give him a kiss between his huge ears and put him down.

"Can't believe you're going to be all the way out there," Elena says as we're gathering our stuff and getting ready to leave. "That sucks."

It does, but I try to look on the bright side. "It's only an hour away. And we'll both be driving soon, right?"

"Yeah, but still. It's going to be so weird that I can't just ride my bike over to your place or something."

As much as I want us to swear to each other that this isn't going to change our friendship at all, we both know better. We've had friends move away before, and even though they cry buckets at first and swear they'll stay in touch, they get absorbed in their new lives. And the emails and texts slow down and then stop. And just like that, they're little more than faces we used to know. Ghosts lurking in the corner.

I want to give Elena a hug and reassure her that won't happen to us, but I'm already looking at the back of her denim jacket. She's headed out the door fast, and I hurry behind her as her mother's car pulls into view.

Chapter Four

EXPLORATIONS

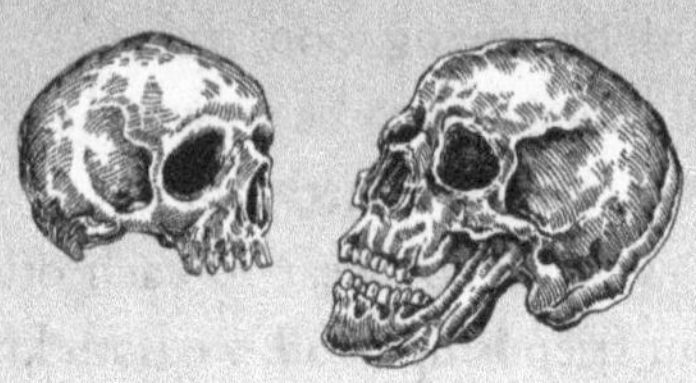

When school is over for the year, Mom and I pack up our little apartment with Geoff's sweaty, earnest help and move to Morgan House for good.

I've never really seen the outside of the place in the daylight, and Geoff shows it off when we get out of the car, using words like *pediments, mansard,* and *balustrades* as he points out the windows, the roof, and the terrace on the second floor. The white paint on the pillars flanking the front door and the porch railings is graying and chipped. Mom's mentioned redoing that as a "fun" summer project. She and I must have a different definition of that word. Nothing about breathing in paint fumes in summer heat and humidity sounds fun to me.

Even in the daylight, my stomach flutters a little when I look up at Morgan House's arched windows. They still give me that sense that something's in there staring back at me.

"Why'd you get such a big house when it was just you?" I ask.

Geoff looks startled by the question for a moment, and then a grin spreads across his glistening face. "Well, heck. This place was a steal, and it had a lot more character than those generic big box houses going up all over, right? And I figured I'd fill it with a big family, of course!"

After we've unpacked a little, Mom offers to let me pick something to place in the living room so it'll feel more like my home, too.

"Like what, Mom?"

"It's your choice. Geoff said it was okay."

The whole idea sounds weird, but it seems important to Mom. I take a purple glass skull Dad bought me for my tenth birthday and place it on Geoff's bookshelf. Which is kind of a misleading name, as it contains almost no books. A small painting of a black horse, a couple of self-help books, a silver beer stein, and a hunk of raw amethyst sit on the otherwise empty shelves. The amethyst, which looks like a ripe purple fruit that's been ripped open, is Mom's. She wears crystal pendants and places stones in strategic areas of different rooms to influence the energy in the air. I know from overhearing her with Gram that she's careful never to use the word *witchcraft* around Geoff.

"Whoa," Geoff says when he gets a good look at the skull. "That's kind of intense-looking, Rach."

"Mom told me I could put it there."

"Oh, no. It's fine. I'm just saying." Geoff shrugs. "You ladies like your purple, huh?"

"It's a powerful color."

"Sure. It's a nice color." But his smile doesn't quite reach his eyes.

Upstairs, I do my best to make my bedroom resemble the setup I had back at the apartment. I put away the blue quilt on the bed and replace it with my thinner purple blanket. I drape black lace over my dresser and put a framed photo of me, Mom, and Dad on top of it. The three of us are outside on the terrace at the Kennedy Center on the afternoon of my eleventh birthday when they took me to see a matinee of *The Phantom of the Opera*. Dad's shielding his eyes from the sun, Mom's holding a hand up, trying to keep the breeze from blowing her hair in her face, and we're all laughing. Whenever I look at the picture, I want to tell my little red-haired self, *Enjoy all that. It's not gonna last much longer.*

I stuff my books into the battered wooden bookcase I've had for almost my entire life and line up my collection of Funko Pops on the shelves. The wooden desk and chair I've had for five years sit facing a window that overlooks an expanse of barren gray trees, and my fluffy purple rug livens up the dull, scuffed wooden floor. The room feels a little more like mine now, but I wonder how long it will take for Morgan House to truly feel like home. Or if it ever will.

There are three other upstairs rooms here besides mine and the master bedroom. One has been set up as a guest bedroom. The doors to the other two rooms have been shut since we moved in. Out of curiosity, boredom, or maybe a little of both, I decide to check them out the day after we move in.

The first room is completely empty, but several large stains stretch across the dusty wooden floor. They spread out from a spot right by the window, and the one closest to me looks long, brownish, and narrow. If I squint, it resembles a sprawled body. I shudder at that thought and leave the room, closing the door behind me.

I open the second room and shriek. Something bright whirls in the corner, and I'm sure somebody's in there.

But when I look again, it's only sunbeams shining through floating dust motes. Feeling stupid now, I walk further into the room and sneeze. Geoff must not have dusted in here in a while.

The walls have been painted a vivid sunflower yellow that still looks clean and lively, very unlike the faded and peeling wallpaper in other parts of the house. The closet door hinge squeals when I open it. Several pink plastic hangers dangle from the rod, but the closet is otherwise empty. This room looks like it's been lived in, and maybe not that long ago.

"Something you need, Rach?" Geoff's voice makes me jump. I didn't even hear him coming. He's peering around the open door, his eyes narrowed.

"Just looking around. Was someone staying in this room?" The bright paint and the pink hangers look extremely out of place in Morgan House.

"Nope. Used to stash some old clothes in here before I got rid of them. I've told you before, it was just me here until you and your mom moved in." He shakes his head. "If you want something, let me know. You don't have to go poking around."

Irritation heats the back of my neck. What's the big deal about me looking in an empty room? "I'm not poking. I live here now, too, right?"

"Of course you do. But you've already seen all the important spots. Like I said, just ask me if you're looking for anything in particular." He gestures to the hallway, and after I leave the room, he closes the door with a firmness that's just short of a slam.

HE SWEARS we'll all have fun once we're settled in, but I learn Geoff's idea of *fun* involves rules—lots of them.

There are the obvious ones that don't bother me that much: *Don't leave dirty dishes in the sink; take off your shoes before putting your feet up on the furniture; finish off what's in one container of food before opening another one.* Not a big deal.

But then there are the strange ones, like *don't go in the basement.* I mention storing boxes of stuff I don't use much down there so they won't clutter up my room, and Geoff says he'd rather I didn't.

"But why not?"

Geoff reaches around and rubs the back of his neck. "I've got a bunch of my woodworking projects down there. It's a little cluttered." He grins. "There are planks of wood all over. And there's my table saw. Wouldn't want you bumping into that."

He lowers his arm before continuing. "And there's nails and other hazards on the floor. I can get kinda messy when I'm working on things. I'd rather you didn't go down there. If you need something out of your way, I'll take it down. I'm used to ducking around all that stuff."

"I almost stepped on a nail down there one time," my mom chimes in. "Let him take the risk. It's *his* mess." They both laugh at that.

That doesn't make much sense to me. Can't he just move his things out of the way? Is it that hard to clean up if you're going to have other people living there? I let it go for now.

But on a Saturday morning a week after the move, while Mom and Geoff are taking a walk on the trail that winds through the woods behind the house, I decide to check it out for myself. I don't even know why I care, but I want to see what's down there now that Geoff's made such a big deal out of it. Especially if he doesn't want me to. He and Mom can't keep telling me this is my house too and then expect me to stay out of big parts of it, can they?

Geoff keeps the basement door locked. He fished a key out of a kitchen drawer once when Mom needed a few boxes taken down there, and so I rummage through that same drawer, pushing pens, rubber bands, and random utensils around until I find a key attached to a round white cardboard tag. "BASEMENT" is written on the tag in Geoff's spiky handwriting.

As I head towards the basement door, I notice more of those strange stains on the wooden floor in the living room, as if someone dropped bottles of wine and did a crappy job of cleaning them all up. The stains are much fainter down here than in the upstairs bedrooms, but they extend out from under the furniture. An especially long, streaky stain leads from the living room right to the basement door. Something about it makes me shudder, but it's not enough to deter me from my current mission.

I take a deep breath, insert the key in the lock, and turn it. The deadbolt slides back with a *click*.

The basement door creaks as I peek inside. Smells of mildew, paint, wood, and earth meet my nose as I look down the staircase. Dingy wooden steps lead down into a large, dark space with shelving, worktables, and yard accessories lining the walls. A large table saw is against one wall, and a half-finished table—upside-down with two legs sticking up in the air as if it's dead—sits nearby. Planks of wood are piled up by the saw.

After hesitating for a moment, I head down the stairs. The further down I go, the hotter it gets, and the stronger the mildew smell grows. But this isn't clammy, humid summer heat. It's dry and intense. My skin is damp by the time I reach the basement floor, but that's not just from the temperature. It's nerves. I feel like someone's been watching me since I opened the door. I want to turn around and run back upstairs before the door slams shut and traps me, but I have to see what's down here.

What could Geoff be hiding?

The only light comes from a high window in the wall, and there's not much of it because the day is overcast. But it's enough for me to see I'm the only one down here, even though it doesn't feel like it. The smell of mildew is obliterated by an odor of smoke so strong I almost choke on it. And there's a metallic stench underneath that.

A sharp object jabs into the sole of my bare foot. I remember Geoff's warning about nails on the floor and wonder if I've just given myself tetanus. I shake my foot and the thing rolls loose.

Another tooth, smaller than the last one, and it's gray and brown and jagged.

I'm about to scream when I hear a faint sound, like someone crying in another room—only there aren't any other rooms down here. My pulse races as if I've had too much coffee. The sound continues, a high and keening wail as if the crier is in agony, and that thrumming sensation starts in my head and chest again. Another sound, something like heavy breathing, surrounds me as I stand frozen.

Nothing down here makes sense. My eyes tell me I'm alone in a normal basement with a lawnmower, paint cans, yard implements, random boxes, and Geoff's woodworking projects everywhere. But I hear people I can't see, my head swims in the baking heat, and everything inside me screams to get the hell out.

What is this place?

My lips are just about to form the word *Hello?* when the front door swings open upstairs, and feet sound in the foyer.

Panic jolts me into action. I hurry back up the steps and lock the basement door just as Geoff and Mom enter the hallway, holding hands and laughing. I fold my arms so they can't see me holding the basement key.

"Started raining out," Geoff says. His green polo shirt is speckled with drops.

"It's a shame we had to cut things short. That's such a beautiful trail. You okay, sweetie?" Mom narrows her eyes, looking at my face. I give her a smile that I'm not feeling at all.

"You guys surprised me. Wasn't expecting you back this early."

"Hope we weren't interrupting anything," Geoff says with a wink.

They head upstairs to change out of their damp clothes, and after returning the key to the kitchen drawer, I put an ear to the basement door. But I can't hear any crying now. I breathe slowly, waiting for my heart to stop pounding.

What the hell is going on down there? Whatever it is, Geoff doesn't want me trying to find out about it, which means I need to know more. About it. And about him.

In my bedroom, I do web searches on his name. Nothing turns up but work-related sites that don't tell me anything I don't know. I think about his weird, fake cheerfulness and the terrifying basement, and I trust him less than ever.

Chapter Five

NICK

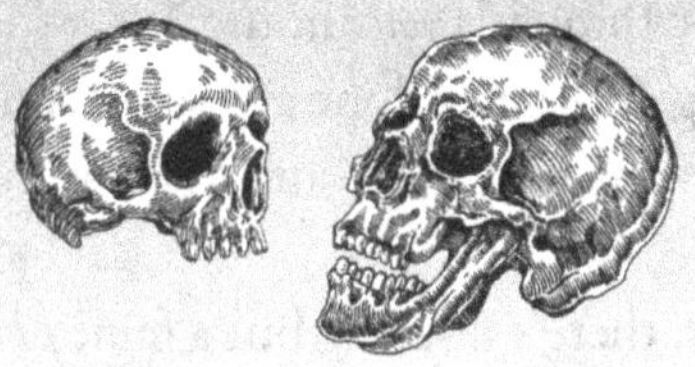

THAT AFTERNOON, Geoff starts in on my hair.

We're sitting in the living room while Mom works on a painting in the parlor. The smell of linseed oil fills the air. It's been quiet between us, but Geoff glances up from his tablet and looks at me in that narrow-eyed way I'm coming to realize means he's got something on his mind.

"What?" I say when I can't stand it anymore.

"Who does your hair?"

"I dye it myself."

Geoff shakes his head. "Not here, you don't."

"What? Why not?"

"Because I don't want black dye all over my bathroom."

I can't understand why he even cares. The porcelain in the old upstairs bathroom looks permanently grungy no matter how much I scrub it, and the floor is tiled in an eye-bleedingly ugly color combo of yellow, green, and faded black. A few splats of black hair dye would be an improvement if they'd even be noticeable among the clusters of everyone's stuff on the counter.

Mom drifts in from her studio to listen, still wearing her paint-smeared smock.

"She's careful with the dye, Geoff. She knows to put down towels."

"And besides, isn't it *my* bathroom too now?"

Geoff raises an eyebrow. "Are you making the house payments?"

"No." Heat spreads inside me, and Mom starts picking at her cuticles again.

"Then I hardly think it's *your* house."

"Fine." I shrug. "I'll get it done at a salon somewhere. It'll cost a lot more money that way, but I sure don't want to mess up *your* bathroom."

For a moment, there's nothing but a faint *pick-pick-pick* sound as Mom digs at the skin around her fingernails. That's going to start bleeding if she doesn't quit it. Why isn't she saying something? She's never had a problem with what I do to my hair.

Geoff takes a long, deep breath as if it's all he can do to keep himself under control before trying again.

"Ever think about going with a different color?"

This isn't what I expected to hear. "What do you mean?"

"Well, that black is so *harsh*. Don't you want to look nice when you start at your new school?"

My ears begin to burn. "I think the black looks nice."

"For heaven's sake, Geoff, it's hair color. It grows out," Mom says.

"Tara, somebody's got to be honest here." Geoff turns his hands out in a *I'm just being* ***real*** fashion that makes me want to hit him. "She looks cheap. And don't kids usually outgrow this phase?"

What phase? What would he even know about what I like? My throat tightens, and my pulse pounds as I jump to my feet. I'm not sure who I hate more right now: Geoff for being an ass, or Mom for sticking me with him. I know one thing—I can't bear being around either of them for one more second.

"We aren't through here, Rach," Geoff says as I storm out of the living room.

"My name is *Rachel*. And you're not my dad. So, keep your opinions to yourself."

Mom says something, and Geoff talks right over her, but I don't care. I grab my purse, storm out the door, jump on the red hybrid bicycle Mom bought me so I could explore St. Mary on my own, and speed off. I half expect Geoff to rush out after me as I pedal away.

The rain from the morning has stopped, but it's still warm and soupy outside. I tear up the long path towards the town center, trying not to cry. Who the hell does this guy think he is? How long has he been stewing over my hair, waiting for his chance to lay into me? He has no say in what I do with my hair—or anything else.

"*Asshole*," I tell the woods as I pedal. Sweat beads on my forehead and runs into my eyes.

I speed through the McMansion neighborhood, dodging joggers, SUVs, dog walkers, and kids on their own bikes. The houses here all look alike, big brick boxes with attached garages. What would it be like to live in one of these places, in a busy neighborhood with other people? Are the kids here afraid of what's in their basements?

There's one last hill to climb to get to the Old Town section, and my thighs burn as I pedal hard up to the main street leading to all the shops and restaurants.

White lights twine around the streetlamps and the storefronts. Boutiques, bars, and restaurants line the sidewalks along the main street, and they're all busy. Voices, music, and the garlicky, peppery smells of different foods carry through the air. The sidewalk teems with groups of people talking, laughing, and enjoying the warm afternoon.

It's alive and busy here, yet I feel incredibly alone in the middle of it all.

A big bookstore with a red and white awning reading MILLEDGE'S BOOK COMPANY sits across the street from me, and all I want is to run inside. I've always loved burying myself in books at the library, hiding from the other kids and teachers, and losing myself in one world after another. And I really need to do that right now.

Shoppers lug big bags along the sidewalks, ducking around outdoor tables where others eat late lunches. Good thing nobody here knows me. My face is soaked with sweat, and I can feel how flushed I am from the exertion and the humidity.

Milledge's Book Company awaits. I lock the red bike up outside the store and swipe the back of my hand over my forehead.

A bell jingles when I open the front door, and there's a *click clack click clack click clack* on the wooden floor. A big yellow lab with a purple collar hustles over and nudges my hand with a damp nose.

"Well. Hi there, guy."

"That's Toby." A heavyset Black woman with short burgundy curls waves at me from behind the register up front. "He's our greeter." The woman's smile is warm and welcoming, and I feel at ease for the first time since we moved here.

"He's a sweetie." I rub Toby's head and scratch behind his soft, warm ears, grateful for the friendliness.

"I'm Mrs. Milledge. You looking for anything in particular?"

"Sort of. I'm Rachel, and I'm just trying to escape."

Mrs. Milledge chuckles. "Well, Rachel, we've got plenty of escape hatches around here. Let me know if you need help finding something specific."

Toby clacks off to a large blue cushion, and I turn around, taking in the store. It looks way bigger in here than it did from the street. Wooden steps lead down to a basement level and a high ceiling with a skylight arches over the main floor. White walls contribute to the bright, airy feeling. Big plush green and blue armchairs have been placed strategically around all the shelves and stacks of books, and the intoxicating scent of fresh coffee drifts my way from a counter in the back. People roam the aisles, choose books, and settle in the overstuffed chairs while they read. Classical music plays over the sound system.

I can imagine myself spending a lot of time here.

My phone buzzes in my pocket. Mom's calling. I hit *decline* and pocket the phone again after muting it.

A large community bulletin board hangs by the entrance, and I glance over all the notices. Someone is running a book club. Someone else is offering daycare.

But something less welcoming hangs there as well: a slick-looking flyer featuring a color school picture of a girl who doesn't look much older than me.

HAVE YOU SEEN ME? MELISSA ANN SIMMONS.

Melissa Ann is brunette, blue-eyed, and seventeen—or at least she was. According to this flyer, she's been missing from St. Mary for almost eight years. My skin prickles. The flyer looks pretty new, and I'm curious who's still looking for her after all this time.

"Looking for something to do in the community?" Mrs. Milledge asks.

"Um, not yet. But...this girl's been missing for that long?" I wonder if my question is obvious: *Do people still think they're going to find her?*

"Oh yes. Such a sad thing. Her poor parents put up new notices year after year, and I'm always happy to let them put one up here. I mean, I can't blame them. If it was my daughter..." Mrs. Milledge turns her hands up and shrugs as if to say, *We all know it's pointless by now, but what can you do, right?*

When I turn away from the bulletin board, my eyes snag on someone who stands out just as much as I do in this town. All the other men I've seen around here so far look like Geoff, with short haircuts, polo shirts, and khakis. This guy's wearing a black T-shirt and faded black jeans, and his long dark hair falls loose around his pale face. He might be my age, maybe a touch older. His brows are knotted over his long nose as he studies a large book in the History section. He looks like he should be walking the halls of abandoned castles and hunting vampires, and I want to be with him while he's doing it. I'd have seen him right away if Toby hadn't distracted me.

Crap. I stormed out of Geoff's crypt in my slobby hang-around-the-house clothes with my hair in a messy ponytail, and now I'm all clammy and slick from the bike ride. I'm debating whether to sneak out of the bookstore and go find a place that sells makeup when he looks right at me.

Those deep brown coffee-no-cream eyes feel like they're burning holes into mine. He must have noticed me staring at him like a dumbass. I decide that greeting him with a small smile and a wave won't seem too overeager.

"Hey," I say.

He nods. "Have we met?"

Don't I wish. "No, I don't think so."

His face remains completely blank, and now I want to die.

"Haven't seen you here before," he says at last.

"I just moved here with my mom. We're stuck at her idiot boyfriend's house. Lucky me, right?"

His mouth turns up in a small smile, but he doesn't say anything.

"Glad I found this place. I like books," I blurt, and then I wonder if I'll ever be able to say anything non-stupid to him.

"That's nice." He looks like he might be wondering the same thing, and it's time to end this before I embarrass myself even more.

"Well. See you around."

I need coffee right now, and the scent drifting over from the little counter in the back is amazing. Glistening, super-caloric pastries sit in a glass case on the wooden bar, and several high stools are lined up against the pale wooden counter. An older woman with a long blonde ponytail stands behind the register.

I order a latte and climb onto one of the stools. My phone buzzes. Mom's left a voice mail. Do I care enough to hear what she has to say about what went down earlier?

Not now. Maybe later. Maybe this place has better WiFi, and I can have a decent text conversation with Elena for once. Geoff installed a new router in Morgan House when we moved in, but the signal is still sporadic.

"So why is your mom's boyfriend an idiot?" The deep voice right behind me makes me jump. The boy slides onto the seat next to mine.

I shrug, hoping he doesn't notice the red flush spreading over my cheeks. "Because he acts like he thinks he's my dad. But my dad died three years ago, and I'm not looking for a replacement."

The woman puts the latte down in front of me, and it's creamy and foamy and delicious when I take a mouthful.

"He kind of sounds like a jackass."

I snort. "There's no *kind of* about it. He's a total jackass."

He studies me for a moment before sticking a hand out. "I'm Nick Alexander. And you are..."

"Rachel. Rachel Morley. Nice to meet you." His hand is firm and dry, and I hope I'm de-humidified by now. The overhead light glints off a silver chain that hangs around his neck and leads to something under his shirt. I look back down at the counter so he doesn't think I'm checking him out.

"Welcome to St. Mary, Rachel Morley. Honestly, it's not such a bad place."

"Parts of it look okay. This store seems pretty cool."

"Yeah. Mrs. Milledge is great."

I know it's not St. Mary's fault that Geoff's so annoying, but it's hard not to hold that against the town anyhow. I struggle to think of something to say as I drink my latte.

"You been living here long?" I ask Nick.

"Yep. Pretty much forever."

"Do you go to the high school here?" It'd be nice to have a friend at St. Mary High when I start in the fall.

"Well, I *did*."

He must have graduated already. "What's it like?"

Nick smirks. "Let's put it this way: what year are you going into?"

"I'll be a junior."

"Then it'll be over in two years. That's about all I've got to say for the place."

I laugh. "What do you do now?"

"I have a couple of part-time jobs here and there. And my friends and I are trying to get a band together."

I should have guessed he was a musician. I can see him playing guitar on stage with lots of screaming people at his feet. Like me. "A band? That's awesome. Can I hear you play sometime?"

He cringes. "No way. We're not really together yet. And we kind of suck, except for the 'kind of' part."

I like the way he blushes when he says that. "So, what is there to do around here?"

"There are a few okay places in town and beyond if you feel like exploring. Have you been to St. Mary's Cemetery yet?"

"No. A cemetery? Why would you think I'd go there?" I fold my arms over my chest and raise an eyebrow in mock offense.

"I...um...." Nick glances down and away from me.

"Just kidding. I like old cemeteries." Was that funny? I hope he thought it was funny.

He looks up and chuckles. "I just thought..."

"The hair, right? And the black clothes?"

"Well, yeah."

I roll my eyes. "That's what Mom's boyfriend was being an idiot about today. Told me I should try a new hair color that *looks nice*."

Nick smiles. "Not that you asked, but I like the black. It suits you."

Something warm and happy spreads inside my chest, and I hope I can keep from blushing. "Thank you. Like it's his decision anyway."

We sit together in silence as I finish my coffee. I can't fathom what's going on behind those dark, intense eyes or what kind of impression I might be making. He didn't have to come talk to me,

I remind myself. He must have seen something he liked. My face starts heating up.

"Well," I say at last, "I should head out. My mom's probably having kittens because I stormed out on everyone."

He briefly glances down at the counter and swallows before meeting my eyes again. "If...if you ever want to check out the cemetery with someone, I'd like to show you around."

It takes everything in my body to not collapse in giggles on the bookstore floor as I type my number into his phone. I haven't been on many dates. I certainly never imagined I'd show up somewhere looking gross and sweaty and get asked out.

I leave Milledge's thinking that if Geoff did one thing right, he pissed me off enough to send me here. To Nick.

Chapter Six

THE UNEXPECTED VISITOR

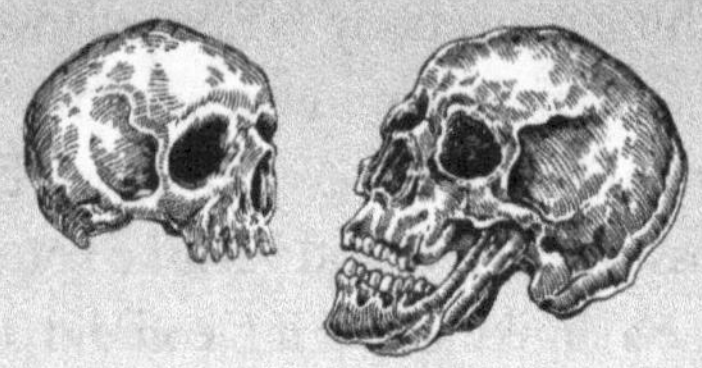

I COULD TAKE off and soar through the air as I pedal home while biting back giggles, barely able to believe I met Nick and actually got his number. I hang on to the sensation as long as I can. When I get back to Morgan House, the static I'm sure I'll encounter will take care of my good mood soon enough.

But when I get home, Geoff's silver SUV is gone. Inside, Mom's curled up on the sectional in the living room. Her cuticles are raw and red again. She fidgets with a chunk of obsidian hanging on a leather cord around her neck, rolling the cylindrical crystal between her fingers, something she does to draw out negative energy.

"I'm sorry about before," she says by way of greeting.

I sit in the armchair across from her. "Why? You didn't do anything." And that's pretty true. She didn't do or say much of anything. At all. A simple *Hey, she's* my *daughter—back off* would have been nice.

"I know Geoff can come on strong. But he means well, Rachel."

"I don't care what he means. He's not my dad. And Dad wouldn't have given me a hard time about my hair anyhow." I don't want to let my rising anger extinguish the spark from meeting Nick, but Mom is making that harder.

"He knows that, sweetie." Mom starts twisting a strand of long red hair around her finger, looking away from my eyes. "I had a good long talk with him after you left. He promised he'll do better."

I'll believe that when I see it. "Where'd he go, anyway?"

"He met some friends for a few rounds of golf." *Golf.* It's the most boring, pointless "sport" I've ever heard of. Of course, Geoff likes it.

"So, what have you been doing all day?" I ask.

Mom shrugs. "I'm almost done with Mood Board #18." Mom likes making large, elaborate canvases full of splats of colors and shapes representing whatever she's feeling at the time. They don't usually look like much of anything other than someone hurling paint around, but the ones she made after Dad died were all dark screaming faces and crimson splotches that tore me up inside because they looked so much like how I felt.

I'm curious to see what Mom's St. Mary mood board looks like so far, but Mom doesn't like people looking at her work before she considers it finished.

"And then I thought maybe we could run to the grocery store. Pick up a few veggies. Cook a nice dinner."

I like to cook, but I haven't done it much since Geoff came into Mom's life. Geoff is all about eating dead animals. His first words upon learning that I was a vegetarian? *Hey, Rach, I've got a great recipe for tofu: Throw it in the trash and buy a steak instead.* Hilarious.

"I'm not cooking meat, Mom. I don't care if you guys eat it, but I'm not fixing it for you."

"You don't have to, sweetie. You can do pasta and vegetables. But I thought it would be nice to do something together."

Mom's face is a question, and I know there's only one answer I can give.

"I met someone," I blurt out instead.

"What? Already?" Mom raises her eyebrows.

"Yeah. This guy, Nick. At the bookstore."

"Oh. Well, how about that?" After appearing to think it over for a minute, Mom beams. "That's nice. Is he cute?"

The funny thing is that I'm not sure. He's got one of those faces that Elena and I would debate for hours: *Is* he cute? His large nose dominates his features. His eyes sit close together, and his long black hair doesn't entirely hide his big ears. And yet, somehow, I don't want to stop looking at him. Or replaying our conversation. Or rolling his image around in my head as if it's a picture I'm sneaking out of my pocket to peek at.

"I dunno. I guess?" I shrug. "He said he'd show me around the town sometime. He likes St. Mary's Cemetery."

"Mmm. I've heard that's an interesting place." Mom uncurls herself and relaxes into the black leather for the first time since I got home.

And maybe for a little bit, things feel normal. Geoff doesn't come home for a while. Mom and I go to a nearby grocery store, and I pick out an eggplant and some portobello mushrooms. I love cooking eggplant—cutting it into cubes and roasting it in olive oil until it's buttery soft and caramel sweet. Mom taught me how to cook, and the two of us used to have a grand old time on Saturdays, making a mess out of the kitchen as we got dinner ready or getting dirty in Mom's garden as we picked herbs and vegetables in the summer. Sometimes, I've even thought about going to culinary school once high school's over and becoming a chef.

I miss the Mom who loved making messes with me. Where did she go? Did Dad take her with him when he died? I thought we were getting back to our normal routines after his death, and then Geoff came along and turned everything upside-down again.

Geoff arrives home shortly after we return from the store. He's red from the sun and looks like a glazed ham, and my good mood dissipates the minute I hear him in the foyer.

But he's decided to put everything behind him.

"Look, Rachel, maybe I got a little carried away this morning." He tries an ingratiating smile, and all I can think is, *Maybe?* "I'm sorry. You're right—your hair isn't my business. Tara said if dyeing your hair is the worst thing you ever do as a teenager, you're doing okay, right?"

As apologies go, that one's pathetic. Even so, Mom's standing behind Geoff's shoulder shooting me a wide-eyed look that practically screams *Please, sweetie? Please?* Besides, we've had a nice afternoon after the bad start, and I don't want to drag everything down again.

"Okay. Sure. No problem."

He beams. It almost looks like a real smile, and for just a moment, I wonder if I've been too hard on him. There has to be something Mom sees in him, even if I can't figure out what it might be.

Geoff sets up the grill. Mom marinates chicken breasts, and I make eggplant pasta. The pleasant smells of garlic and charcoal fill the air. The kitchen here is definitely bigger than our old one, but even with all the space, Mom and I still manage to be almost on top of each other. But as we pile plates, cutting boards, towels, and used knives on the counters, it almost feels like old times—like the two of us having fun making messes again.

We eat outside on the wooden porch overlooking the dark woods. Mom lights citronella candles to keep the bugs away. I've never sat out on the porch before, and the evening feels calm and peaceful.

While we're eating, Geoff talks way too much about the day's golfing game and about his marketing work, but he doesn't try so hard to make me like him. He doesn't call me Rach, nag me about something stupid, or tell me how much better his house is than our old place. And somehow, that makes him a little more tolerable.

I go to bed that night thinking maybe this won't be so bad after all. Maybe Gram was right, and these things just take time.

I WAKE up in the middle of the night boiling hot. It's June, and it's been humid outside and inside the stuffy house all week. But this heat feels different. It isn't the typical summer haze that saps all my energy. It's burning. Intense. The box fan in my room does nothing to help. As I sit up in bed, my pulse thuds in my ears.

My throat is dry and parched, and I ease out of bed to find my way to the hall bathroom for a cup of water. Nothing but a sliver of moonlight illuminates the floor.

My lips tremble as I open my door. A rush of even more heat washes over me, and now, a charred smell lingers in the air. *Fire.* It smells like fire, and my heart pounds even harder. Is there a fire? The hallway's dark, but the illumination from the windows overlooking the staircase reveals no billows of smoke, no signs of flame. Everything is normal. Except my pulse.

The floorboards creak as I step into the hallway. The smell of grilled chicken and eggplant from dinner linger in the air, which must be the cause of the smoky smell.

The sounds start as I make my way down the hall.

Muffled crying and jagged gasps freeze me in place. I hold my breath to better hear what's going on. The sobs sound feminine, and I tilt an ear toward the master bedroom, trying to figure out if something's going on with Mom.

But the noises aren't coming from her and Geoff's room. They're coming from the bathroom. I remain perfectly still, watching, waiting, unsure of what to do, until the keening subsides.

The silence that follows is as thick as the baking heat on my skin. I swallow hard, hold my breath, and take slow, cautious steps towards the bathroom. Is Mom sick in there? The crying didn't really sound like her, but what else could be happening?

With a trembling hand, I flip on the light.

At first, I think someone's left a jumbled heap of white and red clothes on the bathroom floor. My brain doesn't know how else to interpret what my eyes are seeing. But then I make out pale arms, an old, faded dress, and fanned-out hair. And red. So much red. Everywhere. My mouth falls open.

There's a dead woman sprawled across the floor.

She's black-haired and skim-milk pale, the contrast made more jarring by the waxy texture of her skin. Her chest is torn open from her neck to her belly, maroon spilling out around her body. Her blank eyes are fixed on the ceiling, and her gray lips hang open.

I try to scream. Try to form words to call for help even though this woman is clearly beyond it. But I manage only a weak wheeze as I stagger into the door.

And then the dead woman raises her head, the movement jerky, unnatural. Milky, marble-like eyes fix on my face, and her throat works as she tries to speak.

But as her lips begin to move, her hand flies up and covers her mouth. Deep red streams pour through her fingers. Blood—so much blood—all coming from behind her hand. My knees shake too hard to hold me up. I slide to the floor, unable to make my own mouth move to call for Mom or anyone as my vision goes dim and fuzzy.

I sink into the beige bathroom rug just inches away from the woman's feet. The room around me gets darker and darker. I'm almost relieved as the horrible scene in front of me fades away into the black because I don't want to see those shriveled gray-white toes anymore.

Chapter Seven

IN THE BASEMENT

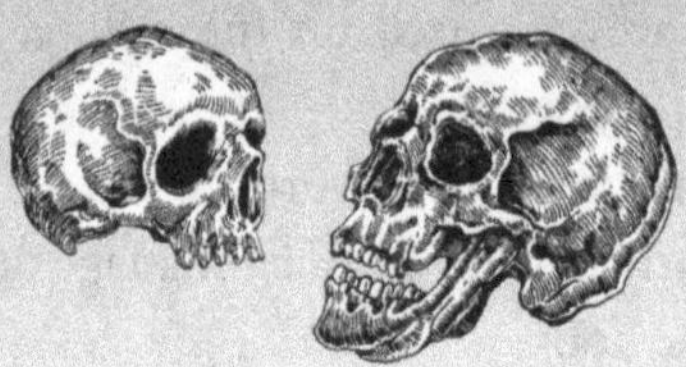

When I come to, the rug is gone. It's still terribly hot, but I'm sprawled on something hard and cool. My arm aches, and my body starts to shake.

"Hello?" I whisper.

At first, the darkness around me is like a blanket over my head, and the only thing I can hear is my own throbbing pulse. But then faint moonlight shines through a window high up on a wall, and a musty, mildewed smell hangs in the air.

I'm in Geoff's forbidden basement again. But I have no memory of coming to this place. Did someone take me here?

Did Geoff?

But he wouldn't do that. He told me straight out he didn't want me down here.

I put a hand on the floor and push myself to my feet. Smells of smoke and iron fill my nostrils, and I hear the cries again, faint but definitely there. Whoever is crying sounds as terrified as I am. I swallow hard, trying not to start crying myself. The air's practically vibrating around me from whatever dangerous energies are inhabiting this place. Something rhythmic and pulsating sounds all around me, like I'm listening to blood rush through veins.

I press my lips together and will my body to be still, to make my heart and breathing slow down. Geoff will be pissed if he catches me, but I'm even more worried about who—or what—brought me down in the first place and what they want to do to me.

The cries fall silent, and I don't hear anything else. But I still feel as if someone's down here with me.

Watching me.

That thought gets me moving, and I stumble around, trying to find the stairs and hoping I can remember the layout from the one time I'd briefly ventured down here. I move my hands around in the dark, trying to avoid Geoff's unfinished woodworking projects all over the floor. How is my pounding heart not waking everyone up? It thunders in my ears.

I walk straight into the stairs and crack my right shin. Stars of pain burst in front of my eyes, and I bite my lip, my leg throbbing as I climb towards the basement door. Every step makes a pop or a groan that shatters the silence. I expect Geoff to appear in the doorway any second now and demand to know what I'm doing down here. Or worse, lock me down here forever.

Halfway up the steps, just when I think I'm almost home free, something *touches* me.

Things that feel like icy fingers brush against my ankle, and I almost chomp my tongue in half, trying not to scream. They sweep against my foot once, twice—as if trying to get a good grip on me and pull me back downstairs.

And that's it. I'd rather deal with a pissed-off Geoff than with whatever's trying to trap me down here. I yank my foot free and kick sideways for good measure, hoping to knock back the thing trying to grab me. Cold fingernails scrape my skin as I hurry up the rest of the steps.

The door is still locked. How? How did I even get in the basement? I find the thumb-turn on the door, twist it with clammy fingers, and finally fly out of the basement. It takes everything in me to not slam the door behind me and wake the whole house up.

My heart bangs like it wants to escape my body as I try to catch my breath.

The leather sectional is in shadows as I move through the living room, and at the sight of it, a wave of fatigue hits me so hard I'm not sure I have enough energy to go upstairs. I'm tempted to just crash there for the night. But that won't be worth the questions if Mom or Geoff find me in the morning, and Geoff's probably got some "No sleeping on the furniture" rule anyhow.

And speaking of rules, there's one more thing I have to do. I find the junk drawer in the kitchen, rummage around until my fingers find the paper tag attached to the basement key, and relock the door.

Upstairs, a light still shines from under the closed bathroom door. I don't want to look in there again, but I have to see. I have to know.

Is she still in there?

But before I can touch the knob, the light goes out, and the door swings open.

I stifle a shriek as Geoff steps out in a white undershirt and shorts. He jumps back a little when he sees me.

"Good grief. You scared the heck out of me. You okay?" he asks in a hoarse whisper. If he's seen a dead woman on the floor in there, he's remarkably calm about it.

"Yeah. I wanted a drink of water," I lie.

"Oh, okay. Well, g'night." He steps around me and heads down the hall, pausing and glancing back at me after a few steps.

"Hey, Rach. Did you leave the bathroom light on?"

Not on purpose, I didn't. "Yeah."

Geoff shakes his head. "Well, don't do that. I can get a night-light for the hall or something if you're having trouble finding your way around."

With that, he goes back to the bedroom he shares with Mom.

I exhale. Finding my way around in the dark hasn't exactly been a problem tonight, but he doesn't need to know that.

The bathroom door hangs open. I take a deep breath, stiffen every muscle, and flip the light switch on again.

The bathroom floor is empty except for the beige rug and those hideous tiles. The gutted woman is gone.

If she was ever actually there.

I make my way back to my room. That intense heat has also disappeared, and I wrap myself in my blanket until the shaking stops. But my head won't stop spinning. How do I explain any of this? The whispers. The dead woman. The basement. Those icy fingers. I'd love to believe this has all been some terrifying dream, but my right shin still throbs from where I hit it on the stairs.

The fatigue I felt downstairs finally catches up to me, and I drop off to sleep as the first rays of sunlight filter through the trees outside my window.

My head feels stuffed with sawdust on Sunday morning. I'd sleep the day away if it was up to me, but Mom raps lightly on the door around nine to make sure I'm okay. For just a few seconds, I forget why I'm so tired, but then it all comes back in a rush.

Downstairs, I rummage through the cluttered kitchen cupboards. Geoff already had a lot of mugs, plastic souvenir cups from college football games, and juice glasses, and Mom brought even more. All I want is the biggest coffee cup I can find, but Geoff's mugs have cutesy sayings plastered on their fronts.

NO SUGAR, THANKS—I'M SWEET ENOUGH!

THIS IS WHAT AN AWESOME GOLFER LOOKS LIKE!

CAFFEINE—BECAUSE MOMMIN' AIN'T EASY!

They all look like they'll make my coffee taste annoying. I dig a plain green mug out from the back of the cabinet and fill it, hoping it will clear the fog in my head and maybe erase the memory of the dead (*not dead—she was trying to talk and coughing up blood—no, don't think about* that *either, not good*) woman in the bathroom.

Geoff eyes the mug when I carry it to the long wooden table where we eat most of our meals.

"Wow, Rachel. That's a lot of coffee."

"I didn't sleep much."

"Well, still." Geoff's bushy eyebrows knot together over his nose. "Not sure it's a good idea for someone your age to drink that much coffee. Or even any at all, to be honest."

Whatever goodwill I might have developed towards this annoying little toad the night before is going away, and fast. Why does his idea of honesty always involve yapping at me about everything I'm doing wrong?

"I've been drinking it for a while, Geoff. It's not hurting anything."

Mom hustles over from the plateful of bagels she's been slicing and toasting. She rests a hand on Geoff's shoulder as she sets a tub of cream cheese in the middle of the table.

"Why didn't you sleep well, sweetie?"

I stare down at the pale blue tablecloth. "I dunno. Weird dreams."

"Don't sleep well in new places, Rach? I have that problem sometimes." Geoff sounds too cheerful again now. "Maybe we could get you a white noise machine or something."

"White noise?"

"Well, I've been thinking. Maybe it's a little too quiet out here for you." He sweeps a hand around at the window overlooking the woods behind us. "Always seemed so noisy out at your apartment. Horns honking, cars tearing down the street all day and night, people walking around and yelling at each other and playing their music right out their windows...might be hard for you to sleep out here where it's actually quiet." It's amazing how he manages to put down my old life even when he thinks he's being helpful.

He takes a sip of his own coffee before continuing. "You're

probably going to need a window AC unit in there anyhow. I bet that'll do the trick. Those suckers are *loud*."

He doesn't know, can't possibly know, what happened to me, what I saw in his house last night. But I'm exhausted and stressed and struggling to hold onto my temper. I stare at the black and white tiled floor, trying to keep from snapping at him.

"Do you know who lived in this house before you?" comes out of my mouth. I didn't know I was going to ask that question until I heard it myself.

Geoff's wooden chair creaks as he leans backward. His eyebrows shoot up.

"No, I do not. This house belonged to the Morgan family a long time ago, but I didn't ask for a list of everyone who's ever lived here. Haven't we already talked about this? Why do you ask?"

My stomach flutters.

"I don't know. It's such an old place. I figure a lot of people must have been here. Right?"

"Well, I imagine so." He doesn't like that question one bit. His mouth is a thin line now as he looks at me. "But the place was empty for a long time before I got it."

"Nobody in town talks about anyone who lived here before?"

He scowls down at his hands. "No, Rachel. It's not something that comes up."

Something about my questions makes Geoff oddly hostile, and now I want to pick away at this the way Mom picks at her cuticles, digging until I uncover whatever it is that's raw and red under Geoff's forced cheerfulness.

But Mom lets out a high, nervous laugh from the counter behind us.

"I think these bagels are big enough for the whole town! Bigger than my head."

She's trying to defuse the tension again. Geoff turns around and winks at her.

"Yep. They make 'em bigger out here in the country." And just like that, his weird, defensive mood vanishes.

My weariness and wariness do not. After breakfast, I grab my iPad and do a search on sleepwalking. There's no known cause for it and no known treatment, nor do any of the websites I read offer any real insight into why someone might start doing it.

Even so, I close the iPad cover, telling myself that this has to be how I ended up in the basement. I had a bad dream, bad enough to make me walk in my sleep. And the lock on the door must have been broken somehow because sleepwalkers can't pass through a locked door.

It's sleepwalking. That's all.

And when you get right down to it, that's bad enough.

Chapter Eight

THE CITY OF THE DEAD

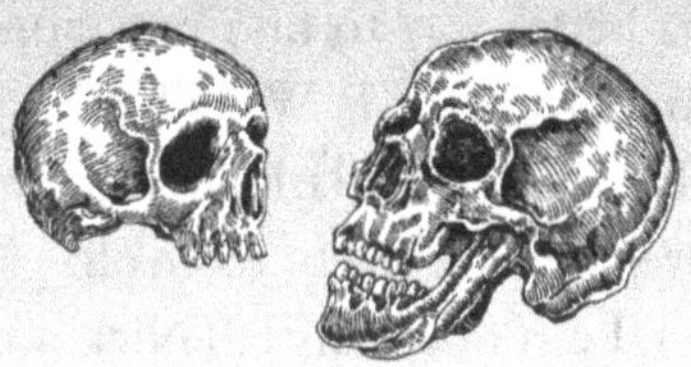

NICK DOESN'T TEXT me for a week after our first meeting at the bookstore, and this shouldn't disappoint me as much as it does. Except that Elena isn't answering my messages much either, and when I look at her social media, I see that she's volunteering at her church or hanging out with people from my old school. Are we already growing apart? She said we wouldn't, but maybe I should have known better.

I try searching for Nick Alexander on every social media site I can find, but it's an annoyingly common name, and I can't find any accounts that might belong to him, not even when I narrow the search down to St. Mary.

My heart leaps into my throat every time the phone beeps. And on a Saturday morning, the message is from him at last.

Want to go see the cemetery today?

Part of me really wants to say *no.* I haven't seen or heard anything unusual in the house since the previous weekend, but I'm not getting much sleep. Closing my eyes every night makes me fear what I might see when I open them again. I'm always tired, and I'm not sure I'm up for trudging around a graveyard.

And Geoff's started nagging me about getting a job, joining a club, or otherwise getting out of the house. A *club*! What the hell, does he think I'm eight? My parents were always okay with letting me take it easy over the summer, but Geoff views the idea of someone relaxing as a personal insult.

"I don't even know what's around here," I say after one such conversation.

"Well, what's a better way to find out more about the town than looking around for HELP WANTED signs, hmm?" The idea that maybe I don't particularly care to find out any more about St. Mary never seems to occur to Geoff.

As tired as I am, I can't possibly tell Nick no. I put my hair up in a messy bun that takes me several tries to get just right, and then I look for an outfit that falls in exactly the perfect spot between too casual and trying-way-too-hard. I settle on black cargo pants and a white Sandman t-shirt.

Geoff's sitting on the sectional in the living room with a cup of coffee, staring at his iPad. He looks up when he sees me heading for the front door with my purse.

"Where are you going?"

"Meeting a friend."

His eyes narrow. "Oh? Who?"

"Just someone I met at the bookstore the other day." My shoulders tense up. I don't know if he'll give me crap about meeting with a guy, and I'm not in the mood for another argument.

He looks like he's considering asking more questions but finally says, "Okay, then. Good to hear you're making friends here."

I leave before he can say anything else.

Outside Milledge's Book Company, I chain my bike up. Ms. Milledge waves from behind the cash register as I scratch

Toby's head and listen to his happy panting. The smell of coffee from the bar in the back makes me crave a cup, but I rule it out. I'm already nervous about hanging out with Nick.

"Hello again, Rachel. Will we be seeing you more often?" Ms. Milledge asks.

"Yeah. My mom and I moved here so she could be with her boyfriend."

Mrs. Milledge picks up on the way I say *boyfriend* and wrinkles her nose. "Who's the boyfriend?"

"Geoff. Geoff Barber."

"Hm. Don't recognize the name."

"There are hardly any books in that house at all, so I guess he doesn't come here much."

She shakes her head. "Well, that's a shame. A home without books isn't much of one, in my opinion. Where's he live?"

"All the way out there." I point in the general direction of Geoff's place. "Big house in the woods."

"Goodness. You mean Morgan House?"

"That's the one."

Ms. Milledge rubs her chin. "Don't know if I'd like being all the way out there in such a big house. Especially one that old. Maybe if I had Toby to watch out for me..."

A dog. I should ask Mom and Geoff about getting a dog.

The bells on the door jingle, and Nick walks in. He gives Ms. Milledge a quick nod and smiles at me.

"You ready?"

He's looking especially attractive this morning with his dark hair pulled back in a low ponytail. Yes, I'm very ready.

Nick's light blue Honda hatchback sounds like it might stall out at any moment; it's rickety and shaky and nothing like Mom's Volvo or Geoff's SUV.

"Sorry," Nick says, not meeting my eyes. "Not much to look at, but it gets me around."

"I don't care." I shrug. "Flashy cars bore me. People seem to think they're a substitute for an actual personality or something." That makes Nick chuckle.

I glance around inside, but there's none of the clutter I'm used to seeing in other people's cars. A faint scent of something like wood smoke hangs in the air, but nothing gives me any clues about what Nick might be like, what he might be interested in, or what he does when he's not around me. I guess I'll have to find out more about him the old-fashioned way: by asking him.

The blocks of trendy boutiques and restaurants lining Old Town end, and I spot a few stores that look a lot less fancy: A bait shop. A pawn shop. A gun shop.

"So, how's it going with you?" Nick asks.

"It's so freaking good to get out of that house."

"Where do you live?" he asks.

"Some big old creepy place out in the woods. It's called Morgan House."

Nick makes another turn, and we pass by a park with a large three-level fountain in the center, surrounded by trees. People throw Frisbees to their dogs.

"I know where Morgan House is," Nick says. "Never lived in a house that had a name."

"Me neither. And I can't say I care for it. I liked our apartment."

"Because idiot boyfriend wasn't around?"

I roll my eyes. "God, yes. I swear, I have to hear something else he doesn't like about me every day. But even if he wasn't annoying, I'd still *hate* that house."

"Yeah? Why's that?"

I don't know him well enough to risk telling him the truth. Not yet.

"Well...because he's there." We laugh. "But it's just musty and humid. And we can barely get a good WiFi signal out there, so it's hard for me to talk to my old friends. And something about being that far out in the woods just gives me the creeps."

"I bet." We approach a pair of big iron gates, and Nick slows the car.

"Here we are."

Letters spelling out ST. MARY CEMETERY are worked into a wrought iron arch that sits above a long, winding gravel path.

We climb out of Nick's car, and I stare at the scene that greets me. Rows of tombstones, some looking hundreds of years old, stretch back as far as I can see under the overcast sky. The landscape of stones is broken up only by the gravel path and the occasional bundle of balloons or withered flowers. Green trees dot the landscape here and there, casting some of the tombstones into shade. I've watched at least two movies called *City of the Dead*, and now I feel like I'm in a city of the dead myself.

"That's a lot of graves," I mutter.

"St. Mary is a pretty old city." Nick shrugs. "Lots of people have lived and died here."

Our feet crunch the gravel path as we walk through the gates. Nobody else is around, and the warm, moist air hangs heavy, making the surroundings feel stifled and still. Crows call to each other from the treetops. My forehead dampens as we walk, and I hope I won't turn into a sweaty mess.

Old tombstones so worn and dirty they're barely legible sit next to crisp new granite markers. Most of these people died at ages I consider unsurprising. It's hard to get too broken up over *Edward Philip Montgomery, Beloved Husband, Father, and Grandfather, 1902-1991*—eighty-nine years is a decent run by anyone's standards. But the ones who weren't that old when they died start getting to me. *1968-2014. 1913-1930.* Some graves are surrounded by artificial flowers or balloons. Others have smaller stones placed on their surfaces. But most of them have nothing at all.

It's been ages since I've seen my dad's grave. I picture it completely bare, and hot guilt floods my chest.

"There's a bunch of fancy tombstones up the hill," Nick says. "Angels and all that. Rich people's graves. They're pretty neat." And then his eyes widen as he looks at my face. "Hey, you okay?"

I stare down at the gravel. "I don't know."

"What's up? I thought you'd like it here. Is it creeping you out?"

"It's not that," I say.

"Then what?"

"My dad died a couple of years ago. This is making me think about him."

My father was tall and dark-haired and skinny and weird and smart. When I was thirteen, he took a trip to Tokyo, and when he came back, he was carrying something extra: a blood clot that traveled into his lungs and killed him. We didn't find out until after his death that he had a genetic tendency towards forming clots more easily, and a long sedentary plane trip had been asking for trouble.

The idea made the skin at the back of my neck prickle. Did I have that faulty gene too? Could staying completely still actually kill me? I'd lie immobile in my bed for hours, wondering if I'd die just like he did, wondering if the idea even bothered me in a world where he wasn't anymore.

How Mom could go from someone like Dad to a guy like Geoff is another complete mystery, as baffling as his sudden death. Dad never talked to me like I was some five-year-old idiot. Dad didn't complain about Thai food, or snark about the Internet. He was amazing. But now he's gone.

"Oh. Oh damn." Nick winces. "I'm sorry."

"Not your fault. I told you I wanted to come here."

He's even paler than usual. "We can go somewhere else. There's this place—"

"No. Let's go look at the angels." I trudge up the hill, moving so fast that Nick has to hustle to keep up.

"I know how you feel," he says from behind me.

"Oh yeah?"

"Both my parents are dead."

That stops me in my tracks, and I turn back to him. "My God. What happened?" And then, "Sorry. That's kind of nosy."

He catches up to me. "My mom died when I was only three. In childbirth. The baby didn't make it either."

I suck in my breath.

"And then my dad died in an accident when I was twelve."

"That's horrible! What did you do?"

"My dad's brother took me in. But he, uh, wasn't happy about it. Still isn't, even now. I try to stay out of that house whenever I can. He doesn't like me being around too much. Says I get in the way of things." He sweeps back a lock of black hair that's fallen from his ponytail.

Get in the way of things? I wonder what the heck that even means. "Now I feel bad, complaining about my father."

He frowns. "Don't. It's not a contest, Rachel."

"I know, but geez. I lost my dad, but at least I've still got my mom." *For now. But what if?* If I've learned anything in the last couple of years, it's that nothing is promised. Things can always get worse. And for the moment, I'm stuck with Geoff, too, and the thought doesn't improve my mood.

We stop in front of a grave featuring one of the angel statues Nick mentioned. The tip of its left wing has broken off, and the angel looks very sad about that as it stares down at the grass.

Nick scrutinizes my face, and it occurs to me that I barely know him, yet I'm telling him some fairly personal stuff. Something about him makes me feel comfortable sharing all these dark, heavy things. Maybe it's his deep brown eyes. They're warm and full of concern as he listens to me.

"Sorry," I say. "I didn't mean for things to get all depressing."

"It's okay. Kind of hard to be lighthearted in a place like this, right?"

I chuckle. "No kidding."

"And anyway, it sounds like you could use a friend in town."

"Yeah. Maybe I could." And maybe something more than

that. I glance up to see him smiling down at me, and his dark eyes warm me.

"So, when did your mom get together with the idiot?"

I roll my eyes. "It's only been about a year now. I don't know what the rush to move us out here was about."

"Hm. So she must care for him, huh? People will do desperate things for love."

I frown. "Well, I wouldn't call her *desperate*."

"Sorry." He winces. "I didn't mean it that way."

"Doesn't matter. They'll just break up sooner or later anyhow. And what's the point? Nothing really lasts, does it?"

He looks at me sharply. "Do you seriously believe that?"

I raise my chin as I stare back. "Well, it's hard *not* to."

"Things don't have to end."

"Well, I wouldn't mind if things ended with the jerk boyfriend."

"That's not what I'm talking about, though."

"I don't know, okay?" I turn away from him. "My favorite teacher died of cancer when I was in third grade. And then my dad died. And then my mom just yanks me away from everything and everyone I know to live here."

I shudder at the memory of Miss Snider, who was warm, funny, and kind to me and everyone else in my third-grade class. One morning, she told us she was sick and that although she might look bad for a while, that meant that the medicine she'd be taking to fight her illness was working, and we shouldn't worry about her.

But she *dwindled,* little by little, shrinking and withering until I wondered if one day, she would just vanish completely right in the middle of teaching class. A substitute named Mrs. Mueller came in to cover our grade, and Mrs. Mueller, who had the warmth and humor of a metal pole in the winter, never left. And then, the principal came in one morning to tell us he had sad news.

I ran home that day and buried my face in Dad's chest.

"Are you going to die too, Daddy?" I asked.

"Not for a long time, kiddo," he said.

But he lied.

Something hot prickles behind my eyes, and my throat tightens. I take a deep breath, trying to calm down. I don't know Nick well enough to cry in front of him. Not yet.

He puts a hand on my shoulder. "Rachel. It doesn't have to be that way."

"Of course it does." I squeeze my eyes shut for a second to keep the tears back. "That's just how things are. Nothing good ever stays that way."

"It can."

I look up at him.

"Once I like a person, I stay with them," he says. "And I like you."

I'm flushed now, warm from something that has nothing to do with the day's humidity. "I like you too."

He gives me a soft smile. I giggle and immediately hate myself for it. It sounds just like my mom's nervous giggle, a high-pitched *aheeheeheehee* I've heard way too much lately whenever she's trying to smooth things over between Geoff and me.

"And you're wrong, Rachel. Good things don't have to end. I believe the people you love the most can always stay with you."

"Yeah, I know." I try to keep the sarcasm out of my voice, but I heard this one a lot after Dad died. "They'll always be in our hearts and minds." This never made me feel better. I didn't want Dad in my heart or mind; I wanted him alive and with us.

"But what if they could really stay with you? Forever?"

I arch my eyebrow. Nick sees the look I'm giving him and says, "What?"

"Is this when you tell me you're actually a vampire?"

The corner of his mouth turns up in a half-smile as he points at the sky. "We're in broad daylight. See how I'm not burning up?"

"So? Dracula could go out in daylight in Bram Stoker's book."

"He could? Really?"

I nod. "*Nosferatu* started the whole fatal sunlight thing." And then I press my lips together to stop myself from nerding out on him even more.

He chuckles. "Do you *want* me to be a vampire?"

"Ugh, no. Why would anyone want to be a vampire?"

Nick rolls his eyes. "Gee, I don't know. Being young and hot and living forever? Who'd want *that*, right?"

"Okay, but the whole blood-drinking thing is a major turnoff. I'm a vegetarian. No blood for me, thanks."

He shrugs. "So, forget vampires. But I'm telling you: Death isn't the end. At least, it doesn't have to be."

That's crazy, I think. But I don't argue. I just want to be out here with him as we walk. I wonder what this odd yet good sensation inside me is, and it hits me: Happiness. I'm starting to feel happy, maybe for the first time since we moved to St. Mary.

Chapter Nine

A VERY HASTY ENGAGEMENT

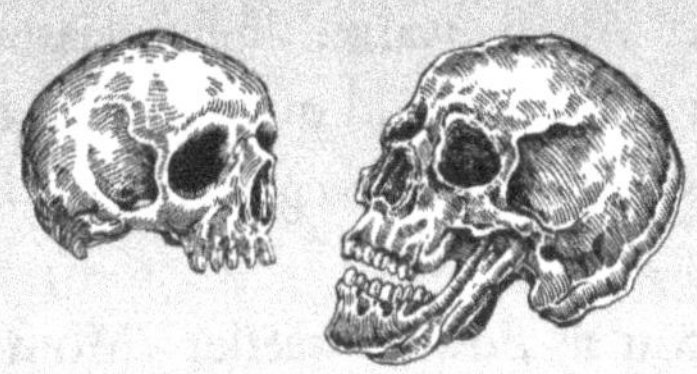

Nick drops me off in front of Milledge's and squeezes my shoulder before I get out of the car. I act like I'm studying the display of Sue Grafton books in the window, but I'm really watching the reflection of Nick's car as he drives off. When I can't see him anymore, I unlock my bike from the rack and get going.

I replay our conversation in the graveyard over and over. He likes me. He even said so and didn't make me guess how he felt. I wasn't expecting anything like that, and especially not this soon. But for the first time, I'm not sorry I'm in St. Mary. If I'd known Nick was going to be waiting for me, I'd have begged Mom to move here ages ago.

Maybe I can even get used to Geoff. Everyone deserves someone who makes them happy, I figure. Mom gets Geoff, I get Nick. Fair enough.

My good mood lasts all the way down the winding gravel path through the trees leading to Morgan House, and then it goes to hell.

Mom and Geoff are at the kitchen table with an open bottle of champagne and two flutes between them when I walk in. Mom's rosy-faced and giggly, and Geoff sports that smug, pleased look that never means anything good. They look up at me and trade sneaky glances like I've caught them in the middle of something they didn't want me to see.

Nobody drinks champagne in the afternoon for no reason. My muscles tense up.

"Hey there!" Geoff's grin looks big enough to split his face in half, and I think he might have even grown extra teeth since I last saw him this morning. "Nice time in town?"

"Sure, I guess." All the warm, tingly pleasure I felt from the time with Nick is vanishing, and quickly. The air in the house is humid and oppressive, and I take a glass out of the cabinet and get a drink of water.

"Why don't you sit down, sweetie?" Mom says. "We've got some news for you."

Oh, this is so not good.

Mom wouldn't be drinking if she was pregnant, so it's not that. But still, I don't want to hear this news, whatever it is. I know I was just wishing them happiness, but right now, I want to take that back. I take a seat at the wooden table, though I want to kick the chair over and run away screaming.

"What's up?"

Mom opens her mouth, about to answer, but Geoff pipes up first.

"Well, this afternoon, I asked your mom if she'd make me the happiest man in the world. And she said yes."

The happiest man in the world. Oh, no. Mom holds up her hand with an excited grin like she thinks I'll be happy to see this. The diamond ring on her wedding finger sparkles and glimmers in the kitchen light.

This isn't a total surprise. They've barely been together a whole year, but there was nowhere else a move out to Geoff's house in St. Hole in the Wall was going to go.

But even so, the floor drops out from under me and makes me remember being a little kid at the beach getting knocked over by the occasional big wave while I played in the ocean. I'd tumble and roll in the murky salt water for terrifying seconds, completely unable to tell which end was up before I finally surfaced again.

My dad always dried me off and comforted me when that happened. But Dad can't do anything about this, and the wave isn't letting up. Mom's going to marry Geoff. If she does, we won't be getting out of Morgan House any time soon. And I can't see daylight.

"Now, I know this must seem sudden to you," Mom starts, but Geoff isn't going to let things get too serious.

"You know what?" He gives me a conspiratorial look. "Sure, the drinking age is twenty-one, but this is my house and my rules. Want a glass of champagne? No reason you shouldn't get to celebrate with us."

I drank a beer at a cast party after the school play last year. I hated the weird, bitter taste, but the alcohol made me forget how much things hurt inside me for an hour or two. And the wave that knocked me down is still tumbling me around, and I'm whirling and disoriented. Maybe the champagne will make it stop. Or maybe it will make me not care. Either sounds pretty good.

"Sure. That'd be great."

"All right!" His smile gets even wider. If I wasn't freaking out about the engagement right now, I might think the way he lights up whenever I agree to one of his ideas is kind of nice.

Geoff gets up and rummages through a cabinet, and Mom comes over to me and hugs me. I want to congratulate her or at least say something, but words won't come when I open my mouth.

He fills a flowered juice glass half-full of sparkling amber liquid and passes it to me, and I concentrate on the rising bubbles while he refills his and Mom's glasses.

"To a whole new life together!" Geoff says, raising his flute high. Mom lets out a high, tense giggle and raises her flute, too.

I want to scream, to run, to smash the juice glass on the floor, and I watch in horror as my hand reaches out and clinks glasses with theirs. What the hell am I doing?

Nobody warned me that champagne would have such a sour tang. It makes me wince, and the bubbles fizzle in the back of my throat and nose. I'm not sure why this stuff should represent things like joy, luxury, or celebration.

"So," Geoff says. "We were thinking of doing something fairly small. Like, justice of the peace small. I mean, your mom's done this before, and I sure don't need a big splashy spectacle. Seems to me like all those major productions do is waste lots of money and drive everyone bananas." Another big grin.

"I guess so." Why is he telling me this? Does he think I've got a long history of planning weddings? I swallow more champagne, hoping the reality-blurring effect I remember from that beer will kick in soon.

Mom is still studying my face. "No matter how small it is, though, we want you to be a part of it," she says.

What choice do I even have? "Sure." I take another sip, and the waves recede just a little bit.

Nick. Remember Nick. Remember how he said he liked you.

"Hey! Is that a smile I see? Looks good on you." Geoff laughs.

"Can I have some more champagne?" I've finished the little bit Geoff gave me, and I'm not close to being numb enough to handle all this.

"Whoa! I think you need to slow down there, Rach. It's not like you're gonna drive anywhere, but still."

"I know!" Mom says, clapping for emphasis. "Let's all make a nice dinner together. That'll be a fun way to celebrate."

"No way, Tara. Tonight we're going out to eat. I already made reservations at Lund's Steakhouse. Best place in town."

Mom's smile wavers as she looks at me. "A steakhouse?"

Geoff waves a dismissive hand. "Don't worry about that. They've got plenty of non-meat stuff. I'm sure she'll be fine. They might even make her something off the menu if she asks nicely."

If I were even remotely hungry, I'd be pissed that Geoff expects me to go to a steakhouse. But right now, a cold brick is sitting in my stomach, and I don't care where we go.

"What do you say we all go get washed up?" Geoff says. "Don't know about anyone else, but I like to spruce up before I go to a fancy restaurant."

"I should go call Mother and tell her the news," Mom says.

I blink. "Gram doesn't know yet?"

Geoff shows me more teeth. "I kind of sprung this on your mom a little."

Mom and Geoff get up and head out of the kitchen. I snatch the bottle of champagne and fill the little juice glass, drinking it down fast before I get caught.

UPSTAIRS, I'm sprawled on the bed, all swimmy-headed and loopy from the champagne, not getting ready to go out. Maybe I'll tell them I'm sick.

I text Elena the news, looking for sympathy, but I don't get any reply. Should I text Nick? Nah. I don't want to seem like I'm already getting clingy.

Mom raps lightly on the door, pokes her head in my room, and I flip my phone over.

"Sweetie? Got a minute?"

"I've got nothing *but* minutes." I think the champagne is making me a little goofy.

Mom raises her eyebrows before turning my desk chair to face me and sitting down. She's pink-faced under her freckles, and she winds a strand of hair around her finger as she talks. The diamond ring on her left hand sparkles.

"Are you okay with this?"

"With what? The steakhouse?"

"Be serious. You know what I mean."

I'm going to say *Sure*, but what comes out instead is, "I don't know. Does it matter?" We both look surprised at those words.

"Well, of *course* it matters. You're still the most important thing in the world to me." Nice to hear her say that. It hasn't felt that way for a while.

"And I know you aren't crazy about Geoff."

That's an understatement. "I barely *know* Geoff, Mom. Do you?"

"Of course I do. He's a good man who wants a happy family. He didn't get that growing up. He wants to have one with us."

"Why didn't he get that growing up?" And why do we have to be the ones to give it to him now?

"He hasn't talked about it too much." She glances away from me for a moment. "But his father was apparently a real disciplinarian. 'Children should be seen and not heard.' That kind of thing."

"Is that why he gives me shit about my hair? And about what I'm doing every second of every day here?" I must have had a little more champagne than I realized, and Mom must be incredibly happy because she lets that *shit* go without a scolding comment.

"I've talked to him about that, sweetie. Yes, he was raised that way. It's hard for him to turn it off now because it's all he knew. But I know he'll try. For both of us."

Oh good. He'll *try* not to be a controlling asshole. The more I think about this, the less I understand what my mom is thinking. She's done impulsive things before, but they've never been this life-changing. Especially not when it comes to my life.

Mom's pink-faced cluelessness is making something hot and ugly brew inside my chest. Mom and Geoff will run off to get married whether I want it or not. I didn't want to move out here with Geoff, and it didn't matter then. What I want won't matter now, either. Why is Mom even pretending like I have a say?

"But Mom, this is so fast. I mean, if I wanted to marry a guy I'd barely known a year, I don't think you'd like it."

Mom starts picking imaginary bits of lint off her beige pants.

"Well, maybe it seems fast to you. But it doesn't to me. It's been so hard without your dad around." *Pick. Pick. Pick.*

She has been happier—much happier—since she got together

with Geoff. Before that, I'd often catch her crying when I got home from school. There were days I'd have to remind her to eat.

Even so, there's a hot, ugly thing inside me gnawing at my ribs now, and I wonder what will happen when it finally chews its way out. Will it ruin everything? Do I want it to?

Mom takes a deep breath, raises her head, and looks me in the eye. "Rachel, tell me the truth. If you really don't want me to do this, I won't."

I gasp. "Are you serious?"

"Completely." Mom's tone turns grave as she looks at me. "You've been through a lot these past few years. I don't want to subject you to anything else you aren't ready for. I love Geoff, but he can wait."

"Come on. I can't make a decision like that for you, Mom."

"You don't have to say anything right away. But think about it."

Mom has to know I'm not on board with this marriage. And why is she even putting this on me? This is completely unfair. If I put a stop to things, Mom and Geoff will be miserable, and it'll be my fault for spoiling their plans and making them unhappy. My head whirls as I consider all my options.

Is there even any point in telling her to put things on hold? Sooner or later, as long as they don't break up, they'll just go and get married anyhow.

And Mom's been through a lot too. Doesn't she deserve someone who makes her happy? Geoff obviously does that, even if I don't understand why.

Can I learn to live with this for a couple of years until I leave for college, even if I don't like it? Is there a door in this situation that *doesn't* have a tiger behind it? If so, I can't see it.

"Well, if you're happy, I'm happy." That's total crap, the kind of thing people say when they aren't happy but know arguing about it is pointless. Mom studies my face a little longer before talking again.

"It's not going to be easy. I know that. I know you miss your father, and so do I. Every day. But don't forget: You're the most important thing to me, okay? I want you to talk to me if you're ever in danger of forgetting that. We can make this work. All three of us."

"I know."

"Do you?"

"*Yes.*"

Mom looks into my eyes as if she can see whatever is brewing in there, and for a moment she hesitates, a slight frown knotting her eyebrows. And then it's as if she decides not to see anymore. She gets up and smiles at me.

"Well, let's go get ready for dinner. Love you, sweetie."

"Love you too."

Mom kisses my forehead before leaving the room.

The hot, angry thing inside me wants to kick furniture over, scream, and claw at my own face until I'm raw and bleeding. Mom says she cares what I think, but she doesn't. Not really. Or else we'd never have moved out here.

I bury my burning face in my pillow and grab fistfuls of the comforter until the rage inside me subsides.

That night at the steakhouse, I pick at a baked potato and a salad drowning in sickening-sweet dressing while Mom and Geoff giggle and smooch and eat bleeding steak and drink red wine that stains their teeth purple. The champagne's long since worn off, and now my head's pounding. My potato's undercooked, but it doesn't matter. The odors of seared meat and frying onions turn my stomach, and I'm not hungry at all. A faint stench of cigar smoke lingers under all the other smells, dating back to the days when people were allowed to have those things in here. The walls are dark red, the lighting is dim, and piano music plays just loudly enough to make conversation difficult. That makes it easier for me to hide.

When we get home, I tell them I'm not feeling well and head to bed. I think about texting Nick but decide against it. Walking with him in the cemetery feels like it happened decades ago already.

SOMETHING STARTLES me awake in the middle of the night. I sit up, my heart pounding, wondering if it's Mom and Geoff talking somewhere. There are moaning sounds coming from somewhere outside my room, and I cringe, thinking, *Oh, come on. Please, no. There's not enough brain bleach in the world for* that.

But when I listen more closely, it's not moaning. It's sobbing. Even though the evening's warm, a cold pit forms inside me as my pulse speeds up. I squint, trying to see if there's anyone—or anything—in my bedroom.

"Not again," I whisper to the darkness. "Not tonight. Please, no. I can't take it."

And then my room fills with that familiar baking, burning heat. A long, repetitive *shhh-shhh* sound begins down on the floor as if something is being dragged towards me. I hold my breath and look.

A shape crawls across my bedroom toward me. Its long arms pull the rest of it across the floor as if its back legs don't work. I shrink away and put my hands over my mouth as the thing coughs and makes a moist, splattering sound on the wooden floor.

I want to turn on the light.

I don't dare turn on the light.

If I can't see it, maybe it isn't there.

But the sounds of limbs dragging across old hardwood get closer and closer to my bed—to me. I tremble hard enough that the bed quakes, and I'm sure the thing on the floor can hear it.

The sobbing morphs into wheezing, as if whoever's making the sound has lost the strength to cry. A hand with long, bony fingers reaches up from the floor, sliding up the side of my bed towards my feet. Cold, dry, tendril-like fingers close around my ankle and squeeze.

I kick and thrash, but the chilly fingers tighten like a snare. The darkness in my room grows heavier and heavier, as though it's a tangible thing, and I've got that feeling again—the sensation of being knocked over by a wave—tumbling and twisting and unable to come up for air.

The blackness closes around me, smothering me.

SOMETHING'S hard against my left side, and my shoulder throbs. I can tell from the dampness and the musty odor that I'm in the basement again, but something's different this time. Instead of the suffocating black, there's a faint glow in here, barely enough for me to see the shape of a door outlined in a rectangle of pale, flickering light in the far wall. A faint voice mutters words I can't make out.

Was that there before? I squint, but it doesn't help me see more clearly. My head swims, and it's hard to focus as my eyes water. I can't figure out who's talking. Is it Geoff? I don't think so. The voice is too deep. But whoever it is sounds angry.

The sound of dragging starts up again. It's as if someone's crawling on the floor—or hauling something around behind that door.

Something, or someone.

Oh God. Whoever is in there and whatever's going on, I absolutely do not want anything to know I'm down here.

And I have to get out of here, fast. I'm about to push myself to my feet and hope my shaking legs will carry me up the stairs when the dragging sounds stop. There's a jarring thud, and that strange door bangs open.

Heat radiates from the open space, and someone strides out, a shadowy shape smelling like fire and iron and wrapped in an air of intensity. I can't see his face, but in the shadows, he's tall and lean and fast. And he's walking right towards me. I struggle to pull myself away, thinking *oh god, no. Don't let him see me. Please, no. Don't let him see. Don't let him hear—*

"*Rachel!*" Someone grabs me by the shoulders, and I scream.

My throat is raw, and I realize I've already been screaming. I thrash around, trying to break free from whatever's got me.

"Rachel? What are you doing down here?"

It's Mom. At first, I think this whole thing has just been a vivid nightmare. But when I pull away from her, the concrete basement floor is still hard under my back.

"She do this kind of thing a lot, Tara?" It's Geoff, and there's an edge to his voice.

"Of course not. Nothing like this has ever happened before."

The basement light clicks on, and the sudden searing brightness makes me close my eyes. When I open them again, Mom's kneeling on the floor, leaning over me.

"Why in the world are you down here? What happened?"

"I don't know. I ... I had a nightmare." And then I do what I've been wanting to do ever since I came home and found Mom and Geoff celebrating in front of their champagne: I burst into sobs.

"Oh, sweetie. It's okay. *Shhh.*" Mom wraps her arms around me, rocking me.

"No," I manage in a whisper. "This isn't okay. At all."

"We need to get her out of here, Tara." Geoff's voice is as cold as his eyes.

Mom stands up and helps me to my feet. She keeps an arm wrapped around me and leads me around the junk in the basement and all the way up to my room as Geoff trails behind us.

"Are you sick, sweetie? Maybe the champagne didn't agree with you."

I sniffle. "It wasn't the champagne. I had a nightmare."

Geoff slams the basement door behind us. The bang makes me twitch.

Once in my room, I lie down on my bed, pulling the purple bedspread over myself even though it's humid. Mom puts a damp, trembling hand on my forehead.

"What were you doing in the basement, Rachel?" Geoff leans

in the door, his gray eyes fixed on me. There's nothing fake-cheerful in his tone now. His arms are folded over his chest. He's angry.

"I don't know. I woke up down there."

His eyes narrow as he turns to Mom. "Does she sleepwalk?"

Mom holds her hands out. "She's never done it before. Not that I know of anyhow."

My heart and head pound, and even though I'm no longer even remotely tired, I need them both out of my room.

"I'm fine. It was a bad dream, that's all. I'm sorry I scared you. Go back to bed now."

"Goodness. After that, I don't think I'm getting much sleep." Mom holds a hand against her chest to demonstrate.

"I'm sorry," I say again. Why won't they just go?

"It's okay. I'm just glad you're all right. Can I get you something?" Mom's hands flitter around uselessly now. She fusses with the purple bedspread and then smooths my hair.

God, please *go*. "It's okay, Mom. I'll yell for you if I don't feel good or something."

"Well... all right. If you're sure."

Mom kisses my forehead and heads out of the bedroom. But Geoff watches Mom walk down the hall before turning back to me. His eyes are like chips of ice, and all his toothy happiness from the afternoon is nowhere to be seen now. He moves to my bed and leans over me.

"What are you trying, Rachel?" There is no trace of his usual obnoxious pep. And I've never heard him sound so stern, so cold, not even when he's nagging me about something stupid. This is different. He's seriously pissed.

"Excuse me?"

"That basement door was *locked*. You want me to believe you can pick locks in your sleep?"

A flash of anger overrides the weariness I've been feeling. "I don't care what you believe. I don't want to be down there any more than you want me down there."

"Who did you see in town today?"

His abrupt topic shift confuses me, and my fingernails dig into my palms. "I told you. A friend. What the hell does that have to do with anything?"

"Don't curse at me. And who put you up to that stunt downstairs? Because I want it to stop. Now."

The fear I'd been feeling is now eclipsed by anger. "What are you even talking about, Geoff? Who do you think would have put me up to this? Now get out of my room."

The silence stretches between us until it feels like something is about to snap. Geoff finally straightens up, but those stony gray eyes don't leave my face.

"It's not your room."

He leaves, closing the door loudly behind him. And now I know for sure: He's hiding something. And someone out there must know what it is.

Chapter Ten

A SAFE PLACE

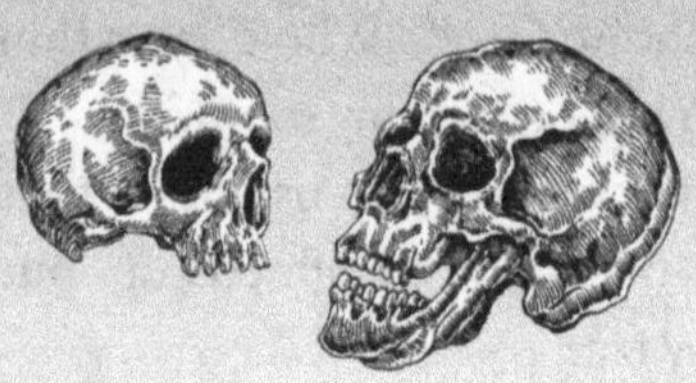

At nine the next morning, I abandon the prospect of rest and haul myself out of bed. My body feels like I've been hollowed out and filled with cement. The sunlight streaming through the window feels like fire on my head and my eyes.

Mom and Geoff are talking downstairs, and Mom's voice is high-pitched and tense. I pause at the top of the steps to listen.

"But I felt it too, Geoff. There's bad energy down there. My skin was crawling."

"Tara, this is a really old house. Lots of people must have lived here, so sure, someone might have died in here, too. That basement gives me the creeps too sometimes, to tell you the truth."

"Really? Why?"

"I don't like being in closed-in spaces like that. Feels like I'm in a tomb. But I asked her not to go down there."

The steps creak as I head down, and their voices break off.

"Oh, sweetie," Mom says when I walk into the kitchen. "You look awful."

"Thanks, Mom." I roll my eyes and head for the cluttered brown cabinets. Geoff's mugs and their stupid sayings don't improve my mood.

"You sure gave us all a scare!" Geoff sounds like his usual jolly, upbeat self again. As if I'm going to forget how callous he was the night before.

Something about one of the obnoxious mugs suddenly strikes me as odd. I take out "CAFFEINE — BECAUSE MOMMIN' AIN'T EASY!" and hold it up.

"What's this about, Geoff?"

He gives me a blank look. "It's a coffee cup."

I know that, you ass. "Yeah, but *mommin'*? You're not a mom. Why'd you get this one?" Now, Mom herself is looking at the mug, an eyebrow raised.

Geoff looks at us for a second and then barks out a laugh. "Well, heck. The mugs were five for a dollar at the community yard sale when I was moving in. I didn't exactly stop to vet all the sayings before I stocked up. That one can be your mother's if it's such a big deal to you."

That reply seems to satisfy Mom, who busies herself with toast and a jar of raspberry jam. But I'm not buying the cheerful act. I fill the plain green mug with coffee. I need a little strength for my next question to Geoff.

"Who do you think I've been talking to?"

His heavy eyebrows shoot up. "Sorry?"

"You heard me. You accused me of talking to someone last night."

"I wasn't trying to accuse you of anything..." He spreads his hands out as Mom watches us, her toast forgotten.

And I'm not letting him off the hook. "Yes, you were."

"What's going on?" Mom asks.

"Geoff accused me of talking to someone who put me up to everything that happened last night."

"Geoff!" Mom bangs the jar of jam on the table.

Geoff puts his hands up. "Look, I'm sorry. She really scared me when we found her in the basement like that, and I might have overreacted." He's using a jovial tone again. "I thought maybe she was pulling some kind of prank. Like maybe some kids in town put ideas in her head about this house or something."

"She wouldn't do something like that." Mom folds her arms over her chest.

"*What* kids in town?" That ugly, clawing beast inside my chest is rearing up again, and while I don't usually like losing my temper or making scenes, I'm not inclined to try to restrain it. If Mom could see him the way I saw him the night before...

He scowls. "I don't know. Who'd you meet up with yesterday?"

I glance away from him and down at the wooden table. "Nick. I met him a while ago at Milledge's Book Company, and we hung out."

"Uh-huh. And where did you hang out?"

None of your business. "St. Mary Cemetery."

Geoff lets out another booming laugh. "Well, *there* you go, for heaven's sake. Hanging out at cemeteries? No wonder you were having bad dreams. What kind of a weirdo takes someone to a place like that on a date anyhow?"

"I go to cemeteries all the time, Geoff. They don't scare me. I even sit in them and draw headstones sometimes. That wasn't what caused last night."

"Ah. Well." Geoff's still smirking.

"Are you sure you don't know anything about who lived in this house before you?"

The smirk vanishes. "How many times do I have to tell you, Rach? I don't know for sure. Definitely no Lizzie Borden types, if that's what you're getting at. Nothing like that's ever happened in St. Mary." He meets my eyes again. The ice chips from last night are gone, but he's still cool. "I'm sure there's plenty of information about Morgan House on the internet if you're curious."

"You know, that's an excellent idea. Looking stuff up online. I think I'll do that." I study him to see if that gets any reaction, but he looks away and takes a long drink of his coffee.

"Why do you want to know who lived here, sweetie?" Mom's toast sits untouched in front of her.

"Because I think something bad happened in this house," I

say after a pause. "Something terrible. And now something else—maybe some*one*—is trying to scare us out of here. You felt it down there too, Mom. I heard you talking about it."

Mom's eyes widen, and she's about to say something when Geoff interrupts.

"Oh, come on now. There's no such thing as haunted houses. And if there were, this isn't one."

The tips of my ears start to burn. "How would you know? You keep telling me you have no idea who used to live here."

He waves a dismissive hand. "I know you like your spooky stuff, but things like that aren't real."

"Last night wasn't the first time I ended up in the basement."

"What?" Mom's mouth drops open, and when Geoff looks at me, those icy gray eyes are back. There he is—the real Geoff, rising to the surface from beneath all those fake grins.

"I thought I told you to stay out of the basement, Rach."

"And I thought I told *you* my name is *Rachel*."

"You two—" Mom's sounding alarmed now. She's never liked it when people fight around her, but I'm not backing down.

"And for your information, I don't go in that basement because I want to. Something's pulling me down there. I can't control it."

Geoff pauses for a moment and then lets out an overly hearty laugh that makes me want to shove him off his chair. Just like that, he's back to his fake cheery façade.

"Look. I know what this is really about, okay? You don't have to do this, Rach*el*."

"Do what?" I blink, genuinely confused. The way he's able to switch back and forth between cold fury and that cloying cheerful act makes my head spin.

"I'm sorry. I truly am." Warmth comes back into his eyes as he leans towards me. "Maybe I sprung the whole marriage thing on you and your mom a little too fast. Maybe I should have given it more time. I was thinking about myself and what I wanted, and that wasn't fair to you."

"But that's not—"

"See, I just want us all to be happy together. But I promise you: I'm not trying to replace your dad. I know nobody could. Especially not me."

"No!" I slam a fist on the table. "This has nothing to do with that."

Geoff and Mom stare at each other before Geoff speaks up again.

"You know, I've never been a big believer in family counseling, but I wonder if it would help here. Might be someone in town we could talk to."

When Mom nods, something flares in my chest. I just heard her tell Geoff she thought the basement was creepy. Why is she pretending this is some family issue now?

"Jesus. Mom? Geoff? Are either of you listening to anything I'm saying?"

"Of course we are, sweetie." Mom looks like she's about to start crying. "And I think Geoff's right."

A pulse throbs in my head. "I'm not making this up. This is *happening!*"

"Whoa, whoa, whoa." Geoff puts his hands up again. "This isn't about anyone making stuff up. It's just about us trying to find our way together as a family."

If I don't get out of here right now, I'll start screaming and never stop. I run upstairs to my room. Mom calls out behind me, but I'm pretty sure I hear Geoff say, "Let her go."

UPSTAIRS, after giving the door an extremely satisfying slam, I throw myself on my unmade bed. My throat's tight, and heat surges behind my eyes as I hold back tears. I don't want to give either of them the satisfaction of seeing me cry. It doesn't surprise me that Geoff wouldn't believe me, but Mom? Is it wrong for me to expect her to be on my side? Why does she let Geoff steamroll over both of us?

I have to talk to someone, so I pick up my phone. My fingers are shaking so hard I can barely type. My texts to Elena don't get a response.

But then another text bubble comes in.

Hi. You up yet?

It's Nick.

Oh god. I never slept.

Why not?

Can you meet me at Milledge's? I need coffee. And a Toby fix.

I tell Nick I'll see him soon, then wash up and pull on a purple T-shirt and a long black skirt. Mom comes upstairs as I'm sweeping my hair back in a ponytail.

"Rachel? Do you want to talk about what happened before?"

"Not in the slightest. I'm going out."

"I'm not sure that's a good idea right now. We shouldn't avoid talking about things that are upsetting us." Mom tugs at a strand of her hair as she talks.

"I don't want to be in this place right now, Mom. And what's the point? You don't believe me anyway."

Her shoulders sag. "Sweetie, nobody said that."

"Geoff sat there accusing me of making this all up because you're getting married. And you didn't say a word. You keep letting him talk over me and shut me down. I think you just don't want to hear what I'm trying to tell you. And that counseling thing? He's trying to make this into some family dispute I'm causing, and you're just going along with it." I fix Mom with a glare.

"Look, I'm sorry." Mom turns slightly pink. "This is all so devastating. I honestly don't know what to do here."

"Being on my side instead of his would help," I snap, shoving past Mom and down the stairs before she can say anything else. Nobody tries to stop me as I hurry out into the humid morning, grab my bike, and ride off.

TOBY GREETS me as I walk into the bright, airy bookstore, and I kneel to hug him. He pants happily as I rub his soft ears.

"Hi, buddy. It's good to see you today," I murmur into his fur.

"Hello again, Rachel," Ms. Milledge says. "I think your friend is waiting in the back."

Sure enough, Nick's sitting at the pale wooden counter with a cup of coffee and a latte in front of him.

"This is what you like to drink, right?" He pushes the latte towards me as I slide onto the stool next to his.

"God, yes. Thank you. It's perfect." I take a sip as he studies my face.

"What's wrong?" he asks.

"You should ask me what's right. It would take a lot less time to answer *that*."

And everything spills out, starting with the surprise engagement yesterday afternoon. Then the sounds, the visions, and the waking up in the basement. Mom's inability—no, *refusal*—to believe any of it, and the way Geoff acted towards me when Mom wasn't around. I didn't want to tell Nick about any of this yet, but once it starts, it rushes out in a tide that I can't stop.

Nick's eyes get bigger as I talk and talk, and I can't tell what's going on behind them. Will he think I'm a freak and run out of the store? Well, better to find out now.

"Do you think I'm faking this too?" I ask him when I'm finished getting it all out.

He stares at me with those wide dark eyes for a minute, his lips slightly parted, and I'm sure his answer is going to be *yes*.

"No. Of course I don't." He reaches out and squeezes my arm, and I want to cry but don't dare do it in front of him.

"I mean, all this crap with Mom and Geoff would be bad enough without the damn house getting into things too, you know?"

"Yeah." He shakes his head. "That's so bizarre. And nothing like this has ever happened to you before?"

"Never. Okay, I snuck down to the basement once before just to see what was down there after Geoff told me to stay out." Nick chuckles. "I didn't see anything that time, though. And besides, how am I getting past a locked door in my sleep?"

"I don't know. Did someone maybe leave it unlocked by accident?"

I stare down at the counter. "Mom said they had to unlock it to get to me."

Nick tilts his head, looking thoughtful. "Any idea who these people you've been seeing are?"

"No." But then I think about it. "Maybe. There's something kind of familiar about the man who came out of that room, but he was all in shadow."

Nick frowns. "You should have called me last night."

"To do what? Ask you to come scare the ghosts away?"

"I don't know." He looks down at his hands. "I just wish there was something I could do."

I smile. "You're doing it now. It's so good to talk to someone who doesn't think I'm a deranged liar, you know?"

His hand tightens on my arm. "I believe you, I swear. Whatever it is that's going on, you know you can talk to me about it."

At his words, all the anger and pain inside me start to lift like storm clouds parting to reveal the sun. At last, someone's on my side in this stupid, dark, scary place.

"So, what else is there to do around here?" I ask at last. "I don't know if I want to go to the graveyard again, but I don't want to go home yet, either. Like, at all."

He grins. "Have you been to Rocket Pop?"

I haven't. He takes my hand and leads me out of the bookstore and down the street.

Rocket Pop makes me think of Willy Wonka's factory. Glass bins and holders full of candies of every different color and shape line the walls. The shelves are stuffed with candy toys, bags and boxes of jellybeans, taffy, and chocolates. Pop songs from the fifties play on the sound system, and the scent of fudge hangs heavy in the air. I want all of it at once, but I'm too embarrassed to buy a ton of candy in front of Nick. Still, he makes me laugh when he buys an oversized swirled rainbow lollipop and presents it to me with a flourish as if it's a bouquet of roses.

He holds my hand as we walk down Main Street, and I squeeze his fingers. Someone wants to be with me. Someone knows about all the scary, bizarre stuff going on in my life and still cares. It makes me feel safe—like I mean something to someone and have a place in the world.

Gram said Mom feels that way about Geoff, but how can she? He's annoying and loud and fake. He's nothing like Nick.

Then, up ahead, I notice a small group of people in lavender shirts standing by an old stone building, holding candles and signs. Flower bouquets line the grass where they stand. A woman holds up a poster with a girl's face on it, and as we draw closer, I recognize her. It's Melissa Ann Simmons, the girl from the missing person flyer in the bookstore.

"What's that about?" I ask Nick.

"Well, that girl disappeared from around here a while ago. Her family holds a vigil every year on her birthday to remind people to keep looking for her." He shakes his head, rubbing the back of his neck with his free hand.

"Did you know her?"

"Nah. I might have seen her around town, but I never met her or anything. I didn't know who she was until she was gone."

"That's really sad." We walk past the group of people. Nick stares at the ground, and I stop talking as we pass. It seems like the respectful thing to do.

"Hey—have you been down to the river yet?" he asks.

"No."

"I don't know about you, but staring at water always makes me feel better when I'm having a crappy day. I don't know why or how, but it works." He smiles down at me. "Want to check it out?"

"That sounds amazing."

We head to his car, and he drives us through a part of town I've never seen. We pass houses that look nothing like the perfectly matched McMansions in the neighborhood near Morgan House. Small, dilapidated older houses sit next to larger, newer-looking ones. Nick turns onto another gravel path and coasts down to a parking lot where a few other cars sit.

"Here we are. Follow me."

He helps me out of the car and leads me to a gravel path between a clump of trees. The path leads downhill, and the tree roots sticking up through the ground give me visions of tripping and falling down the hill. But Nick reaches back and takes my hand before that can happen. His warm fingers closing around mine make me feel supported.

I hear the river before I see it: Water rushes past and laps up against the banks, and birds call to each other. The trees thin out as we walk further downhill, and then the river is in front of us, blue and wide. Kayakers paddle through the water while people climb over the huge rocks that line the shore. The sun sparkles off the river's surface. There's a warm, earthy smell in the air.

We walk to a bench by the water and sit close together.

"I just like it here," he says, shrugging. "It's peaceful. Even when lots of people are around."

"Yeah. It's so beautiful." And it is. He knew exactly what I needed right now. The sun shines down on us, and the warmth of his hand in mine makes me forget about Morgan House's basement.

"Rachel?"

When I glance at him, he's studying my face closely.

"What's up?" I ask.

He smiles, and for a moment, time slows down. It feels like the entire world around us—the kayakers, the stones, the river itself—fades away, leaving just him in front of me with his eyes fixed on mine. My heartbeat sounds in my ears.

Nick leans in and kisses me. It's a cautious, gentle kiss, as though he isn't sure how I'm going to respond. His lips taste faintly of salt, and my heart skips a beat. Then it soars as I lean in and kiss him back.

"Sorry." He pulls away quickly and looks down at his hands, and his dark hair falls over his face. "I guess I got carried away."

"It's fine. Extremely fine." Everything inside me tingles as I watch him.

"It's just..." He sighs, shaking his head. "I lost someone. Someone I cared for."

"You lost? You mean..."

"Miranda. She had pneumonia. And she died before I got a chance to tell her how I felt."

I reach out, touch his hair, and brush it back from his face so I can look into his eyes.

"I'm so sorry, Nick. God." I hurt for him and all the loss he's already suffered.

"It's not something I talk about much." He raises his head and meets my eyes at last. "But when I meet people I like, sometimes I move a little fast. And I've wanted to do that ever since I first saw you."

"You thought that when you saw me all sweaty and gross at the bookstore?"

That makes him smile.

"You didn't look sweaty or gross to me." My ears get hot at his words.

We watch the river together, our fingers entwined and my head on his shoulder, not saying anything else. I replay that kiss in my head over and over again. I like that he didn't just grab me and ram a slobbery tongue down my throat the way Adam White did on one of my only dates.

Nick makes me realize how unusual it is to find people who know how to sit with someone and *not* talk. Almost anyone else would be running their mouths, embarrassed by the silence, thinking they had to say something. But Nick and I sit side by side, enjoying the sunlight and the rushing water, warmth spreading through me as he holds my hand. He knows he doesn't have to say a word. And he doesn't make me feel like I have to talk, either.

And then my phone buzzes in my purse. I groan and pull it out.

Sweetie? Can you come home soon?

It's Mom. I roll my eyes and ignore the message.

"What's up?"

"Mom wants me back at the house."

"Eh. Tell her she can wait." Nick squeezes my hand a little harder.

But the phone buzzes again, and I check.

Someone's coming who really wants to see you.

It's probably Gram. Mom's been known to pull her into fights before.

"Sounds like my grandmother's on her way over. And it would be nice to see her. She's not full of shit like the rest of them are." Unless they've gotten to her, too.

We leave our bench and trudge uphill through the trees to Nick's car, and he drives me back to where my bike is chained up outside of Milledge's. I drop the giant rainbow lollipop in my bike basket before heading home. He gives me another quick kiss before driving off.

"This better be extremely good, Mom," I mutter as I ride down the bike path back to the house. I'm still warm and happy from the kiss, but the good feelings I had from being with Nick fade away as I make my way down the gravel drive and parts of Morgan House appear through the trees. It's as if the place is hiding behind them and peeking out, watching for me. Why is it always so ridiculously dark back here? The trees are so thick it feels like night, even in the middle of the day. I think again about the basement, wondering what's lurking in and around this place.

But when I finally reach the house, I see it at once: A red Lexus SUV sitting outside on the gravel drive, bright in the gloom. That's not Gram's car. That's ...

My heart leaps as I drop the bike off outside and hurry through the front door.

Elena and her parents are sitting in the living room.

Chapter Eleven

BACKGROUND CHECKS

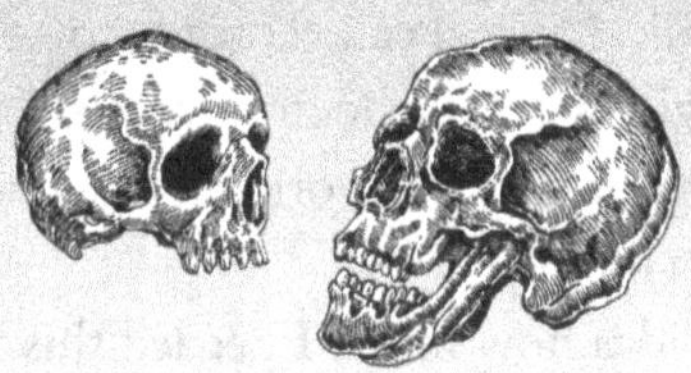

"LANEY? OH MY GOD." I've always found Elena completely adorable with her masses of curly brown hair and huge hazel eyes. But she's never looked as good as she does right now in Geoff's living room. I drop Nick's giant lollipop on the coffee table and run to throw my arms around my best friend.

"Hello, Rachel." Dr. Garcia stands and gives me a bright, friendly smile as he holds a handout. The overhead light shines off his glasses as if his eyes are twinkling. Mrs. Garcia's standing behind him, sleek and elegant. She's had her blonde hair cut into a bob since the last time I saw her, and even the simple black T-shirt and pale blue jeans she's wearing look expensive. Mom lurks behind them, brushing lint only she can see off her gray yoga pants. Geoff hovers behind Mom, looking pleased with himself again. I ignore him, focusing on the Garcias. All three of them light this miserable place up and banish all the gloom, rendering Morgan House's dark aura harmless.

"Sweetie?" Mom's still looking tense. "The Garcias were kind enough to ask if you wanted to stay with them for a couple of days."

"God. Of course I do. Are you serious?"

"We thought perhaps a little change of scenery might be in

order. And my Elena misses you." Dr. Garcia gives me another kind smile, and I could cry.

I know I should be embarrassed. Mom must have called the Garcias while I was gone and told them I was acting unhinged, and now they're here to collect the runaway brat.

But Elena's all bright and happy and I don't care what they think might have happened if it means I can get out of this house, even for a little while. "Sure. I can get ready to go now!"

"Sounds like just what the doctor ordered!" Geoff crows, and I wonder how long he had that cornball line ready to go. I hurry upstairs, and Elena follows.

"You have no idea how much I needed this." I rush back and forth between my bathroom and the bedroom, grabbing clothes, pajamas, my toothbrush, and my laptop and shoving them into my overnight bag.

"Rachel, slow down." Elena laughs at my haste. "You don't have to pack, like, everything you own. It's only for a couple of days."

"Can't it be longer? You're sure I can't move in? I'll live in the hall closet or something."

Elena steps closer and lowers her voice, her eyes wide. "I don't blame you. This place is so freaking creepy. Mama didn't even want to come inside."

"How much do your parents know, Laney? About what's going on here?"

Elena shakes her head. "Your mom called my mom this morning. Far as I know, they just think you're having a rough time accepting Geoff."

I snort, tossing deodorant into the bag. "Well, that much is definitely true. But I seriously wish that's all it was."

Elena pivots, looking all around my bedroom and stretching her arms out. "This house sure is big, though. I think you could fit three of your old places in here."

"Size isn't everything." I yank on the zipper until it finally closes. "Let's get the hell out of here."

MOM AND GEOFF walk us outside to the Garcias' SUV. Mom hugs me harder than usual before turning to Elena's parents to thank them again so profusely that it gets a little embarrassing. She's acting like I'm a complete trainwreck, and they're kind enough to take me off her hands. Is that the way my mother sees me now?

"You girls have a good time now. And don't do anything I wouldn't do!" Geoff chuckles as if he invented that line as we climb into the car. He's grinning like he just won the lottery, and it occurs to me that he's probably as happy to see me go as I am to get out of here.

Glad I'm finally doing something he approves of.

As Dr. Garcia drives down the gravel path away from Morgan House, I turn to watch it disappear behind the trees with no small amount of satisfaction. The worn bricks and the weird arched windows disappear from my view. *You have no power here, Morgan House.*

"Oh my god. That guy is such a dork," Elena says. I laugh.

"*Elena.*" Mrs. Garcia turns around from the front seat to glare at her.

"What? He is."

"I imagine the poor fellow's doing the best he can. This sort of thing can be a difficult transition for everyone," Dr. Garcia says.

The morning with Nick and then Elena's unexpected appearance had put Geoff out of my mind, but now he returns with a vengeance. I won't forget his steely eyes as he asked me who I'd been talking to. Nor do I buy the excuse he cooked up about being freaked out by finding me in the basement. Something's not right about how he's been acting, especially when Mom isn't around to see.

So, what do I do about it?

ELENA'S HOUSE isn't much smaller than Morgan House, but it's vastly different both outside and inside. The brick exterior and pale trim look bright and well-kept, and the huge windows let in lots of sunlight, amplified by the pale yellow walls. Paintings and sculptures in vivid primary colors decorate the wide-open rooms. The air feels crisp and cool from the central AC and always carries a slight scent of potpourri. There's none of the stuffiness and mustiness I've come to associate with Morgan House.

I love Elena's house, Elena's big noisy family. Sure, Elena's little sister Laura, a clone of Elena but with lighter hair, gets on my nerves the way she always buzzes around us like a gnat. And maybe it bothers me a bit that her older brother David barely registers my existence most of the time. David's curly black hair and piercing dark eyes make me think of Nick with a slightly guilty twinge. I had a crush on David way before I met Nick, which only intensified at Elena's quinceañera last year when David kept up a sarcastic commentary about the other guests that had me dying of stifled laughter. David's still cute as hell, even if he'll never see me as anything more than his little sister's little friend.

But the idea of having a rowdy, happy family in a house full of light, noise, and love always spurred a stupid sense of longing in me. And now the house feels like it's my last remaining true home —a place where I remember feeling safe and content. My childhood house was sold long ago, and I'll never, ever consider Morgan House mine.

We eat a quick lunch of hummus, pita bread, and carrots in the sun-drenched kitchen and head down to the basement to watch the latest superhero movie with Laura trailing after us. I've been getting a little bit tired of those movies, but Elena keeps talking about how funny this one is. Maybe a few hours of hot guys in tight costumes will help get my mind off everything else.

We settle into the overstuffed purple sofa in the finished basement as Elena pulls the movie up on the TV.

Before the movie starts, I send Nick a quick text.

I'm out of town for a couple of days with a friend of mine from home. See you when I get back?

He takes a minute to text back *OK*.

And that's it.

That's *it?* That feels so cold and abrupt, and something sharp stings in my middle for a second. But then Elena starts the movie, and I decide not to worry about it. I feel better than I have in ages, like I'm finally getting over being sick for weeks. The sofa is lush and comfortable.

I'm confused when I realize Elena and Laura are staring at me, and the movie's end credits are rolling.

"Uh oh. What'd I miss?" I didn't even realize I'd fallen asleep.

"Like the *entire* movie," Laura says.

"Ugh. I didn't sleep much last night." I rub my eyes. "The house didn't let me."

"That's stupid," Laura declares. She's three years younger than us and believes she knows everything. "How can a house keep you awake?"

"You didn't see that place, turdbrain," Elena says. "It's super creepy. I can't imagine anyone wanting to live there on purpose."

"That's Geoff for you." I shake my head.

THAT NIGHT, the Garcias take us all out to dinner at Dave & Buster's, and I play video games and skee ball with Elena and David while Laura hovers around us.

When we get back to the Garcia house, I'm not the slightest bit tired. The stimulation of the arcade lights and machines, and the excitement of being out of Morgan House and away from Geoff, have me all wound up.

I sit cross-legged on an inflatable mattress next to Elena's bed and open my laptop. Elena flops on her Hello Kitty bedspread and looks over my shoulder.

"Whatcha doing?"

"I want to find out more about the jackass. I don't think Mom actually knows very much about him."

"Aw, come on." Elena swats my shoulder. "Do you seriously have to do that right now? The whole point of this was getting you away from that guy for a little while."

She's right, and I feel a little stab of guilt. "I'm sorry, Laney. But the connection out there's still crappy. And I want to do it when they can't catch me looking because Geoff would get pissed off if he knew I was doing this. This won't take long, I promise."

She scowls, propping her chin on a hand. "Okay, but it better not."

I open Google and type *Geoff Barber* into the search bar. The first results are his LinkedIn profile and bio page at the marketing firm where he works. Both websites sport the same professional photo of him with his big fake smile, and I shudder at the sight.

"Don't they have sites where you can download personal info about people? Like criminal records and stuff?" Elena asks, scooching closer to lean over my shoulder and look at the screen.

"Maybe. You need a credit card for those, right?" Mom would have questions, and lots of them, if something like that showed up on the card she lets me use for emergencies. But Mom marrying Geoff *is* an emergency as far as I'm concerned.

"No idea," Elena says. "I'm not exactly an expert at doing background checks."

"No time like the present to learn." I keep scrolling. A few other Geoff Barbers pop up, but they're all too young or too old or too blond or brunette or otherwise wrong. The one I'm stuck with seems to keep an annoyingly low profile on social media.

I go back to the search bar and type "Geoffrey Barber."

At first, that turns up the same pages I found with the last search, and maybe Elena's onto something with the background check sites. I'll figure out how to explain that charge to Mom later.

But then something catches my eye as I click through the screens of search results.

"GEOFFREY AND CHELSEA — MYSPECIAL-DAY.COM."

Something tingles inside me as I click on the link. But it pulls up a *404 Not Found* page.

"Huh. I guess that one's a dead end," Elena says.

"Not necessarily."

A few months ago, my Ancient History teacher tried to show us a museum exhibit web page that led to a broken link. She'd used a site called the Wayback Machine to get a cached version of the page.

I copy the URL of the My Special Day page, pull up the Wayback Machine site, and paste the URL into the search bar.

A timeline of cached versions pops up, and I click on the oldest one. And as the page comes up, a header reading "*Geoffrey and Chelsea —June 23*" appears.

The main photo on the page remains an empty square for several seconds. I drum my fingers on my laptop, hoping it isn't a broken image. After what feels like forever, the picture finally loads. And we both gasp.

A bride and groom stand together under a floral wedding arch, beaming like the entire world has just been handed to them. The woman has a blonde updo, a flowered headband, a simple white dress, and a radiant smile.

And the groom is unmistakably the same Geoff Barber my mother is going to marry.

Chapter Twelve

SPEAK NOW OR FOREVER HOLD YOUR PEACE

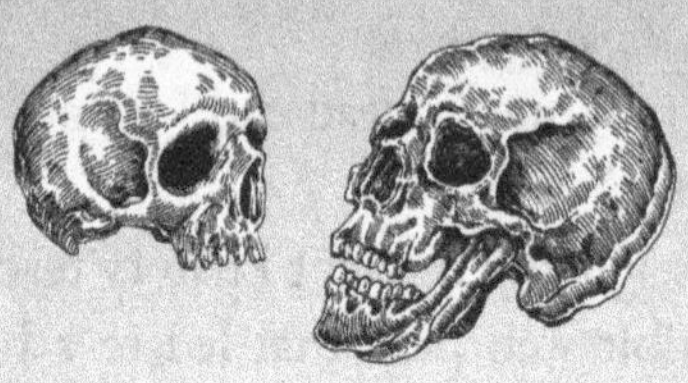

"OH MY GOD," I whisper. I'm shaking from a wild combination of relief—I *knew* he was hiding something—and rage.

"*Whoa*. Does your mom know he was married before?" Elena scoots even closer to me, and now we're both whispering, which doesn't make sense. Geoff and Mom aren't here, and it's not like Elena's parents or her siblings are going to care about any of this. But now I've uncovered something truly shocking, something to be spoken of only in hushed voices.

"She's never mentioned it." And what had Geoff said just yesterday about the wedding? *Your mom did this before.* Implying that he *hadn't*.

"That *slimeball*," I mutter. "I knew it. I knew something was going on with him. He's so fake. And no wonder he gets so pissy whenever I ask who lived there before. He must think I already know." Even his smile in the wedding photo looks sneaky, like he's getting away with something. I've never hated Geoff quite as much as I do right now when he's proven all my suspicions right.

Chelsea looks beautiful in the picture, smiling and happy. Wherever she is now, I hope she's okay.

"Is there anything else about them on that page?" Elena asks.

I click on the Wedding Day tab.

Geoffrey Barber and Chelsea Whittaker Barber became husband and wife on a beautiful early summer day. They were married at All Saints Chapel outside St. Mary, VA; Chelsea's daughter Amber Marie Whittaker was an attendant. The family is planning to live at Geoffrey's home in St. Mary.

"Amber. Which one's Amber?" I scan the page until I see a photo of Geoff and Chelsea with their arms around a teenage blonde girl in a pastel pink dress. The girl's smile looks pasted on, not even close to genuine. She looks a lot like Chelsea with her long face and bright blue eyes, and in the picture, she appears to be about the same age I am now.

"That freaking liar," I say, staring at the pictures. "Look at that."

"Are you positive he never told your mom?"

"She's never mentioned it. And he's been filling her full of crap about how he had a tough childhood without a loving family, and he wants one now. This should have come up."

"Maybe," Elena says, fiddling with her pendant again. "God, this is weird. What are you going to do?"

"I'm telling Mom."

"What if she already knows?"

I shrug. "Then she won't be surprised. But if she doesn't know, then she deserves to hear it before she marries that lying little creep. And I want to know where this Chelsea ended up."

I type *Chelsea Whittaker* into another Google search bar.

The first thing I turn up is the My Special Day page. The next site is a bio page for a real estate agency, but when I check, it's not the same Chelsea.

I try *Chelsea Barber* but get no hits on any woman who looks like the woman in the photos with Geoff.

"Ugh. Why are all these people so damn hard to find?" I ask Elena. I'm not really expecting an answer, and she shrugs.

I go back to Google and do one more search: *Amber Whittaker.*

Most of Amber's social media accounts are private, but I find one that isn't. She's called AmbrosiaGurl, and I recognize her from her user picture. I can't figure out much about Amber from the feed. It's mostly reposts of cat pictures, *Supernatural* memes, or someone trying out new eye makeup.

"Doesn't look like she uses it that much," Elena says.

"Definitely not. But this might be worth a shot. Let me just shoot her a message, and then I'm done here."

Asking a complete stranger about something so personal feels weird, even creepy, but I can't let this go. I need to find out what Amber knows about Geoff, so I take a deep breath and write a direct message to her.

> I know you don't know me, and this is going to seem weird, but my mom is about to marry Geoff Barber. I saw that your mom was married to him too. He's never said anything about her, and I wondered if something happened there that he's not being honest about. If this is too strange for you and you don't want to answer, that's fine, but if you could fill me in about anything I might need to know, I'd really appreciate it. Thanks.

If Amber's still using that account, she's probably going to think this is a joke. But it's worth a shot, and I hit *Send* fast before I can chicken out.

With that, I put down the laptop.

"How are you going to tell your mom about this?" Elena asks in such a low voice that I have to lean closer to hear her.

"Hmm, I don't know. Do you think putting a giant billboard on the front lawn with a printout of that wedding page would be too much?" I smirk.

Elena bops my shoulder with a pink throw pillow. "I mean, it's going to be awkward. Especially if Geoff is right there. Maybe you should get her alone before you tell her anything."

"Oh, no. I want Geoff there. I want to see that smug little

asshole's face when I bust him." In fact, I could scream that I've only found out about all this at Elena's, where I can't march right down to Morgan House's living room, thrust the wedding webpage in Mom's face, and say *How do you like your Mr. Wonderful now?*

"What do you think your mom will do?"

To me, there's only one possible answer to that.

"Hopefully, she'll realize that this guy can't be trusted and get the hell out of there. Anyway, I don't want to talk about him anymore. What's been going on here since I got dragged off to the Hellmouth?"

Elena fills me in on what everyone has been up to over the summer. The kids at the day camp where she's been working are total brats. David has a new girlfriend, news that I would have found depressing if I didn't have Nick waiting for me back in St. Mary. I wonder what Nick might say when I tell him what I've found out about Geoff and his past.

Then Elena talks about our classmates and people she's seen at church or at parties over the summer. I didn't care about my old high school much at all while I was there. It was something to be endured until it was time for college.

Now I can't believe I won't be there when school starts up again in September. Sometimes, I pore over everyone's social media, commenting and participating as if I can will myself into being with all of them again. But people don't respond to me the way they used to. I'm lucky if my comments get a few "likes."

Out of sight, out of mind.

But maybe not for much longer.

We eventually drift off, and I sleep soundly, secure in the knowledge that I won't hear dragging noises in the middle of the night or wake up in Geoff's basement. And when Mom finds out what I know, we'll move away, and I will never have to deal with any of those things again.

For the first time since we moved, I truly believe everything is going to be okay.

THE NEXT DAY, Mrs. Garcia takes everyone to Six Flags Amusement Park. I text Nick a picture of myself strapped into a roller coaster. But he doesn't respond. After swallowing a rush of hurt feelings, I try not to dwell on it. He must be busy with the band. Or one of his jobs.

The day after that, Dr. Garcia and Elena have to take me back to St. Mary. Even though I feel like I've got the upper hand—something Geoff doesn't know I know about him, something which might be enough to undo everything that's happened in the last few months—I still don't want to go back there.

"You're sure I can't live in your room or something? I promise I won't eat much," I say to Elena. And I'm not even kidding. If the Garcias offered to let me stay, I'd unpack my bag again without being asked twice.

But of course, they don't ask. My mood sours as we cross the state line between Maryland and Virginia. Well before it's actually in sight, Morgan House looms larger and larger in my head like it's reaching for me, darkness rushing towards me in the daylight, anxious to drag me back within its walls.

Mom runs out of the house to hug me when I get out of the car as if I've been gone for years rather than a couple of days.

"Did you have a good time, sweetie?" Mom asks, searching my face.

"Oh yes. The *best*." Mom looks satisfied with my big smile.

Mom invites the Garcias in for coffee, and Geoff's in the kitchen setting the pot up when we all walk inside.

"Hi there, Rach! Good to see you again."

You might not think so when you find out what I know about you, you shady little creep.

"Thanks," I tell him. Elena and I smirk at each other. Geoff hums and scoops coffee into the pot, oblivious.

We all sit in the living room, clutching our cups. After a few days in Elena's bright, happy house, everything in here is so dim and depressing. Mom can't thank Elena's father enough, and Dr. Garcia insists it was no trouble. I'm welcome any time, and he hopes the break has helped things.

"I hope so, too," Mom says, shooting a sideways glance at me.

Oh, it has, Mom. It's helped a lot. You have no idea. But you will.

I walk Elena and her father out to the car when they leave. Elena hugs me tightly before getting into the SUV.

"Be careful," she whispers.

I stare up at Morgan House after the Garcias leave. It towers over me, as dark and unwelcoming as ever, even in broad daylight.

But I have a weapon now, and the house doesn't scare me the way it did before.

GEOFF HEADS out to the grocery store right after the Garcias leave, announcing that he wants to grill something as a special meal for my return.

Mom and I wash the coffee cups together, and then she gets some chocolate ice cream from the freezer. She takes two small purple dishes from the cabinets.

"Dessert in the middle of the day?" I ask. "That's decadent."

She grins. "Hey, dinner's not for a while. Let's go crazy." She opens the ice cream carton and scoops it into our dishes. "Besides, I wanted to talk to you about something."

I should have known there was a catch. "What's up?"

"Let's sit down." She carries the dishes to the kitchen table and pats the chair across from hers. We sit, and she spoons a little ice cream into her mouth before talking.

"Did you have a good time at Elena's?"

"Yeah. It was great."

She's trying to act casual, but she starts picking at her cuticles when she puts the spoon down. Which means something's up. And now I don't want the ice cream anymore.

"Are you sure?"

"Of course, Mom. Why?"

"You've seemed a little tense since you came home. Like something's on your mind."

Am I being that obvious? "Everything's fine."

"Well, okay. Just wanted to check."

Neither one of us is eating now. Why is she only now noticing that I'm tense when I've been that way pretty much the entire time we've lived in this house? "Mom? Is something going on?"

"Nothing bad, sweetie."

"Then what?"

She dabs at her mouth with a paper napkin before answering. "Geoff's planning to go to Baltimore and get our marriage license this week."

No. Already? My heart sinks. "Baltimore? Why?"

"He's always liked that city, and so do I. The harbor is so pretty. We were thinking about getting a couple of hotel rooms overlooking the water. One for us and one for you."

I wring my paper napkin. If I want to tell Mom about Chelsea Whittaker, this is a perfect opportunity to do it.

"Mom ..." I start. But I didn't really plan what I was going to say when the time came, and the right words aren't coming now.

She clears her throat. "Sweetie, I just wanted you to know something. I don't like that basement, either. I unlocked the door and did a banishing spell down there while Geoff was out golfing. I might have to do it a few more times, but it should help get all that bad energy out of there."

She means well and believes in her spells, so I fight the urge to tell her I seriously doubt her crystals and incense are a match for the things I've seen and felt in that place.

But then Geoff returns from his supermarket trip. He's ridiculously excited about the steaks he bought, and he brandishes a plastic package of veggie kabobs for me.

This doesn't seem like the time to blurt out his big secret.

But then when, Rachel? Speak now or forever hold your peace.

Geoff was married before. And I'm pretty sure my mom doesn't know about it.

Wow. What a creep, hiding that.

I'M in my bedroom texting with Nick, hoping he'll have some good advice about what I should do. He's been a lot more talkative now that I'm back in Morgan House, and I want to know: When should I drop the bomb?

I need to tell Mom. But I'm not sure how.

Just be careful.

I frown at the screen as if he can see me.

This is being careful. She should know about all this before she actually marries the lying jerk.

Right. But if she didn't know this, it's going to hurt her a lot, and you don't know how she'll react. What if she goes into denial and all you do is piss the guy off? And what do you think the idiot boyfriend might do while you're still in the house?

That's something I hadn't considered. I'll probably still have to live in Geoff's house, at least for a little while, after telling Mom about his past life.

> Maybe Mom will just dump him on the spot and move us out. Besides, he wouldn't hurt me. I don't think anyhow.

> You don't think!? You said you barely know this guy. You can't be sure what he might do, right?

I bite my lip.

> But that's all the more reason to clue Mom in, isn't it? He's talking about getting the marriage license this week.

> Look—just don't just go blurting it out without having any idea of what's going to happen next, OK? Be careful. You should have a plan.

Nick's raised a disturbing possibility in my head, and I finally allow several thoughts I'd been suppressing to come to the forefront of my mind:

The voices. The dead woman in the bathroom. Geoff hiding a previous marriage. His weird, hostile attitude when he found me in the basement. And the way he gets irate when I ask who lived in the house before him.

What's he hiding?

What *did* happen here?

What does he know about it?

On my phone, I check my messages to see if I've heard back from Amber Whittaker. There's nothing yet.

Then I open Google and type *Morgan House, St. Mary, VA* into the search window. The phone takes an annoyingly long time to pull up any results, and it doesn't have that many to show. There are a few sales listings about Geoff buying the place and one random blurb from several years ago that catches my eye.

> *Jenna Rollins, 18, was last seen with an unidentified male heading to the south side of St. Mary in the vicinity of Morgan*

House. The police searched the vacant property but no indicators were found that Rollins might have been there.

Jenna Rollins has wavy brown hair and a big smile in the one picture I can find of her. Another missing girl like the one whose vigil I'd passed with Nick—and this one was even seen near Morgan House. My pulse quickens.

But the article says Morgan House was vacant when Jenna disappeared. Geoff hadn't even moved here yet. And now I don't know what to think.

"Rach?" Geoff calls up the stairs. "Chow's on!" I swear, if he calls me Rach one more time, I'm going to call him Chelsea and see what he does.

We eat outside on the back porch. It's a pleasant summer evening, a rare non-humid night in July. A breeze ruffles the trees, making a steady and soothing rustling sound. Dinner is calm at first, even though I'm jittery and unsettled inside, waiting for just the right time to tell Mom what I know.

As I reach for another veggie kebab, Geoff starts again.

"You know, growing girls need lots of protein and iron. You sure you're getting that with just vegetables and tofu?"

He has got to be kidding me. It's like he just can't help himself. "Do I *look* like I'm starving?"

"Geoff," Mom says. "Come on. Not tonight."

Geoff ignores Mom. "It's none of my business, I know. But you look pale and tired all the time. I'm not saying you have to have steak every night. Even *I* don't do that." He laughs. "But maybe you ought to hold your nose and choke down a little meat once in a while. Might even help with that sleepwalking thing."

"I'm *fine*. I don't need meat. Nobody needs meat. Some cultures don't eat it at all, and they're way healthier than Americans." The sensation that there's an angry beast inside me, something trying to claw its way out, flares up again. Something's growing and pulsing inside my chest, taking up room, squashing my stomach. This knowledge I've been hiding wants out, and it wants out now.

And Geoff won't shut up.

"And honestly? It's kind of a pain for us to have to buy and cook different meals for you. When I was growing up, everyone ate the same thing, or they didn't eat at all."

Mom shakes her head. "Geoff, she's fine. She's almost never sick, and her doctor said she's in perfect health. If anything, *we* ought to be doing what *she* does."

"Heh. Not likely." Geoff shakes his head, smirking. "I can't believe a little meat once in a while would be that big of a deal. I mean, I've seen you wearing leather shoes. Didn't an animal die for those, too?"

Somewhere inside, I feel a slight surge of pleasure that Mom's taking my side for once. But the beast is angry and insistent. It wants out. It's not going to be denied this time. My blood roars in my ears.

"We were having a nice night, Geoff," I say, keeping my voice even. "Do you want to do this?" It's a warning. His final warning.

"Do what?" Geoff's eyes widen. "So, I'm not allowed to have an opinion now if you don't like it? We're going to be a family. Things won't work that way."

And that's it. I surrender, unlock the cage, and unleash the starving beast.

"Okay, fine." I take a deep breath, and my lips curl into a smirk. Here I go. "I'm very curious about something. What's your *opinion* on men who were married before and don't tell their fiancées about it?"

All the color drains from Geoff's face as he blinks those gray eyes and stares at me.

Holy shit. He didn't tell Mom. He really didn't, and now look at him.

It's as if the entire area around us, and maybe the entire planet, freezes in place. Mom's hand stops as she's reaching for the pepper grinder. Geoff is slack-jawed, that inane grin finally wiped off his face. Even the rustling trees in the woods fall silent. The only thing I can hear is my pulse pounding in my ears.

For a split second, I wish I could take it back, unsay what I said, hit a cosmic rewind button, and stuff the words back in my mouth. Nick was right. I've started something new—something big and more than a little scary. Something I don't have a game plan for.

Mom's mouth falls open, and she lowers her hand. "Rachel! What on earth was that supposed to mean?"

I draw another long breath, hoping it will slow down my thundering heart. "Why don't you ask him? In fact, why *didn't* you ask him about this before?"

Mom glances between me and Geoff, who's still white-faced and silent.

"Geoff? What's she talking about?"

He opens and closes his mouth a few times before managing an answer. "You *have* been talking to someone." He points at me, but I'm not having this.

"No, Geoff. I found it out all on my own. You told me to look stuff up online, and I did. The wedding site was still cached. You didn't cover your tracks as well as you thought."

"I don't have any tracks to cover." Those ice-chip eyes are back now as he stares at me.

"Found *what* out?" Mom's voice is loud and shaky, and once again, I briefly wish I hadn't let Geoff needle me into losing it. But there's no taking anything back now.

"Geoff was married before, Mom. Didn't he tell you? No, forget that. He obviously didn't. But don't you wonder why he'd keep that from you? I sure do."

Mom looks like someone slapped her. Something's burning in my midsection, and it's no longer the beast inside. It's guilt. I knew this would hurt Mom, but seeing the anguish in her eyes as she looks between me and him is a lot harder than I imagined.

"Geoff? Is she telling the truth?"

"I can show you their wedding webpage, Mom. There are pictures. Her name was Chelsea. Chelsea Whittaker."

"Don't do that, Rachel." At least Geoff is calling me by my actual name now, though his tone is sharp enough to cut.

"Why not? What don't you want her to know about?" I raise my chin and glare at Geoff.

Mom's eyes shimmer with tears as Geoff glances between her and me. I take some small satisfaction that he's not going to smarm his way out of this one, even as watching Mom's face crumble makes everything ache inside me.

"I was going to tell you, Tara." His face flushes pink. "I didn't want you to find out like this."

Mom slams her napkin down on the table.

"When were you going to tell me? Why did I have to find out from my daughter?"

Geoff can't meet her eyes. "Because it's still hard for me to talk about. It was a tough situation. That marriage didn't end well."

"And you thought I wouldn't understand that?" Mom's crying openly now. "Trust is a huge thing with me, Geoff. You know that. And you know why. Or at least I *thought* you did."

Trust? Something about that exchange piques my curiosity.

Geoff reaches a hand towards Mom's shoulder, but she shrinks away from him. "Tara, I was going to tell you. It's just something that's still very painful. And I'm sure you know what that feels like."

Mom studies her half-eaten steak for a minute before standing up.

"Where are you going?" he asks.

She glares at both of us. "I need some time to think." Geoff starts to say her name, but he's not fast enough. She spins around and slams back into the house. The door bangs shut behind her, rattling the porch.

You didn't do anything wrong, I tell myself as something throbs behind my eyes, and my face burns. *Not to this lying idiot, anyhow.*

"Well, I sure hope you're happy now." Geoff's face is deep red as he glares at me.

"No, I'm not. And this isn't my fault. Did you actually think you could keep this a secret forever?"

"It wasn't your place to tell her." His voice is as frigid as his eyes. His body is half out of his chair, leaning towards me, and a wild thought flashes through my head: *Hit me, asshole. I dare you.* My heart's beating almost out of control. The air around us feels like it's crackling with furious energy.

"She's my mom. I have to look out for her. She's all I have. And I'm all she has."

Geoff shakes his head. "It doesn't have to be that way. I could be there for both of you if only you'd give me a chance."

"Not when you're keeping the truth from us, you can't." I try to hang on to that feeling of righteous rage, of letting Geoff know he can't boss me around and deceive us without facing consequences.

"If there's anything else you want to know about me, Rachel, I'd appreciate it if you'd just ask." His eyes and voice feel like a blast of winter on this warm summer evening.

I muster up one last bit of courage and meet his stare. "Okay. Are there any other ex-wives we don't know about yet?"

And again, for just a second, those eyes flash something besides cold. I hold my breath, waiting to see what he'll do now that his cheesy, nice-guy act is falling apart. *Show me who you really are*, I want to tell him.

He stares at me for another long moment before shaking his head. "No, Rachel. There are not. You can search the entire internet if you want. Hire a detective, even. I don't give a damn."

I exhale. The beast is gone now. All that's left is shame.

Geoff's shoulders slump as he backs away from the table.

"You can clean up the dishes," he says in a voice like frost. He slams the door hard enough that the noise echoes through the woods.

Chapter Thirteen

THE ROAD TO HELL

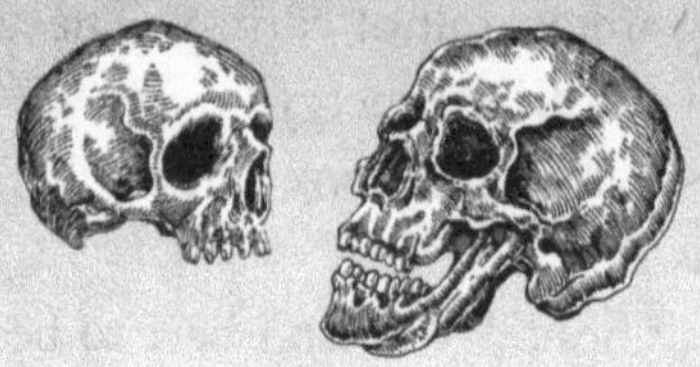

"Oh my God, I'm so stupid. I don't know why I didn't listen to you. You and Elena both tried to tell me and now look."

Nick and I sit on a wrought-iron bench outside of Barkley's Drugs after meeting on Main Street. I'd grabbed my bike and fled Morgan House right after putting all the uneaten food away and cleaning up the dishes.

It's still a warm, pleasant summer night, filled with the sounds of acoustic guitars and the smells of fried food from nearby restaurants. People sit at outdoor tables, talking and laughing, but my guts are churning, and the only thing keeping my food down is my not wanting to get sick on the sidewalk right in front of Nick.

"Well, it's done," Nick says, sounding grim. He rubs my back as I sit bent over, my head in my hands. I can't get any enjoyment from his touch this time. Maybe I don't deserve it. Not after the pain I just caused Mom.

"I swear, I wasn't going to do it that way. But he's just such an ass. We were having a nice dinner outside, and then he started nagging me about eating meat. If he could have just left me alone for one freaking minute, I wouldn't have lost it on him."

I can focus anger on Geoff all I want, but it's the memory of

Mom's devastated face that's making my stomach lurch. I hadn't thought through how Mom would receive that news. Maybe if I had, like both Elena and Nick told me I should have, I'd have been more cautious. Or maybe my motives weren't quite as pure as I told myself they were. I'd been savoring the thought of knocking that smug asshole down a few pegs. Was that maybe more important to me than saving Mom from making a mistake?

"Well, he should have told her. It's not right that she had to hear that from you," Nick says as if he knows exactly what's bothering me.

"Thank you."

I stare at the pavement under my feet for a moment before speaking again.

"What do you think I should do now? Assuming they don't just throw me the hell out?" Maybe now I really can live with the Garcias. That idea doesn't bother me at all.

"I don't know, Rachel. Parental drama is unfamiliar territory for me, you know?"

I wince, remembering how young he was when he was orphaned. "I know. But you were right that I should have thought things through before dropping the bomb. I figured I could at least start listening to you. Now that it's way too late to matter." I wipe my watery eyes and let out a grim chuckle.

Nick rubs his chin and glances away from me for a moment before answering.

"I'd say you need to go home soon and try talking things out with your mom. I mean, he should have told her about his last wife. You should never have had to do that. But maybe tell her you wished you'd been a little more...discreet?"

"Yeah. That's fair." I lean back on the bench, feeling drained and still hot with shame.

Nick starts stroking my hair.

"So, your hair is red naturally?"

"Hm? Oh, yeah." Great. I hadn't thought my roots were bad

enough that anyone would notice them yet. "I haven't been able to dye it again. Geoff won't let me do it in *his* house."

"The red is a pretty color," he says, and then we don't talk for a moment. He's still good at the not-talking thing, as if he senses I need to work things out in my head.

"So, what's going to happen now?" he asks at last. "You think your mom might dump him?"

Something tells me I won't get that lucky, but a girl can hope.

"I don't know. She told him trust was super important to her and that he knew why." I break off for a moment and frown, remembering that. It was a strangely specific thing for Mom to say, and I have no idea what it might mean.

"Well, trust is *always* important in a relationship. Right?"

"That's exactly why it's such a weird thing to have to tell your partner. It should go without saying, shouldn't it?"

"Definitely."

I sigh. "Then again, what the hell would I know? I've never been in a relationship."

He raises his eyebrows. "Seriously?"

Now I'm blushing, but at least the squirmy feeling inside isn't from shame over Mom and Geoff anymore. "I mean, yeah, I've gone out with guys. But a relationship? I never got to the boyfriend stage."

Nick smiles. "Do you want a boyfriend now?"

When I look at him, he leans over and kisses me. His lips are salty and sweet, and it's like he's pulling all the shame and embarrassment out of me as I turn my face up, pressing my mouth harder against his, savoring this moment.

"Are you sure you want to be *my* boyfriend?" I ask when we pull away from each other. "I mean, I'm kind of horrible. I just broke my mom's heart."

Nick shakes his head. "You weren't trying to hurt her. You meant well."

The road to hell is paved with good intentions. Isn't that how the saying goes? I kiss Nick again, but all that soggy embarrassment is back. The road to hell is going to have to take me back to Morgan House, and pretty soon.

When I get back to the house, the lights are on downstairs, but the place otherwise looks empty. The unlit dormer windows upstairs still look like a pair of stern eyes glaring down on me and judging me. The trees around the house rustle in the evening breeze.

In the living room, my mother sits at one end of the sectional, rubbing at her red, blotchy face. Several crumpled tissues are piled in her lap, and her obsidian pendant dangles from her neck again. Geoff's in the armchair, his lips pinched in a thin line. He looks up at me, but she doesn't.

"So, now you walk out of here without telling anyone where you're going?" he says.

"I had my phone." I hold it up. "You could have texted me if you wanted to know where I was."

"Sit down, Rachel." Geoff points at the sectional. I want to tell him not to order me around, but maybe I've caused enough trouble for one night. I sit at the opposite end from Mom.

"I already explained some things to your mom. And now I want you to hear them too."

He clears his throat and studies his fingers before continuing.

"So, yes. You're right. I got married once before. And you're also right that I shouldn't have kept it quiet. I won't agree that it was *your* place to tell anyone, but what's done is done."

Mom's still staring down at her lap.

"Anyhow, the reason I don't like to talk about it is because I feel like I failed them," he says. "Chelsea, the woman I married, had a daughter who was about your age. We didn't get along. And I...I was afraid. I didn't know what your mom might think about that, seeing as she has a teenage daughter, too."

"Amber," I say. Geoff's eyes narrow.

"Yes. Amber. You've been talking to her, right?"

I sigh. I've been trying to, but she still hasn't answered my message. And he doesn't need to know about that anyhow. "No, Geoff. I told you I found your old wedding page on My Special Day, and it mentioned her. I haven't ever talked to either of them."

"Oh. Well." He clears his throat again. "Anyhow, Amber had some serious mental problems. She was hearing voices. She hallucinated. She'd wake us all up screaming in the middle of the night."

Something cold starts creeping into my blood.

"And her mother and I tried to help her. We really did. We took her to doctors. Family therapy. But nothing worked. And I started thinking ... well. I started thinking she was faking it all just to split up me and her mom. She didn't like me. She didn't exactly keep it a secret."

He shakes his head. "I didn't handle it well at all. And Chelsea got angry with me, as she should have. And they ended up leaving me."

He sighs, shaking his head. I expected him to be angrier. I don't know what to make of this subdued Geoff. "And then what?"

"I don't know. Haven't heard from them since I signed the divorce papers. You're the internet sleuth. Why don't you tell me?"

I can't tell if he's going for sarcasm or if that's a serious question. "I have no idea where they are now. I couldn't find out anything else about either one of them."

"Well, then." He shrugs. "Maybe you can imagine how it looked to me when you turned up in the basement screaming the other night."

And my mouth drops open. Even Mom's head finally pops up at that.

"I *wasn't* faking that, Geoff." I'm pissed again.

He holds up his hands. "I know. But still. It brought back some pretty bad memories."

"That's what this Amber was doing?" That's the first thing Mom's said since I got home.

"Not exactly. More the kind of thing where she was hearing voices. Having bad nightmares. Seeing things that weren't there."

Like dead women in the bathroom. Oh my god. What the hell is this house? I'm sick and numb inside again, but this time, it's not because of Mom.

"Honestly, I thought she might be on drugs. She ran with a rough crowd." Geoff frowns. "And she was dating some creepy character in town. Still not sure he wasn't giving her something."

"I'm not doing drugs," I say, feeling indignant.

"I know, Rachel." He studies the living room rug for a moment before continuing. "Maybe it's the house."

That's not something I expected to ever hear from him. "What do you mean?"

"Well, like I said before, it's a big change for you. Your old place was in a busy suburb with lots of people around all the time. So was Amber's. Maybe you just aren't getting used to being way back out here in the woods, mostly alone. I could see where that would scare someone, honestly."

I know this is ridiculous. Whatever's happening here, it's not because I'm a scared little girl too afraid to be out in the country at night.

"I told you before, Geoff—I don't like the energy in that basement," Mom says. "Maybe that's what's affecting these girls so badly." She makes eye contact with me for the first time since I came in. Her sad eyes make me think of Toby at the bookstore, and I have an idea.

"Maybe we could get a dog." They're unlikely to want to let me have anything right now, but a dog could be a good ally out here. Maybe a dog would make everyone happy—calm everything down.

"Oh, no." Geoff crosses his arms. "No dogs."

Of course he'd say no. "Why not?"

"Because when I first moved out here, I went to a rescue and adopted a dog. Gorgeous guy. Golden retriever. His name was Rusty. I figured this would be the perfect place to have a dog, you know? Plenty of room to play and run around in."

"So, what happened?" Mom asks. I'm not sure I want to know.

"I could barely get him out of the car. And Rusty was a big fella, let me tell you. I had to drag him into the house." Geoff winces at the memory. "And he howled constantly. *Arrroooo*, all the time. When he wasn't howling, he was whining. Any time I'd take him out for a walk, I thought he was going to dislocate my arms trying to break free from me and run away.

"At first, I thought Rusty was scared of being in a new place, but he never got better. He'd howl all night long and scratch at the doors, begging to be let out. I had to take him back to the rescue."

Mom shakes her head. "But dogs love having lots of space. What was wrong with the poor thing?"

"Poor thing, nothing. He was perfectly healthy. He was just thrilled to be out of here. I thought maybe I got a crazy dog, so I tried again. Exact same thing happened. And this one was a Rottweiler. They're supposed to be tough, right?" He looks around the living room until his gaze settles on the window facing the woods. "Maybe the dogs just don't like it this far out here. They can hear critters in the trees that we can't, you know?"

So, it's not just me who is affected in horrible ways by this place. Amber was, too. So were Geoff's two dogs. Tonight, I've been focused more on the living inhabitants of Morgan House than what might have been here before, but Geoff's story makes a cold pit form in my chest.

"I've heard you never really know what those rescue animals have been through before they get to you," Mom says, but she sounds hesitant, and she's frowning down at her hands as if she's had a disturbing thought she's trying to talk herself out of.

Nobody says anything for a moment. Whatever energy there was in this room when I walked in is gone. Now it's leaden and humid like a rainstorm came through that made the air even damper and heavier than before. Mom continues to rub her eyes and sniffle while Geoff slumps in his chair as if his story about the dogs has taken all the energy out of him. The only sound is the steady hum of the box fan in the corner.

"Well, anyhow. It's been kind of a whirlwind of a day," Geoff says at last. "I think I might turn in a little early. Watch some TV upstairs or something."

I can't meet his eyes, but I'm sensing ice chips again. After he wanders off, I steal a glance at Mom.

"Are you okay?"

"I don't know yet, Rachel." Mom doesn't look at me.

"I'm sorry, Mom. I shouldn't have just blurted all that out like that." I thought I'd tell her about Geoff and she'd whisk us both out of here, grateful that I'd discovered the truth before she actually married the guy. Somehow, I didn't expect her to be quite this hurt.

She scowls. "You're right. You shouldn't have. You should have come to me privately."

"Well, Geoff should have left me alone at dinner instead of picking at me like he always does. And besides, what difference would it make how I told you? I thought you needed to know the truth about him."

"Did you?" Her head snaps up, and she fixes me with her dark blue eyes. "Or were you trying to get back at Geoff?"

My face burns with the unfairness of this. I know she's upset, but I'm not the one who was lying to her. "Why can't it be both? He's been acting shady since we got here. And now we know why. He was hiding things, Mom. And who knows if I've even found it all?"

She sighs and rubs her forehead. "Rachel, I assure you I'll be getting to the bottom of all that. But that's for me to do. It wasn't your place."

Oh, *now* she wants to learn more about Geoff. My fingernails dig into my palms. "If you'd done that before you dragged us both out here, I wouldn't have *had* to."

Her mouth drops open, and she blinks several times. Her lips move as if she's trying to think of a good retort, but maybe she can't come up with one.

Because I'm right, and she knows it.

"I'm going upstairs too," she says, getting up. "Good night, Rachel."

Mom's footsteps are louder than usual on the stairs. I sit in the living room after she's gone, my temples throbbing as I listen to the sounds of arguing upstairs. I'm not going up there while they're fighting. What if they draw me into it and demand I explain myself again? I don't want to look at either one of them right now.

Anger and resentment whirl in my chest like the box fan spinning in the corner, until I feel like a drop of oil in a scorching skillet. Why the hell is everyone acting like I'm the villain here? This would never have been an issue if Geoff had been honest with Mom from the beginning. Plus, I have to live with the guy, too. Unlike Mom, I get no say in who we share a house with. It wasn't wrong for me to check him out or to tell her what I found. Really, she's the one who should have discovered this. And yet she's acting like she's just as angry with me as she is with him.

Even now, when I might have saved her from making a huge mistake, she still isn't on my side.

The fighting upstairs subsides at last, but the warring emotions in my mind continue. When I retreat to my room, I prop a chair under the doorknob. Nothing is going to pull me down into that basement this time.

But the chair can't prevent everything. As soon as I turn out the light and climb into bed, low sobbing sounds from the hallway break the silence, broken up by gasps and sighs. It might just be Mom, still distraught. Even if it isn't her, it can't be that different from how she must feel right now.

My own eyes flood with tears as I pull the purple blanket over my head and cry over everything that's happened since I was first brought to Morgan House. Because on top of everything else, now I know it's not just me who experiences terrifying things in this place.

But it doesn't happen to everyone. Mom and Geoff can't see just how wrong this house is. Am I going to be accused of trying to wreck their relationship if I get hauled down to the basement again?

The sliver of moonlight on the ceiling fades into darkness, and a vision of that basement door pops into my head. The knob is made of ornate, tarnished metal. Gothic-looking scrolling patterns cover its surface. A red glow surrounds it, outlining it against the concrete wall. Shadows pass underneath the door, and that male voice whispers again, low and ferocious. The words are incomprehensible, but a chill spreads through me nonetheless. I want to move closer, to examine that door, open it, and find out where it leads and who's lurking behind it.

But I'm still in my own bed when the sun rises.

Chapter Fourteen

UNTIL DEATH DO THEY PART

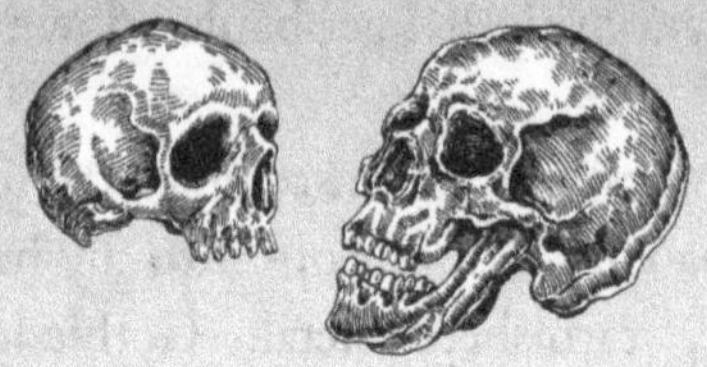

THE NEXT FEW DAYS REDEFINE "AWKWARD." Any rest or feelings of well-being I got from being with Elena and Nick are long gone. The sounds of Mom and Geoff bickering in their bedroom at night carry through Morgan House's walls, but when we're all together, we have almost nothing to say to each other aside from the occasional "Pass the salt."

And it hasn't stopped raining since the night I dropped the bomb, so whenever I try to flee Morgan House on my bike, I get splattered by the giant mud puddles the rain leaves in the long gravel drive. Rumbles of thunder roll through the sky regularly as if reflecting all the free-floating anger in the house.

The only good news is that Morgan House itself has been bizarrely quiet through all this. Nothing comes to my bedroom. I don't end up in the basement. I don't see any dead women in the bathroom. It almost feels like the house is waiting to see what will happen next.

On Tuesday morning, Geoff's already at work by the time I get up, and Mom's in the shower. Not knowing what to do with myself, I text Elena, who's sympathetic and hasn't said "I told you so" even once through all of this.

After she signs off, I decide tea sounds better than coffee

today. In the kitchen, I fill a white enamel kettle with water. A faint whiff of gas floats up as I turn on the burner and place the kettle on the blue flame.

The Lazy Susan cabinet by the stove is cluttered with boxes of crackers and cans of coffee. When I find the Lemon Zinger tea and turn around, Mom's standing in the kitchen doorway with damp hair, her face flushed, her hands on her hips.

"So. We need to talk." She isn't exactly cheerful, but she doesn't sound as pissed as she's been lately.

Even so, I swallow hard before speaking.

"What about?"

"Things have been so tense here for too long. It's time we started moving past that, isn't it? I know Geoff can be overbearing, but he's willing to work on that. Are you?"

"Am I willing to work on what? Doing everything he says?"

She sighs. "On giving him a *chance*, Rachel."

I want to scream. There's only one reason she'd be asking me to do this. "So, you've forgiven him then?"

"Yes. I have."

Something hot flares behind my eyes. "Are you serious? Come on, Mom. If he hid a whole family from you, what else could he be hiding?"

She shakes her head. "He explained why he doesn't like to talk about his ex-wife or his stepdaughter. Weren't you listening?"

"Yeah, but..." This is all happening too fast.

Mom rubs a finger over her chin as if considering what to say next. "He didn't go to work today. He's going to Baltimore to get our marriage license. We have to wait forty-eight hours after he gets it, but we'd like to get married on Saturday."

Saturday? Is she *kidding?* An icy brick drops in my stomach.

"You said if I asked you not to marry Geoff, you wouldn't."

She frowns. "That's right, I did."

"Well, I'm asking you now. Don't do it, Mom. Not until we're sure he isn't hiding anything else."

Mom shakes her head. "If you'd asked me that earlier, I'd have done it without question. But not now. I'm not going to give you unlimited time to play Harriet the Spy and try to dig up something else you can use to humiliate him."

"Something else? Like what? Are you worried he's hiding another ex-wife?" The teakettle begins rattling behind me as the water heats up.

"*Rachel.*" Mom's face is as red as her hair. "Do you think you're the only one who knows how to use the internet? I've done a lot of searching of my own this week. And I found the woman you're talking about. But I didn't find a single thing about him and any other women. Or any other negative information. Did you?"

I didn't, of course, and Mom obviously knows it.

"I didn't find much of anything about him, Mom. Isn't that kind of weird?"

"What's weird about it? He's not a teenager. He doesn't live on social media the way you and your friends do."

"So, you're just going to marry this guy, and tough shit if I don't like it?" I thought the beast inside me was gone for good after I'd spilled the beans about Chelsea, but it's back, kicking and clawing behind my ribs. Wanting out.

Mom folds her arms and scowls. "Watch your mouth. I'm going to marry him, and I'm hoping that you and Geoff will do your best to try to get along with each other. I love both of you. I truly believe we could have a good, strong family together if we can stop the fighting and work at it."

The teakettle interrupts us with a high, piercing whistle. I turn the burner off and take one mug out of the cabinet. Normally, I'd offer to fix Mom a cup too, but after this, she can make her own damn tea. I'm so angry my hands are shaking, and it's all I can do to pour water over a teabag without spilling it all over the counter.

"You know what, Mom?" I turn back to her. "I didn't take you up on your offer right then because I didn't want you to be unhappy. And it'd be really freaking nice if, once in a while, you'd care about *my* feelings the way I cared about *yours*. Just saying."

Her nostrils flare. "I *do* care about your feelings. I just wish you'd been honest with me about this before."

"Why? I knew you'd end up marrying the guy sooner or later anyhow. That was another reason I didn't bother with your offer."

"Rachel—" Her shoulders sag as she looks down at the floor. She's hurt again. And this time, I couldn't care less.

"Anyhow, congratulations on the wedding, I guess." I pick up my tea and storm right by her and up to my room. She doesn't follow me.

And that's it. I'm stuck in Morgan House with Geoff, and even though Mom told me I was the most important thing in her life and that my feelings mattered, it was a lie, too. I check my messages for any response from Amber, but there's nothing. Which is just as well. At this point, nothing Amber could tell me about Geoff would make any difference.

GEOFF LOOKS wary when he returns home from Baltimore, but after Mom kisses him hello, he's all smiles. Of course he is. Why wouldn't he be? He's won. I hit him with my best shot, and it barely left a mark. I don't know why I even bothered.

He's got the license. They've hired a minister. They've booked hotel rooms for themselves and for me.

"Now look, Rachel," he says, sitting next to me in the kitchen with the most serious face he can manage. "I know this has all been rough on you. I know I can be a little much sometimes. People at work let me know that kind of a lot."

He gives me one of those extra-toothy smiles before continuing. "But I really want this to work. I love your mom. I'd like to give her back the sense of family she lost when she lost your dad.

And I want you to be part of that. Not because you have to be, but because you *want* to be."

Mom's peering around the kitchen door, her presence reminding me that what I want doesn't matter. I *want* to tell Geoff to forget about it—if they want to go through with this joke, that's fine, but I'm not playing along.

But what difference will it make? Mom made it clear. She's doing it whether I want it or not. I rub my forehead.

"Fine," I say. It's not fine. At all. But he's not getting anything more from me.

"And hey, Baltimore's a fun place. We'll find somewhere nice to eat afterward. Somewhere that has plenty of rabbit food, okay?"

"Sure. Sounds great." Another lie. Right now, I wish they'd stop pretending to care about me and go back to leaving me the hell alone.

I FEEL like I'm moving underwater over the next two days. We drive to Baltimore on Saturday morning, and I slump in the backseat, defeated and detached from myself the entire time. The only good thing about this week is that the house has continued to be quiet. I haven't heard anything, seen anything, sensed anything.

We check into the hotel suite early so Mom and I can set up flowers, put out some cake, and put on the outfits Gram helped us pick out two days before the ceremony. Mom wears a pale green wraparound dress with her red hair in a loose bun on top of her head, and I'm in a lacy purple sundress. Geoff wears a blue suit and tie, his brown hair newly trimmed for the occasion.

A minister Geoff hired pronounces Geoff and Mom husband and wife on their suite's balcony, which overlooks the harbor. As they trade vows and kiss, I study the crowds of people walking around the pavilions along the waterfront until the mercifully short ceremony is over. Geoff and Mom let me have a glass of champagne for a toast. They look ridiculously happy, and I try not to hate them both. The champagne doesn't make the hurt go away. It just makes me numb.

After a lavish dinner at an Italian restaurant, we return to the hotel. I'm thankful that my room is a few doors down from theirs. I *really* don't want to accidentally overhear whatever they might be getting up to on their wedding night, thanks very much.

I drag an armchair over to the window and stare down at the people wandering around Inner Harbor, the boats on the river, and the Domino Sugars sign reflecting off the water. I don't realize how tired I am until I drop off, still in the armchair.

MOM AND GEOFF are going to go on a little honeymoon trip to Bethany Beach in Delaware. They offer to take me along, but staying by myself in this haunted hell hole somehow sounds more appealing than having to be around either one of them.

"You sure, sweetie? I know you aren't crazy about this house," Mom asks. She's been extra nice since the wedding. Now that it doesn't matter anymore, she cares about what I want. I fight the urge to flip her off.

"It's fine, Mom. I'll be okay for a couple of days. If something happens and I need help, I can call Gram."

Mom studies my face. "You haven't had any more of those nightmares lately, have you?"

"No." If I think about it, it's a little weird how quiet the house has been lately. Maybe Mom's banishing spells actually worked.

"We'd love to have you along if you want to go, Rachel," Geoff chimes in. He's been super nice since the wedding, too. Everyone's been nice. Even the house. So why do I still feel so unsettled?

"Nah. You guys have fun. I'll be fine here. Thanks."

Mom doesn't look like she's too sure about that. She leaves

me detailed instructions on where she and Geoff will be and extracts a promise that I will call her if I have any more nightmares. It's as if Mom's finally developing a conscience again after blowing off all my unhappiness prior to the wedding.

I reassure them I'll be fine. And I will be. Not having to deal with either of them for a few days sounds great.

As soon as their car is out of sight, I ride my bike up to Barkley's Drugs and get a box of Black Sapphire hair dye. Back home, I put towels down all over Geoff's precious bathroom and take care of my annoying red roots. Part of me wants to splatter black dye all over the walls and ceiling and fixtures, but I don't want to deal with the fallout when he gets back. I clean everything up and take the garbage bag outside.

After that, I decide there's another way to take advantage of being alone in the house. Even if he's married to my mom now, it's still not too late for me to try and figure out if Geoff Barber has been hiding anything else from us. Mom might think that marriage certificate she was so eager to get will stop any more ugly truths from coming out, but we'll see about that.

I've rarely been in the master bedroom, but I take a deep breath and walk in. The dueling scents of herbal candles and Geoff's bergamot-smelling aftershave hit me. The bed's been made up with a thin green blanket and matching pillows. A painting of a man in a red jacket and white pants riding a black horse hangs on the wall facing the door. Mom and Geoff's shoes are lined up under their dressers. A floorboard creaks under my feet, and I freeze for a second before remembering nobody's here to catch me snooping.

With shaking hands, I pull out the drawers of Geoff's large oak dresser. I don't know what I'm looking for—other marriage certificates? Pictures of mystery women?—but this is the only chance I might have to do this.

The dresser is full of neatly folded and arranged clothing. I try to move things as little as possible, but it becomes clear pretty quickly that I'm not going to find out much this way anyhow.

The man owns more polo shirts than I thought ever existed in the world, but Mom probably already noticed that. And there's nothing in the dresser that strikes me as suspicious. He's kept ticket stubs from football games and a pack of business cards, but those don't prove anything.

His closet doesn't offer much more insight. Pairs of dress shoes and boots are lined up on the floor. His work clothes hang neatly pressed from their hangers.

But when I look towards the back, a large metal safe sits on the closet floor, and now something in me tingles. If he's hiding anything big, surely it's in here. But I have no idea how I'd ever figure out the combination. After twirling the dial uselessly for a moment, I make a mental note to research safe-cracking on the internet. With incognito mode turned on, of course.

And although a big part of me doesn't want to do this, I go downstairs, fish the key out of the junk drawer, and unlock the basement door again. This, after all, is the one place Geoff really doesn't want me to go—and the one place where something else really wants me to be.

The musty, mildewed odor hits me right away, but silence greets me when I get the door open. The stairs creak as I descend, and I tiptoe as if Mom and Geoff might somehow hear me all the way at the beach. At the bottom of the staircase, I catch a faint whiff of sage incense, a remnant of Mom's cleansing ritual.

I snap on the overhead light and walk over to the wall where that door is in my visions, but it's solid in the light. The space feels cold and damp when I run a hand over it. I push on it, but it doesn't give. There's no sign there's even been a door here, and I'm more confused than ever.

Whatever it is that wants me down here so badly, it doesn't seem to know what to do now that I'm here of my own volition. All I can hear is my heart beating as I wait for something to grab me, to show me terrible things. But the house leaves me alone.

With plenty of time and no fear of interruption, I examine the space more closely. What am I expecting to find—evidence of more wives? A bloody weapon? A dungeon key? Unless he's embarrassed by boxes, gardening tools, abandoned woodworking projects, old golf clubs, and other junk, there's nothing down here Geoff should mind anyone seeing.

As I run my hand over a high shelf, something stringy and sticky snares my fingers, and I curse as I swat spiderweb tendrils off my hand. Spiders are fine with me in jewelry form, but I draw the line at encountering real ones. The dust starts getting to me, and after a good sneeze or two, I walk back upstairs and lock the door behind me.

I told Mom I'd be fine in Morgan House alone. And I actually believe I'll be okay until the sun starts going down. The darker it gets outside, the more my body tenses up.

I settle in on the sectional with a bowl of pretzels, intending to spend the evening binge-watching the kind of trashy reality TV shows Mom doesn't allow in her presence. A floorboard creaks upstairs, and I pause *Real Housewives* long enough to listen for footsteps. As soon as I unpause the TV, I hear another creak. Something in the living room wall thumps. The hair on the back of my neck prickles as I huddle deeper into the sectional, wrapping my arms around myself.

This is going to be a long couple of days if I'm wigging out at every sound I hear at night, and even the sight of one housewife hurling a bottle of prosecco at another housewife's head isn't enough to distract me. I text Nick.

You there?

Yeah.

He replies almost at once. That's a relief. I've barely heard from him in the last few days. He's been busy with the band, he says.

Mom and idiot boyfriend–husband now, barf–are out of town. Want to come hang at my house?

Sure. Can be there soon.

I put the phone down before realizing something: I never told him where the house is. And yet headlights spill through the front window not ten minutes later. I make sure *Real Housewives* is turned off before I hurry for the door.

He's warm and solid and strong when I embrace him. I haven't seen him since the night I told Mom about Geoff's ex-wife. He kisses me fiercely as I cling to him, savoring the feeling of his arms around me, making me feel safe. Protected. I think he missed me as much as I missed him.

"How did you know where I was?" I ask after he lets me go.

"You told me you lived in Morgan House. Everyone around here knows where that is." His face is flushed as he glances around the house. "Nobody else home, eh?"

"Nope. I'm alone in the big scary house all by myself." I pout at him. "Until now. Wanna watch a movie or something?"

As soon as those words are out of my mouth, it starts.

The temperature feels as if it's rising several degrees and fast. It's like an oven preheating on the hottest day of summer, and my skin prickles. Nick glances around, frowning.

"Is it getting really hot in here?" I whisper. "You feel it, too?"

"Geesh, yeah."

"Oh my God. This is what it does whenever the bad stuff starts happening."

Nick wipes a hand over his forehead. "Christ, this is weird. I'm getting dizzy."

"Let me go bring down the fan from my room." I try to sound braver than I feel.

"Okay. Come right back." He watches me go to the staircase, looking concerned.

I hurry upstairs and unplug the box fan in my bedroom.

Before heading back down to Nick, I check myself out in the mirror. Nothing's in my teeth. My hair's a deep, glossy blue-black again, no carroty roots showing. I look acceptable.

My heart starts to speed up a little as I think about what I'm doing, and for a minute, I forget about the creeping heat downstairs. I've got Nick in the house alone, and no Mom or Geoff anywhere nearby. For a couple of days, even.

We could do anything together. *Anything*. That thought makes my face in the mirror go pink.

And then my bedroom door bangs shut.

Chapter Fifteen

STUCK

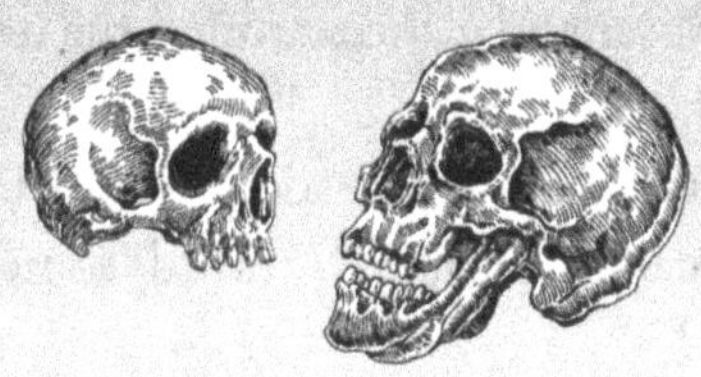

"WHAT THE HELL?" I hurry over and yank on the doorknob. It won't move. I rattle it, but it slips uselessly in my hand as my palm sweats.

"Nick?" He doesn't answer, and I shake the doorknob harder and call again.

"Nick!"

After an eternity, his footsteps sound on the stairs.

"Rachel? What's up?"

"My door's stuck! It slammed shut, and I can't get it open."

"Hold on." He jiggles the knob on his side of the door, but he doesn't have any more luck.

A noise builds in my room, and my skin crawls, the animal part of me clamoring to get away. The sound isn't quite a growl. It's a rumble that rolls around the room and vibrates the floor under my feet. Whatever it is, it began when Nick came to the door, and now it's getting louder. And it sounds angry.

"Nick? What's happening?" I try so hard not to sound frightened as he continues yanking the handle and pushing on the door.

"I don't know. But I'll find an axe somewhere in this house and smash the door down if I have to."

Oh my God, if I have to explain that *to Geoff.* The rumbles get louder on my side, loud enough to shake the walls. I think I'll dive out the window if it doesn't stop. It's swallowing the room and surrounding me. And if I don't do something, it'll devour me too.

The door finally crashes open. I fly into Nick's arms.

"Nick. Something's in here." My voice is frantic and my breaths are shallow. I try not to hyperventilate as we cling to each other.

He pulls me closer and glances around the hall. "What do you mean?"

My head swims, and I take deep breaths, trying to settle myself before speaking again. "I heard something. Some*one*. Didn't you hear it?"

"No. I didn't hear anything."

"We have to get out of here."

His arms tighten around me. "Rachel, there's nobody here. Just us. You're going to be okay."

"How do you know?"

"Because I'm here with you."

He smiles down at me. But there's a sudden sparkle in his eye, and something about that makes me want to shove him down the stairs.

"You were out there holding the door shut. Weren't you?"

"What?" The sparkle vanishes at once. "No. I wouldn't do something like that."

"Then what's happening?" I don't want to cry in front of him, but this house trying to trap me in my own room is almost all I can take after everything I've been through with Geoff and Mom.

"Well, it's an old house, right? Sometimes doors stick in the summer when it's humid," he explains. "The moisture makes the wood swell."

I clench a fist in frustration. Is he someone else who'll ignore what's going on in this place and tell me I'm wrong about it all? What happened to the guy who said he believed me when I told him about the horrible things I was seeing in this house? "Nick,

I've told you. Something bad is happening in this house. Something was in here tonight. I *heard* it."

He takes my face in his hands, which are still warm. "It's going to be okay."

"Can't we go to your place?"

His eyes widen for a second before he shakes his head. "No. That's not a good idea."

"But why?"

"It's my uncle." He rolls his eyes for emphasis. "He hates it when I bring girls over. Says it's not the Christian thing to do. You think Geoff's a pain in your ass? Trust me, my uncle will make Geoff seem like the coolest guy ever."

So, he's had girlfriends before. I brush that aside. Getting out of Morgan House is far more important at the moment.

"Then let's go downtown or something. Someplace away from here."

He shrugs. "Look, let's go back down to the living room. Pick out a movie or a show or something. It's wide open down there. Nothing can shut you in anywhere, and I'll be with you. It'll all be fine. Okay?"

I don't know about this idea or why he isn't taking me more seriously when I say we need to get out of here. But I don't want him to think I'm a frightened kid, so I swallow all my nerves. "Fine."

I grab the box fan, and Nick insists on carrying it downstairs. We settle on the sofa together, and I punch up *Black Mirror* on Netflix.

"Oh, *that* should relax us," Nick smirks.

"That show is a different kind of scary. Not like this place."

I huddle against him, allowing myself to curl around his body despite the heat in here. He slides an arm around me and pulls me closer.

But I keep hearing someone crying, someone not on the TV. I'm sure of it. I glance up at Nick, but he's engrossed in the show, oblivious to the sound. I turn my head and listen, hoping it's something else—anything else—but all I make out is that same quiet sobbing.

I shiver. He looks at me.

"You aren't cold, are you?" He's warm as I snuggle even closer to him. When I look up at him again, he pulls me into a slow, deep kiss.

Before long, I'm lying on the sofa, and he's on top of me. I'm not shivering anymore, and I can't hear anything but my own blood thundering in my ears as he kisses my lips and my neck. His hand sweeps over my chest, stopping at my breasts.

I've never slept with anyone. The guys at school I might have wanted to do this with didn't want me, and I wasn't interested in the ones who did.

Nick works a hand under my shirt, and I shiver again—happily this time—at the feeling of his fingers against my bare skin.

"Have you ever...?" he says.

My face flushes. "No. But I want to."

"Your mom and your stepdad won't be home tonight?"

"Nope." Something warm flares inside my body. Am I actually going to go through with this? I think maybe I am.

He kisses me harder, and his hands start to ease down the waistband of my yoga pants.

"Let me know if you want me to stop," he murmurs. His hand keeps moving, and I can't imagine wanting him to ever stop as an intense warmth begins building deep inside me, but then...

Footsteps. In the foyer, moving fast. My breath catches as my heart bangs in my chest.

"Nick? Someone's in here. I can hear it—"

"Me too." He pushes himself off me. When I sit upright, a figure is in the doorway, and I gasp.

Gram's standing in the living room, holding an overnight bag and looking for all the world like she's trying not to laugh.

"G-gram?" I try to cover myself and rearrange my clothes at the same time, while Nick stares at Gram with his mouth open.

"Oops! Sorry about that, hon. Your mom called me. She was a little worried about you staying here by yourself all weekend. But it looks like you were way ahead of her." Her mouth curls up even more.

"Um, yeah. I didn't think anyone else was going to be here." My face gets so hot I wonder if it might actually catch my hair on fire.

Gram stares at Nick for a second before speaking. Her amused smile fades as she looks at him. "Hello there, young man. I'm Helen Strauss, Rachel's grandmother. And you are?"

"Nick." He smooths his hair down and leaps to his feet. "I should be going soon."

"You don't have to leave on my account," Gram says. Disappointment, sharp and sour, settles into my chest. I would have gone through with what Nick and I started. I'm sure of it. I'm usually thrilled to see Gram, but not tonight.

"S'ok," Nick stammers. "I'll talk to you tomorrow, Rachel. Bye." He darts past Gram and all but runs for the foyer. She doesn't stop watching him until he shuts the front door. His car crunches the gravel as it pulls away from the house. I lean back into the sofa and sigh.

Gram sits down next to me as I swipe the back of my hand over my forehead.

"So. Pretty hot in here tonight, huh?" she says.

"Yeah." In more ways than one.

Gram looks around and wrinkles her nose. "I don't like this house. Not one bit. Feels like I'm in *The Shining* or something. And why in the world is it even hotter in here than it is outside?"

"I don't know. It gets like that in here sometimes."

"Well." Gram turns to me and narrows her eyes. "Are you being careful, honey?"

"We didn't do anything. I...I haven't done anything with anyone yet." My ears burn. "Mom said she'd take me to Planned Parenthood when I wanted to—"

Gram waves a hand, cutting me off. "I know. Tara's told me

about that, and that's great. But I don't necessarily mean sex. I'm talking about that boy. What do you know about *him?*"

I study my fingers. "He's lived around here pretty much his whole life. His parents are dead."

"Oh my. How old is he?"

"Eighteen. I think." I'm not sure I've ever asked.

"That's all?"

I glance up at Gram. "Yeah. Why? Does he look older to you?"

"I couldn't say for sure, but something about his eyes..." Gram rubs her chin. "So, what does he do? Is he in college?"

"I don't think so." My voice goes up at the end of that sentence as if it's a question. Most of our time together has involved me talking a lot about myself. Nick always seems content to listen, and since I sometimes feel like people rarely listen to me, especially lately, I've taken advantage.

"He sure did skedaddle as soon as there was an adult around, didn't he?"

I shrug. "He was probably embarrassed. That was kind of awkward, Gram."

Gram chuckles. "I *did* text you. Guess you were a little too preoccupied to hear your phone."

My phone is still up in the bedroom, where I haven't wanted to go since Nick had to fight to get me out of it. "I guess so."

"Well, just be careful, honey. I know that's easy for me to say, and I realize fast relationships are the popular thing over here these days." She raises an eyebrow as I snort. "But try to find out a little more about him. If he's worth it, he won't mind."

"Don't you like him?"

She shrugs. "Good grief, Rachel. I saw him for about five seconds before he tore out of here. That's hardly enough time to form an opinion of anybody. But I just don't want to see you rushing into things."

Something's gone heavy and leaden inside me. Gram doesn't like Nick. She hasn't said so, but I can tell. Gram's usually a pretty good judge of character, but her intuition must have failed her this time.

"I *am* sorry I spoiled your night," Gram says. "*Black Mirror*, eh? That's romantic." She winks.

"It sounded like a good idea at the time."

Gram flaps the collar of her shirt, fanning herself. "Seriously, though. When is Geoff going to get some decent AC in this place?"

"The house just gets hot sometimes. Really hot."

"Ugh. I knew these old houses were stuffy as hell in the summer, but I had no idea they got this bad. No wonder you look like you never sleep. Have you had any more bad dreams lately?"

I open my mouth and then close it again. I want to tell Gram about what happened with the door tonight, but I don't know if she'll believe me about any of it. And whatever sounds I heard earlier have gone silent now.

"Not exactly."

"Not *exactly?*"

I examine my fingers before speaking again.

"Do you believe in ghosts, Gram?"

Gram bites her lip. "Well, I'm generally open-minded on the subject. The skeptic in me feels duty-bound to say no, of course not. But that's kind of boring, isn't it?"

I stare at the floor. "I think something happened in this house. Something bad. And whatever it was, it's ... lingering. I keep seeing and hearing these horrible things. Dead women. Screams. Cries. Sometimes, I don't even know what's a dream and what's real anymore."

Gram frowns. "And you haven't said anything to your mother or Geoff about this?"

"Of course I did. Didn't Mom tell you? I mean, they've found me in the basement. Mom said she did some banishing spells because she felt there was some bad energy down there, too."

"Hm." The corners of her mouth turn down, and she rubs her chin.

"Geoff gets pissy if I even ask if someone else has lived here. He thinks I can't adjust to being out in the country, so it's making me sleepwalk." I roll my eyes.

"You don't think that's the real problem, though, do you?"

"No way."

Gram looks around, her brow furrowed. "Well, one thing's for sure. I can't sleep in this kind of heat. What do you say we head back to my place? I'll text Tara and let her know where we are. I'll have to clear some things out of my guest room, but at least we won't roast to death overnight."

I do not need to be asked twice, and I nearly trip on the stairs running up to my room. Only after I clear the threshold do I wonder if I'll be trapped in here again. I grab the desk chair and prop the door open while getting a bag ready, but I don't hear or sense anything.

Morgan House is quiet, as though it's glad I'm leaving.

Chapter Sixteen

THE EYE OF THE HURRICANE

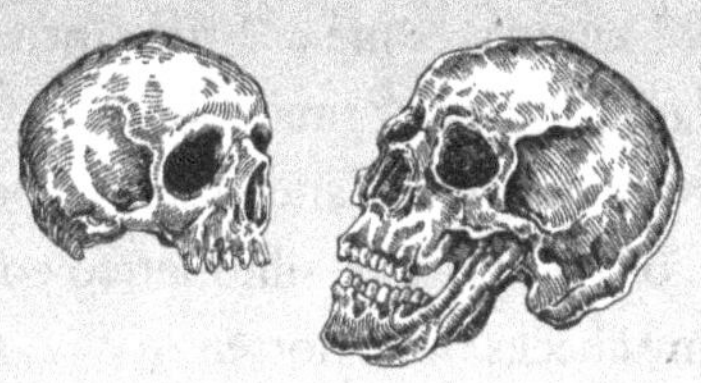

GRAM BRINGS me back to Morgan House the day Geoff and Mom are due to come home. She extracts a promise from me to call her again the minute I have any more problems in this place.

When Geoff and Mom get back from their short honeymoon, everything feels different, as if my revelation about Geoff's previous marriage never happened and they've hit some kind of cosmic reset button.

They're still being nice. Extremely nice. Nice to the point that it makes my teeth itch to be around them, and I wonder if the big smiles make their faces hurt. Geoff and Mom act like they're trying not to overdo the PDA around me. Geoff doesn't nag me about eating meat, or dyeing my hair, or getting a job. Nobody brings up the ex-wife at all. It's like *Chelsea Who?*, as if the last couple of weeks didn't happen.

Geoff and Mom apparently made a pact while they were gone: This Family is Going to Work. I don't know what to think about any of it, but it makes me want to be out of the house more than ever.

On the Thursday after Mom and Geoff's return, I ride my bike to town and chain up outside Barkley's Drugs. The smells of perfume testers and disinfectant wash over me when I walk inside.

Pop songs from the 80s play over the store's sound system. I pass sunscreen displays and American flags as I head to the hair care aisle and dig through all the boxes and loops of synthetic hair until I find one lone box of Black Sapphire dye.

Instead of heading for the cash register, I take a deep breath and walk further back into the store, keeping my eyes on the dingy checkered floor. I beg whatever forces might be listening to make sure nobody I know sees me as I turn into another aisle and stop in front of a large display of small boxes.

Some of the boxes are plain and discreet, others are brightly colored, and some of them depict silhouetted couples and hint at things that make my cheeks burn hotter.

Mom's made it clear that getting birth control is smart and responsible and nothing to be embarrassed about, but even so, I'm convinced everyone in St. Mary somehow knows that the Morley girl is going to the drugstore to look for condoms so she can lose her virginity.

And there are so many *kinds*. I have no idea which ones to get, and it's not like I can ask Mom or Gram for a recommendation—or Geoff, God forbid. My face and ears burn as I look at all the different boxes. Ribbed? *Extra-large*?

I finally grab a box at random and hurry up to the register, refusing to make eye contact with the young male cashier.

I haven't had a chance to have any more alone time with Nick, but if I do, and if things start getting intense again, I want to be ready. I put a couple condoms in my purse just in case, and then I hide the rest in my bedside table.

"IT'S BETTER than them nagging you all the time, right?" Nick asks. We've spent Saturday afternoon browsing and drinking coffee at Milledge's, and we've had grilled cheese at Syd's Diner on Main Street. Now we're nestled together in the front seat of his Honda, which sits outside Morgan House under a threatening overcast sky. I'm in a tank top and black shorts, and the humidity makes my skin stick to the vinyl seat. Nick's body generates even more warmth, but I don't mind that.

"Well, sure. But it's weird. It makes me worry about what's going to happen when the other shoe drops, you know?"

"You worry too much." Nick hooks a finger under my chin and turns my face to his, pulling my lips to his. I'm not sure where Mom and Geoff are. Nor do I care while he's kissing me like this.

"So," Nick says when we finally break for some air. "Want to pick up where we left off when your grandmother walked in?"

And for a couple of seconds, a pang strikes me: Gram didn't trust Nick. She never actually said so, but I could tell.

Well, maybe Gram would have liked him more if she hadn't walked in while he had his hand down your pants, you know? That moment couldn't have been more awkward, but I still wonder why Gram seemed so cool to him.

"What is it?" Nick asks, studying my face. "Don't you want to?"

I think about the condoms in my purse, and I can hear my own quickening pulse in my ears. "Here?"

Nick snorts. "Maybe, but that would be pretty uncomfortable. Are your mom and the idiot home?"

Lights are on in the living room and in Mom's studio. "Yeah."

Nick sighs and looks over the grounds. "We could go into the trees a little bit."

"The trees? And then what?" I frown. "Is there anywhere comfortable there?"

"Only one way to find out." Nick turns and raises his dark eyebrows, and my pulse drums even faster.

We climb out of the car into air that's like wet cotton. But before we move towards the woods, Nick pushes me against the side of the car and kisses me deeply. Just as he leans in for another kiss, I glance up at the house.

There's a flicker of motion in one of the dormer windows as if someone has just stepped out of view.

"I think we might have an audience," I whisper. But when Nick looks up, the windows are blank and empty. He stares down at me.

My face gets hot. "I think someone in there is spying on us."

"Are you sure you want to do this?" he says. "We don't have to."

Am I sure? I want him. I know that much. Do I want my first time to be on the ground by a cluster of trees? But it's not like we can use my bedroom, and Mom and Geoff could see us in the car if they happened to look out one of the front windows. And I wasn't expecting to make this decision tonight, *right now*.

A light rain begins as he leans in and kisses me again. The rainfall rustles the trees as I kiss him back. His hand works its way under my thin T-shirt. The sensation of his fingers against my damp skin does things to me, making a warm energy pulse through my body. The light patter grows steadier and heavier, but I don't care now. I pull him closer, savoring the salty taste of his lips. Suddenly, heading out into the woods for a little privacy doesn't sound so bad. Or maybe we could stay right here in the twilight. If it gets a little darker out and the rain falls a little harder, nobody will be able to see us anyhow, and—

A crash of breaking glass shatters the quiet around us, and Nick and I jump away from each other.

The large living room window overlooking the front yard is now a jagged hole. Shards of broken glass litter the porch and the ground outside, glittering in the faint light from inside the house. My pulse, already quickened from what I was just doing with Nick, starts pounding in my temples.

"What the hell just happened?" Nick says, his voice shaking.

"I don't—"

Before I can finish, Geoff bangs the front door open and storms outside. He looks at me and Nick, and then the window. Even in the dim light, I see Geoff's face turn almost crimson with anger.

"Why in the hell would you do this?" he yells, as furious as I've ever heard.

I hold my trembling hands up. "What? It wasn't us, Geoff."

Mom comes running outside, and when she looks at the broken window, and then at Nick and Geoff, she appears to draw the same conclusion. "Rachel!"

What, her too? "Mom, that wasn't us. Come on. Why would we do that?"

Geoff speaks through clenched teeth, all his sugary niceness of the last several days gone. Because it was fake. Just like everything else about him. "You hate it here. You always did. No matter what I do to try to make it better for you, you're determined to be miserable and make everyone else miserable right along with you." He's so angry it's like the air pulsates around him.

Nick straightens up. "That's enough. We didn't touch your window."

Geoff glares at him. "Why the hell are you even here?"

"He's a friend of mine from town, Geoff."

"And he can get himself *back* to town right now before I call the police."

"But—" The unfairness of all this burns me, and my fists clench. They're not the least bit interested in the truth; they just want someone to blame, and I'm the easiest target. The obvious target.

"Rachel? That's probably the best thing for tonight. And we should get back inside." Mom's holding up a placatory hand as the rainfall grows heavier and thunder booms in the distance.

"Jesus. Of course, you'd take his side. Why'd I think things were going to be different now?"

"This isn't about sides," Geoff shouts. "It's about you vandalizing my house—"

And then Nick strides over until he's inches from Geoff, towering over him. Geoff's eyes widen as he takes a step back. I know Nick's tall, and I'm used to looking up at him. But even so, the way he looms over Geoff is a little shocking.

"Look at the glass, genius," Nick says. The corner of his mouth curls up into a smirk.

"Excuse me?" Geoff looks like he might actually hit Nick, and I half-hope he's stupid enough to try it because I'm pretty sure Nick could flatten the little toad.

"Look where it all fell." Nick sounds as if he's talking to a particularly dim toddler. I hadn't thought anyone could ever sound more condescending than Geoff, but Nick's pulling it off. "It's all over the *outside*. Which is only possible if someone *inside* broke the window. And we are pretty clearly *not inside*."

Geoff's mouth drops open as he looks at the shards on the porch and the grass. Nick's right.

Nick takes another step closer to Geoff. The smirk is gone now, replaced by pure anger. His nostrils flare and his lips are pinched. Mom looks at both of them wide-eyed.

Geoff tries to stand a little taller and raises his chin. "You need to back off."

"You need to apologize." Nick's voice is low and menacing, and his brown eyes look almost pure black in the rainy gloom. I've never seen him angry before, and it's an alarming sight. I hold my breath, wondering what he might be about to do.

"Everyone, please calm down." My mom holds her hands out towards them. "Come on. This was obviously some kind of freak accident. No need to fight over it."

But Geoff and Nick don't move. All of us are getting wetter, and I'm feeling a chill that I don't think is just from being drenched.

Finally, Nick takes a step back and waves a hand at Geoff as if to say *Never mind, you're not worth it*.

"I'll see you later, Rachel." He turns towards his car. "I'd love to hear your stepfather's ideas on how you and I managed to bend physics to make this happen. Be sure to fill me in."

"Nick—" He gets in the car and slams the door shut before I can say anything else, and now I'm pissed off and embarrassed as I watch his car lights retreating down the gravel path.

"Thanks a lot, guys," I say to Geoff and Mom.

"Clean up that glass." Geoff's voice is as sharp as the shards on the ground.

"No."

"Excuse me?" His face looks beet red. I expect the water dripping down his forehead to start sizzling.

"Rachel..." Mom's voice is quavering now.

I straighten up and raise my voice so they can hear me loud and clear.

"Fuck the glass. I didn't do that. I'm not cleaning it up."

Rain falls heavy and fast now. I run into the house and upstairs to my room, slamming the door hard behind me to shut out Geoff's angry voice and Mom's low, placating one.

I kick my wastebasket across the room, but the *clang* when it hits the opposite wall does nothing to soothe my anger. Only then does it occur to me: What *did* break the window? Geoff or Mom wouldn't have done that, which doesn't leave much of anyone else. I get a towel from the bathroom and peel my damp clothes off, waiting for my pulse to slow as I dry off and put on fresh clothes.

The voices downstairs stop, and there's a quiet knock on my door a little while later. Mom lets herself in before I can wonder if Morgan House is acting up again. Her hair is frizzy from the rain.

"Rachel? Are you okay?"

I wrap my arms around myself. "Oh yeah, Mom. This has been an awesome night so far. I'm super glad we moved to this place."

"Sweetie, Geoff was upset. Surely you can understand that."

I slam a hand down on my dresser. "I don't care about Geoff! I'm upset the first thing the two of you did was accuse me. Can *you* try to understand *that*?"

She takes a deep breath. "You're right, and I'm sorry. We heard the crash, and when we looked outside, you two were right there. We jumped to conclusions."

The "sorry" does little to calm my anger. "Why would he

think we'd break the window? That's the stupidest thing ever. I mean, I have to live in this place too. Unfortunately."

She shrugs. "Well, it's not a big secret you don't like the house. Geoff thought maybe you were just acting out."

"But Nick was right about the glass. I couldn't have done that even if I wanted to. Which I didn't."

"I don't know, Rachel." She shakes her head. "Sometimes old houses just...settle."

I roll my eyes. "Really? That window broke because the house is *settling*?"

"Well, I don't have any better ideas." Mom's tone is sharper. "I mean, I believe you and Nick didn't do that. But we obviously didn't, either. So, what else could have happened?"

What indeed? I study my fluffy purple rug, avoiding Mom's eyes.

"Anyhow, I think tomorrow we should all clean the glass up. It wasn't anyone's fault, but it's not safe to have that all over the ground."

"Fine." Maybe tomorrow, Geoff can apologize for accusing Nick and me of something we didn't do. But I'm not going to hold my breath waiting for that.

Chapter Seventeen

DOWN TO THE BONE

A SCREAM JARS me out of a dead sleep. My bedroom is stifling hot, like I'm baking in a kiln. My heart pounds in my ears as I sit up and turn on the bedside light.

The first things I see are tangled red hair and an old, filthy nightgown barely clinging to a gaunt frame. The creature in the gown crawls across the bedroom floor, and I realize it's another woman. Her movements are crooked and stumbling as if one or more of her limbs are broken. The nightgown makes a *shhh-shhh* noise as it trails along the floor. I hold my thin summer blanket to my mouth to stifle the shriek that wants to come tearing out.

The woman leaves a long, smearing trail of blood on the wood behind her. Silvery, clouded-over eyes lift in my direction. As soon as her grayish gash of a mouth opens, one of her white hands claps over it. She shakes her head as if she's fighting to get free of her own hand—to tell me something.

"You're not real," I tell the apparition on the floor. "You can't hurt me."

The woman drops her hand, closes her eyes, and vomits up a gout of thick maroon blood onto my purple rug with a groan. The splattering noise turns my stomach.

The light snaps off, and I cry out. Cold, damp fingers so thin they feel like bones clamp around my wrist, and I roll and tumble through the darkness like I've been knocked over by another wave. *Please, no. Not again,* I think all the way down.

When I hit the basement floor, my hand goes through something dry that snaps under my palm like a twig. The stink of rot in the air nearly brings bile up my throat. That strange, glowing door up ahead provides a small rectangle of light, the only way I can see anything in here.

I crawl forward, and my hand strikes something that rolls away with a dry clatter.

Soft, prickling things move up my arm, making it itch—making my skin crawl. I raise my arm close to my eyes to see what's going on.

Maggots. Swarms of them. Oh, holy shit. I scream and flail my arm and try to slap them away, but there are too many of them, and they keep coming, wriggling over my body.

I sob "What the hell?" through jagged breaths as I scramble to my feet, and more things shatter and squish underneath my toes.

"Please stop." My foot hits something that skitters against a wall, and in the dim light of the room, I see it's a bone. And it's not the only one. Shards lie all over the floor, and smaller things that look like teeth. More teeth.

Even though its flesh has long since shriveled away, a form that's still clearly human lies too close to my feet. I scream again.

"Let me out!" I don't care if I wake up all of St. Mary now. But no one's nearby to hear me.

Tears pour down my face as I get up and stagger forward, holding my hands in front of me, unconcerned with all the sharp things that could cut my feet if it means I can get the hell out of here. But instead of finding the basement stairs, I crash into a wall I didn't see. The impact jars my arms, and I stagger backward.

Where are the steps? Where am I now? There's never been so much ghastly stuff on the floor when I've been down here. I trail my hands around the walls but yank them back in disgust. Unlike

Geoff's dusty, cluttered shelves, the walls here feel warm. Pulsing. Alive.

Then, a faint rectangular shape appears in front of me, outlined in light. A door. I hurry over to it but can't find a knob or any way to open it. My fingers brush over ornate metal scrollwork.

Panic shoots through me as I realize at last where I am: I'm actually *in* that basement room, behind the door that doesn't exist when I've looked for it during the day. Something pulled me back here. What if it never lets me out?

The ornate door bangs open, and he's standing there—the man I saw down here once before—and he's just a hulking silhouette in the basement's lack of light. He clutches a knife in his right hand and points it straight at me as he lunges too fast for me to get away and—

"*Rachel!*" Hands grab my shoulders hard, and I thrash as the shadow man vanishes and the overhead light sears my eyes again. Mom and Geoff are dark shapes bending over me, and the basement floor is stone-hard against my back. There's nothing on the floor around me—no bones. No teeth. No bodies. I want to stop screaming because, Jesus... my throat aches. But I can't.

Mom wraps her arms around me and holds me close to her chest as I realize that nothing's coming to murder me.

Not yet.

I gasp for air as Geoff looms over both of us.

"Is this ever going to stop?" There's no warmth in his voice. No concern.

"Geoff! She's terrified." Mom brushes my hair off my damp forehead and places a hand there as if she's feeling for a fever.

"The door," I say through heavy breaths.

"*What* door?" Geoff sounds disgusted.

I break free from Mom and struggle to my feet even though she's still trying to hold me down.

"There's a door down here. Where did it go?" There's

nothing but concrete where the ornate door should be. How can it be gone again?

"The only door is up there. The one you keep coming through even though I lock it for a reason." Geoff jabs a finger at the basement stairs.

"No. There's another one." I run towards that spot and press my hands against the concrete. It's cold and slightly damp against my warm palms. I pound my fists against the wall.

"What do you want? Why won't you leave me alone?" I cry and beat my aching fists uselessly against the blank space until Mom grips my hands and pulls me away.

"Sweetie, I don't know what you think you saw, but it's not there now. You're okay. You might have had another bad dream. Let's go back to bed."

"It's not a dream, Mom. Something happened here."

"Rachel, nothing is going on down here. No door. No nothing. And I've had more than enough of all this." Geoff pounds the banister.

"Geoffrey, you are *not* helping." Mom wraps her arms around me again and guides me carefully up the narrow steps I can barely see through my tear-blurred eyes.

"I don't understand why this keeps happening," Mom says.

"It's this house." I can hardly talk through sobs. "It's getting worse."

"There's *nothing wrong* with this house!" Geoff shouts. He slams the basement door behind us with a bang that shakes the floor.

Back upstairs, there's no sign of the dead woman who crawled into my room. Mom hustles me into bed, brings me a glass of water I didn't ask for, and pulls my purple blanket over me. Geoff glares at me from the doorway, but Mom leaves and shuts the door behind her, cutting me off from him—from them.

I don't try to sleep. Even if I were tired, the sounds of Mom and Geoff arguing in their room would keep me up. I stick a chair under the doorknob, though I know it won't help if someone wants me to end up in the basement again. After several minutes of lying in bed listening to my heart pound, I grab my phone and text Nick, quietly willing my messages to go through. But if he's getting them, he doesn't answer. Of course not. He's probably asleep like a normal person living in a normal house right now.

Even though the air in my room is sticky and humid, I wrap a thin blanket around myself, desperate to stop shaking.

GEOFF DOESN'T EVEN BOTHER LOOKING up from his breakfast when I come down to the kitchen the next morning and pour myself an extra-large serving of coffee.

"Get any sleep, sweetie?" Mom says.

"No." My eyes sting, my head aches, and my throat is paper-dry when I talk. I'm not sure I remember what sleep is anymore.

Geoff has nothing to say, no matter how much Mom tries to jolly him into talking. He sits at the head of the kitchen table and scowls into his AWESOME GOLFER mug. When he's done smearing cream cheese all over his bagel, he slams the knife down on the table.

Only Geoff could take something like this and make it all about himself and his delicate feelings. My dad would never have reacted like this. He'd have moved us the hell out of any house where this happened to me even *once*, much less over and over again.

I can't imagine eating anything, now or maybe ever. I carry the coffee mug out to the living room. Someone duct-taped a sheet over the hole where the glass used to be, and it's not doing much to keep out the clammy, humid air. This doesn't bother me. My bones are so chilled, I feel like I'll never be warm again.

Mom walks into the living room almost on tiptoe as if she's

afraid I might start screaming again. She sits down on the sofa beside me and clears her throat.

"I've been thinking, sweetie. Maybe we should make a doctor's appointment for you sometime this week." She wrings the hem of her lavender T-shirt as she talks.

"What for?" My ears burn. Behind us, Geoff leaves the kitchen and storms upstairs, but my focus is on Mom.

"This sleepwalking and these active nightmares aren't normal for you. Or anyone."

My fingernails dig into my palms. "That's because *this house* isn't normal, Mom. I know you felt it, too. You were talking to Geoff about the basement that one time. And don't you remember what he said about his stepdaughter?"

Mom shakes her head. "I definitely don't like it down there. But I'm not reacting to it the way you are. Rachel, you've been through a lot in the last couple of years. It's okay if you need some help dealing with it."

"What kind of help?" I narrow my eyes, and Mom glances down at her hands.

"Counseling. Or maybe medication. I don't know."

The beast that's been hiding inside me since I arrived at Morgan House claws at my ribcage again. Do I have to actually die down there before she finally gets it? "Mom, if you really want to help me, please talk Geoff into getting us out of here. Maybe he'll actually listen to you, and then we can move someplace that isn't trying to kill me."

"Sweetie, I don't think—"

But Mom doesn't get a chance to finish that thought as Geoff's voice roars out from upstairs, loud enough to make the walls ring.

"*Rachel!*" Both Mom and I jump.

Footsteps come down the stairs hard and fast enough to rattle the furniture. Geoff storms into the living room, red-faced. He brandishes the box of condoms I bought.

"What is this?" he shouts.

"They're condoms, Geoff." I try to keep my voice from shaking, hoping he can't see the blood rushing to my face. "Why were you in my nightstand?"

"That's not important! What are you doing with them?"

"How is you snooping through my stuff not important? And I haven't done anything with them." Yet.

"Geoff!" Mom jumps up from the couch. "Calm down. Right now."

"I wasn't born yesterday." Geoff's face is raspberry-red.

Maybe he'll just have a heart attack and end all this, I think hopefully. "I said I haven't used any of them yet."

"The box is *open*." He waves it at me to make his point.

"Because I put a couple in my purse. So what?" My stomach churns, but I refuse to let him see me upset. "Again, why were you snooping through my things?"

"This is not happening in my house." There's spit flying from his mouth.

"Geoff." Mom's voice is louder than I've ever heard it get, and even Geoff raises an eyebrow. "I taught Rachel that she needs to be prepared and responsible. I won't have you trying to embarrass her about it."

"She is *sixteen years old*," Geoff says, enunciating every word like he's talking to an idiot.

"Don't you dare talk down to me, Geoffrey Barber." Whoa. I've never heard Mom sound this mad at Geoff, not even when I told her about his first wife. Her face is as red as her hair as she jabs a finger in his direction. "I know how old my own daughter is, thank you. And I'd much rather she use protection than get an STI, have to get an abortion, or need my help to raise a baby when she's still in high school."

"She's too young to be thinking about this." Geoff shakes his head, but his voice is softer. His shoulders sag.

Mom puts her hands on her hips. "She most certainly is *not*. She has a boyfriend. It's going to come up. Maybe it already has."

It's like I'm not here. "Why were you digging around in my room, Geoff?"

He whirls around on me. "It's *my* room in *my* house. When you're under my roof, I have the right to know what you're doing."

"Children have a right to privacy," Mom snaps.

"Oh, really?" Geoff glares at her. "My parents took the *door* off my bedroom when I pulled stunts like this."

"That's awful, and I'm sorry they did that to you." Mom raises her chin. "But Rachel is *my* daughter, and you will respect her space."

"Those weren't even out in the open. They were inside my bedside table drawer. Why were you looking in there, Geoff?" I insist.

He takes a deep breath as if he's trying to keep from exploding. "I wanted to see if you had any drugs stashed away in there."

I almost laugh. "Oh my God. What is it with you thinking everyone's on drugs?"

"You're seeing things. You're hearing things. We catch you freaking out in the basement. The way you're acting isn't normal. I have the right to figure out what's going on." He waves the condom box again. "And I've seen now that *you* can't be trusted. What else have you been up to?" He hurls it on the floor.

Mom takes another step towards him. "She's watching out for herself, Geoff. Just like I taught her. You have no reason to be angry. Don't you dare shame her for this. Don't you *dare*."

Even though Mom is on my side for once, the sight of the condoms on the floor makes my pulse pound in my ears. The purple box, labeled *Pleasure Pack* in huge letters, sits there looking like a sleazy accusation. I never imagined Geoff finding those. And now he knows what I'm considering doing with Nick. What I would have done with him if Gram hadn't walked in. That's personal and private, something Geoff has no right to know. He's my mother's husband, nothing more.

I push past Mom and run upstairs, ignoring Geoff's voice

behind me. After slamming the bedroom door shut, I wedge my chair under the knob again. Mom knocks, and then Geoff pounds. Someone tries the door, but it won't move. I block out all the warnings and pleas as I climb into bed and pull the blanket over my head. I go away.

In my dream, I'm somewhere with Dad. He walks ahead of me fast enough that I can't quite catch him, and he keeps glancing back at me with his sad, dark eyes. If he'd just stop for a second, I could catch up to him, but he won't even slow down, and I can't keep pace. He moves out of sight as tears sting my eyes. And my throat tightens, reminding me of the ache from all the screaming.

A steady knock at my bedroom door penetrates the dream and jars me awake. I roll over, intending to ignore it.

"Rachel? Honey? Would you mind talking to me?"

Gram. I jump out of bed, run to the door, pull the chair away, and fling it open. Gram holds her arms out, and I fall into them in relief.

Chapter Eighteen

THE RESET BUTTON

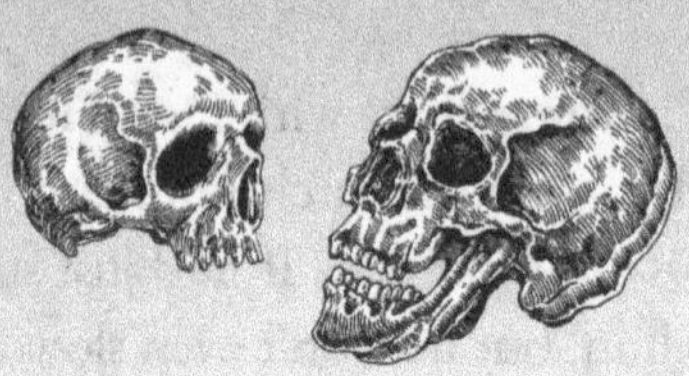

"Now, look. This is a difficult situation, and nobody's at fault here," Gram says, clutching some coffee in the MOMMIN' AIN'T EASY mug as we all sit around the kitchen table. Geoff sits with his arms folded over his chest and his nostrils flaring. Mom sniffles. I just want to be anywhere but here. "You only want the best for each other and for Rachel. But I think everything has been moving way too fast. If it were just the two of you, it'd be one thing."

"We're not getting any younger, Helen," Geoff says, scowling at his glass of water.

"I understand. And I know you both had terrible things happen in your previous marriages. But rushing headlong into another one was never going to undo all that."

"But what can we do now?" Mom asks, dabbing at her eyes.

Gram pushes her glasses up the bridge of her nose and tents her fingers together before continuing.

"How about this? Rachel looks to me like she hasn't slept since she moved in here. What would you think about her staying with me for a week or two? Maybe she got pulled away from her old life way too fast. I'm hoping that giving her a chance to breathe a little will help all of you with what's going on now."

My heart leaps. I'm getting out of here? Out of Morgan House and its horrifying sights and sounds? I'll be close to Elena and my old life again?

But Nick. I'll be away from Nick.

But he can always come to see me.

"I'll bring her back in plenty of time for school to start," Gram continues. "And in the meantime, you two need to talk through some things I don't think you discussed much before." Mom looks down at the tablecloth. Geoff frowns at the wall. "I've never been a stepparent, but I'm sure it's harder than hell. You need to figure out what your expectations are. For her and for each other."

Geoff rubs his forehead. "I feel like this is running away from the problem, Helen."

"Rachel isn't a *problem*, Geoff." She gives him a pointed look. "She's a teenage girl who's endured a big loss in her life, and what's going on here now isn't doing her a bit of good. Or you, either. You'll still have a lot to work out when she gets back, but for now...well, consider this hitting a pause button. I think you could all use it."

Mom's face is splotchy under her freckles. She slumps in her chair.

"Does...does this sound like something you want to do, sweetie?" she says in a small, shaky voice.

Hell yes. Can I move in with Gram right now and never come back at all? I can't say that to Mom's face, but oh, I want to.

"If it's okay with you." I won't look at Geoff. I don't care if it's okay with him. His opinion is officially irrelevant.

"I guess it's a good idea, then," Mom says, staring down at her raw, red cuticles.

"All right, then." Gram nods at us. "I need a night to clean up the condo and get the guest room ready. I've been using it as the junk storage room again." She lets out a guilty chuckle. "I'll be back here tomorrow afternoon to pick Rachel up."

I want to get up from the table and dance all over the kitchen, but I settle for giving Gram a hug. I'm getting away from here. Finally.

What do you mean, you're leaving?

It's for a week or two. Not forever.

NICK'S TEXTS don't sound like he's happy. This pleases me.

So, I'm not going to see you for a week or two?

I'm just going to be in Rockville. It's barely an hour away. You could come visit me anytime. I don't think Gram would mind.

I'm not actually sure about that last part, but he doesn't need to know.

My car's not good on long trips. It's old.

I roll my eyes.

Well, it's not going to be for that long. I doubt Gram would let me move in forever. Not even if I really begged. ;-)

He doesn't reply to that, even after I send a *You OK?* message. Is he seriously mad that I'm going away for a little while?

Well, that's his problem. Nothing, not even Nick, can keep me here any longer than I have to. I practically sing as I pick out clothes and pack them in one of Mom's bright red suitcases.

Mom buys eggplant and fettuccine for a goodbye dinner, and I hum as I slice the eggplant into rounds and put them in a colander to salt them. I can't help but notice that I seem to be the only one happy about the upcoming trip to Gram's. Geoff keeps sighing and rubbing his neck as if he wants to say something but won't, and Mom sniffles and jiggles a leg as we eat. And they don't even look at each other. Other than their sound effects, dinner is extremely quiet.

I head upstairs after we eat to finish packing, my heart still soaring at the sudden, wonderful turn of events. Elena and I are already planning to go clothes shopping for school, even if we won't be together this year. Then we're going to take the Metro downtown to DC to spend the day at the National Gallery. I've missed it all so much. Just one more night here, and then I've got happy times to look forward to.

As I put one last T-shirt in my suitcase, Mom comes into my room, shutting the door behind her.

"Need any help, sweetie?"

"No thanks, Mom. Got a system. Just cram everything in here and hope for minimum wrinkles."

She gives me a faint smile and sits on my bed.

"What's up?" I ask her.

She starts to pick at her already-raw cuticles before answering. "There's something I thought you should know."

That sounds serious, and I put down the makeup bag I'm holding. "What's that?"

She lowers her voice and leans close.

"Look. While you're gone...it's possible I might ask Geoff for a separation. Just for now," she says. I sit down hard next to her and lower my voice.

"But Mom. Already? Why?"

She raises an eyebrow. "I thought you'd be happier."

My cheeks get hot. She's got a point. I thought I'd be ecstatic to hear news like this, yet it feels strange to hear her say it. "But you guys just got married. He and I aren't getting along, but I thought the two of you were doing okay. Mostly." That hasn't been true lately, though.

"Keep your voice down. He doesn't know I'm thinking about this."

"What brought this on?"

She shakes her head. "The way he yelled at you when he found those condoms? That scared me. Things haven't been great between you two, but something about that really bothered me. And he's been so cold whenever we've found you during your... your bad dreams."

Yes, he has. He's always seemed way more upset I'm breaking one of his rules than about something awful happening to me. Even my starry-eyed, newlywed mom couldn't miss how lopsided those priorities are.

"And the thing Mother said about everything happening too fast made me realize there's so much Geoff and I never talked about that we should have." Mom sighs, and her shoulders droop.

I'm getting out of this house, and Mom might ditch Geoff at last? I should go buy a freaking lottery ticket.

"And I'm sorry, Rachel. For a lot of things. I was hoping you and Geoff would get along better once we'd been here for a little while. I just wanted this all to work so much."

"I know you did." Her head sags, and her blue eyes well up. I feel a twinge of guilt over my own excitement.

"Now, I don't know if I'm going to do this or not. If we can talk things out, I might not. But I don't want it to come as a shock if I do."

My heart's beating in my ears, and I don't know what to say. She looks almost as sad as she was after Dad's death. And now I'm starting to feel guilty about leaving her alone at a time like this.

"Do you want me to stay here instead of going to Gram's? This is kind of a big deal."

She shakes her head. "I think it's probably best if you aren't here. It's not your responsibility. And I've been keeping you in this place against your will long enough." She gives me a sad smile. "If I decide to do it and feel like I need backup, I'll call Mother. We can work something out from there."

"Okay. Geez, Mom." I can't bring myself to tell her I'm sorry. There's no point. We both know I'm not.

"Don't worry about any of this now. You finish getting ready for tomorrow. I want you to have a good time with Mother and Elena. You've earned it."

"If you're sure..."

"I'm sure. Love you."

She hugs me goodnight. My head spins from trying to process everything that's happened today as Mom leaves the room.

After I'm finished packing, I settle into bed, turn the lights out, and immediately tense myself, ready to hear crying, crawling, banging. But the house is quiet tonight.

I start to drift off, but intrusive thoughts slam into my brain, jarring me wide awake. I stare at the ceiling and grab my blanket in my fists as my mouth goes dry.

Something bad happened here.

I keep seeing dead women, dead *things*.

Geoff doesn't want me in the basement.

Geoff has a bad temper.

Geoff had a marriage he never told Mom about, and we've only got his word as to what happened or why it ended. Or that he's only had one other wife.

I never heard back from his stepdaughter about what might have happened there.

What if?

What if Mom tries to break it off with him and...

No. *Oh no.* I'm wide awake now, my heart racing.

"I can't leave her alone in this house with him," I whisper to the darkness.

But what can I possibly do? Geoff and Mom will never buy it if I claim I changed my mind and want to stay here. And if I tell Mom what I'm thinking, she might think I'm overreacting. Or paranoid from sleep deprivation.

A plan presents itself as I lie in bed, wringing my blanket between my hands: I'll pretend I'm sick tomorrow and can't go.

And then I'll call Gram, let her know what Mom told me, and tell her what I'm afraid could happen. It might sound bizarre, but I know Gram. She won't blow it off if she thinks we might be in danger.

I consider what would be easier to fake—a sore throat or an impending stomach bug—and fall asleep while trying to decide.

It's still night when someone shakes me awake.

"Wh—" A clammy hand on my mouth cuts my question off, and a dark shape hovers over me. I jerk upright and thrash, trying to shake the hand off. Not tonight, Morgan House. Not now.

"Rachel. *Shhh.*" It's Mom whispering. "Someone's in the house."

My heart pounds even harder. *Oh god. It's happening. Already.*

A *ka-snick* that I recognize from countless movies and TV shows sounds near my bed—a gun being cocked. I bite back a scream, wondering who's in the room with us.

"I'm gonna go find this clown," Geoff mutters. "Give him one chance to get the hell out of here." A small shaft of moonlight from my window glints off the barrel of the handgun I had no idea Geoff owned.

"Oh, Geoff. No." Mom's whisper is verging on too loud. "That's a bad idea. I already called 911."

My brain is still sleep-fogged. Earlier tonight, I'd been so sure Geoff was the one coming for us. What's happening?

"Who knows when they'll get here? You two stay put. And don't make a sound." With that, Geoff tiptoes out of the room, shutting the door behind him. Mom and I huddle together on my bed, trembling.

"Are you sure there's someone down there?" I whisper. After all, I've heard strange footsteps in this house from the very first night I was here.

Mom shushes me. And now I can hear the living room floor creaking under someone's heavy tread. The floorboards squeal.

Geoff couldn't get down there that fast, and he doesn't walk that heavily anyhow. My stomach clenches.

"Hey! What the hell do you think you're doing?" Geoff's voice rings out.

Mom gasps, and I put a hand on her arm. Her skin feels clammy, and she's shaking hard.

Geoff screams as several crashing noises sound from downstairs. Mom wraps an arm around me and holds her other hand over her mouth, but I can hear her breaths coming in sobs now.

Three gunshots sound out from the first floor, so loud they rattle my bones and startle a scream out of me. My head spins, my tense muscles from moments ago liquefying as I fight to stay upright.

Footsteps boom up the staircase, but they're way too heavy to be Geoff's. The thuds ring closer down the hallway, then stop at my door.

The door. It isn't locked. Oh god. An ice-cold sensation spreads over the back of my neck. I get up, but Mom stands, too, and tries to hold me back.

"Rachel! Don't!"

"The door, Mom. I have to—"

The person outside jiggles the doorknob. The door doesn't budge.

Mom and I clutch each other, and she whimpers as the intruder shakes the knob. And then they slam into the door, again and again, like they're throwing their whole body into it. Mom's body jerks with every slam. There's no way that old, faded wood's going to hold up to much of this. Raspy breathing noises sound from the hallway.

"Geoff?" Mom whimpers, a pleading tone in her voice.

"That's not Geoff, Mom. God, it isn't Geoff. Oh my God."

And then that terrifying guttural growl starts up in here again. I look at Mom, but if she hears the growling, she doesn't react. Her eyes are fixed on the door, which shakes a little harder with every slam from the intruder.

I fumble around in my bedroom, trying to find something, anything I might use to hit someone. But it's not like I've got a handy collection of weapons lying around. Could I stab someone with a clothes hanger? Crack them in the face with a shoe? Smash a chair over their head? How many people could be out there?

The growling sound rumbles the floor under our feet now. Are we in more danger if we stay in here or if we get out? I don't know anymore. Tears roll down my face as my eyes dart around the room, searching for something—anything that might stop this person or at least slow them down long enough for us to escape.

And then I hear another sound: sirens in the night, distant at first and then getting louder and closer.

The banging against the door stops. A beat of silence passes before footsteps pound the hallway floor again, away from us this time. As they do, that growling stops, too.

Oh God. Geoff. I'm sick thinking of what might be waiting for us downstairs.

The intruder hurries down the stairs, those heavy footsteps vanishing as the front door slams.

Mom wrestles my bedroom door open with a crash.

"Geoff!" she screams. She tears out the door. I'm a sobbing mess now, too afraid to leave my room. Whatever's down there, I don't want to see it. I'm not ready.

Her footsteps shake the walls all the way down and stop. And then her screaming shatters the silence. Mom calls Geoff's name, again and again, desperation in every cry as she screams her throat raw. The sound is so loud and harsh it could rip the air in half. I don't want to see what's happened, but I have to. I can't hide from this forever.

I force myself to move out of my bedroom into the dark hall, towards the stairs, and down. I cling to the banister so my rubbery legs don't send me tumbling.

Mom is on the floor in the dark living room, huddling over a still shape. She makes a heartrending sound that's halfway between a scream and a sob. The keens come over and over until I think the noise will rip us both apart. And I *know.* I know even before I turn on the light with a trembling hand and see Geoff's blank gray eyes staring at nothing. Blood pools beneath him, staining the floor as Mom bends over him and wails. The sobs become the word *No*, raw and drawn out.

No. No. No. That's not fair. Not again. My legs give out at last, and I collapse on the floor, completely useless. Flashing red lights pulsate through the window, and the police pound on the door.

Chapter Nineteen

LOSSES

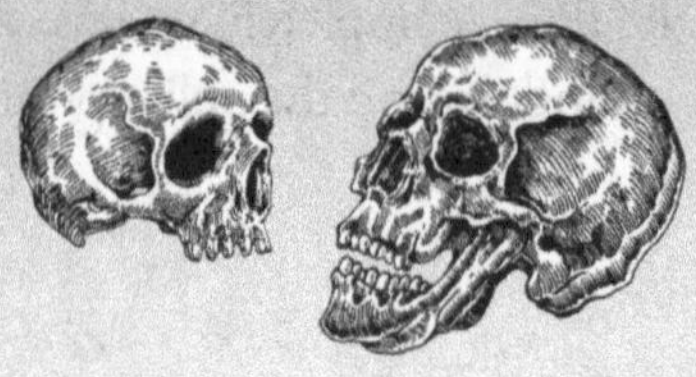

THE WEEKS after Geoff's murder are a haze, and only occasionally does something break through the fog enough for me to remember it later.

The police ask us questions for what feels like days. Did Geoff have any enemies? Had we seen anyone strange around the house? What happened to the front window?

I learn bits and pieces of what happened from Mom. The sheet someone taped up to cover the hole was on the floor. The intruder must have come in that way, as there was no sign of forced entry. The gun was lying in the middle of the living room floor, but the only prints on it were Geoff's. The person who'd wrestled his gun away and killed him with it left absolutely no trace of themselves.

Gram appears at some point and wraps both of us in big, warm embraces, then spirits us away to her condo for a few days until the police are finished examining the scene. *The Scene*. I will never again walk through that living room without mentally calling it the Scene.

Gram hires a company to clean up the Scene, so we won't be heading into something horrible when we return to the house. Mom doesn't want to go back there at all. Neither do I, but we have to. Geoff died without leaving a will, and by state law, that means Mom, as the surviving spouse, gets everything he had: his money, his car, Morgan House, and all the stuff inside it.

I've never liked this house, but it's even more foreboding when we return. It's still damp, creaky, and musty inside, but now there's something especially sinister hanging over us, combining with the grief. It's as if the house knows it's claimed another soul. If I close my eyes and listen, I'm sure I'll hear our screams and the gunshots of the night Geoff died still echoing off the walls.

A company in town fixes the window for free as a compassionate, neighborly gesture. Gram and I move around the house, making sure every window is securely locked, even the ones on the second floor that nobody could possibly reach without hauling a ladder out here. Gram arranges for the installation of a burglar alarm. Why Geoff didn't do that before... well, it doesn't matter now.

Elena calls and asks if I'd like to stay with her again for a few days, but feeling that I should stick close to Mom, I tell her no. Not that Mom, who's pale and distant, would notice if I was gone.

I could cry, should cry, but something inside isn't letting me. Instead, I'm numb and ice cold all the time despite the humidity in the house.

Something isn't letting Mom cry, either. She spends hours slumped in Geoff's favorite armchair like an abandoned rag doll, listless—almost boneless. Her eyes don't look at anything.

She focuses just long enough to ask us to help her with a banishment spell to cleanse the negative energy from the living room. I see the look in Gram's eyes at that request, but neither of us can bear to tell her no.

Mom opens the windows, and we all walk around the Scene in a clockwise circle with sticks of sage incense. When we're finished with that, she sprinkles black salt around the room's perimeter, sweeping it all up an hour later with a handmade broom she bought off Etsy. And then she places pieces of shining black obsidian on the mantel, the windowsill, and the bookshelf. Tears finally flow free from her eyes as she finishes up. I wonder if she has any spells to try to heal herself or if healing this new hurt is even possible.

"Do you think that worked?" I whisper to Gram afterward.

"I have no idea. But if it made your mom feel better, even for a few minutes, it did something useful."

I stand alone in the living room later, hoping to feel something different, something lighter. The spiced smell of the incense lingers in the air, but I don't sense any other kind of change. I think of the odd stains on the floors and wonder if there's a new one, permanently marking the spot where Geoff was killed. That thought makes me head for my bedroom.

My mom tends to focus on positive magic, spells for love and forgiveness and good energy. I'm not sure she has any real idea how to fight against everything that has happened here. Does anyone? I sure don't.

Gram bustles around, arranging for a cremation service for Geoff. She sits in the kitchen with her laptop and phone and tries to track down his family. The only ones that turn up are a few far-flung distant cousins who aren't broken up enough about his sudden, violent death to come all the way out to Virginia to say goodbye. Geoff's co-workers and golfing buddies pay their respects via emails and cards and occasional bouquets that trickle in, but that's it.

No wonder he wanted a family so much. He wasn't kidding when he said he didn't have one. That thought makes me feel sorry for him now that it's too late to make a difference. Was he so desperate for connection—any connection—that he just tried too hard with people?

It doesn't matter now, yet the thought makes me sad.

We have him cremated privately, and his ashes sit in a black lacquer box on the fireplace mantel while Mom decides what she wants to do with them. She's not at all up to deciding yet. She starts opening bottles of white wine at noon. By four o'clock, she's either lost in a haze, staring at nothing with bloodshot eyes, or zonked out cold, snoring as Gram and I quietly box up Geoff's things to donate to whatever charities will send a truck over.

I pack almost all of Geoff's obnoxious mugs, wrapping them in newspaper and leaving just a couple out for us to use. When I finish, I clean his things out of the upstairs bathroom. But even though I never felt close to him, getting rid of little pieces of his life—used razors, his toothbrush—feels odd and wrong. When Dad died, my mom and Gram were the ones who packed or threw things out. I'm not used to the feeling of removing someone's presence from the world.

I help Gram pack Geoff's stuff in the bedroom after Mom picks out what she wants to keep. The safe I found in their closet is wide-open now. Turns out, that's where he kept the gun. I can't help but wonder what might have happened if that gun had stayed locked up. Would he still be here? Or would we all be dead?

Mom tries to help at first, but after picking up a few of Geoff's things and setting them down over and over, she returns to her Chardonnay. I'm not surprised. If I feel weird about getting rid of Geoff's things, I can't imagine what it must be like for her.

"I feel like I should put a stop to that," Gram says to me as we watch Mom slumped in her chair in a wine-soaked sleep one afternoon. "But maybe not yet."

"I don't know," I respond. And I don't. I just know that I should have warned Mom: *Nothing lasts. Don't get attached.* But surely Mom already knew that. She's lost two husbands now.

"Are *you* okay?" Gram asks me. "How are you holding up, hon?"

And I don't know the answer to that either. I can't pretend I loved Geoff or even liked him very much, but I never imagined he'd meet such a sudden, brutal end. The knowledge stings as if I'd somehow wished it on him with all my contempt. What might have happened if I'd given him more of a chance?

I'll never know.

Sometimes, I'll catch a whiff of his Earl Grey-smelling aftershave or his laundry detergent like he's still lingering in the house somewhere. And every time one of his scents drifts through the air, I want to tell him I'm sorry—that even if I never really liked him much, I never wanted *this*.

"I WISH I could stop thinking about it," I tell Nick. We lie together on a blanket in a small, secluded clearing in the woods near St. Mary Cemetery. Trees rustle in the breeze over us. It's an overcast afternoon, and it's the first time I've seen Nick since everything happened. His black hair fans out under his head. I rest my head on his chest and listen to his breathing as we talk. The silver chain around his neck leads to some kind of pendant under his shirt, and it makes an indentation that rises and falls with each breath. I find the up-down-up-down motion soothing to watch.

"Shouldn't be that hard, should it?" he asks.

"What do you mean?"

"I mean ... well, you didn't even like him that much. Did you?"

I raise my head and stare at him. I still feel numb and cold, but the total callousness of his comment makes something flare inside me.

"That's all you can say? Seriously? It's not just about Geoff. Watching my mom fall apart all over again and knowing I can't do a damn thing to help her hurts."

He turns pink. "You're right. That was dumb. Sorry. I don't know what to say, honestly. This whole thing is so weird."

"Yeah." I drop my head back to his shoulder, and he puts a protective arm around me. "More than weird. He was an asshole most of the time, but God. He shouldn't have had to go out like that. If I never hear my mom make sounds like that again, it'll be too soon." I shudder.

"I'm so sorry," he says, rubbing my arm. "I'm just glad

whoever it was didn't get you. The police any closer to figuring out who it could have been?"

"No. Whoever it was got really lucky. No fingerprints, nothing."

We lie in silence together for a moment. I watch his chest rise and fall until something occurs to me, something that Geoff's death made me forget.

"So. Were you seriously mad I was going to go stay with Gram?"

"Not *mad.*" He thinks for a second before speaking again. "But I was going to miss you. That's allowed, right?"

"Sure." I smile. "But I wondered. You stopped texting right after that."

"I didn't mean anything by it." He studies my face. "I just didn't like the idea of you being gone that long."

"I would have missed you too. A lot."

He rolls over on top of me, his mouth finding mine, and I tangle my fingers in his hair, returning his kiss with equal enthusiasm. He works his hand under my shirt and pushes it up so that he can caress my breasts. And then his fingers find their way to the black skirt I'm wearing and pull the fabric up over my bare legs.

My heart beats faster. The awful chill that's taken up residence in my guts and bones since Geoff's death fades now as Nick touches my body.

He moves a hand away and works his jeans open, and I glance around. It's hardly private out here. Anyone could walk by. And this spot is far from comfortable. The blanket does little to blunt the feeling of sticks and pebbles under our bodies.

But if I stop to think too much about things, I might change my mind about what I'm about to do, and right now, I want Nick whether it's a good idea or not.

I'm not sure I'm ready for this. Is anyone, ever? How do you even know?

I reach for my purse and find one of the condoms I'd stashed there, just in case.

Boys will come up with all the reasons in the world why they shouldn't have to wear a condom, Mom told me. *Make them put it on anyway. And if they won't, then don't have sex with them. You can't ever be sure who else they might have been with.*

Nick eyes the blue foil wrapper.

"We don't need that," he says. "I...I'll be careful."

But being "careful" doesn't always work, and besides, it's not only about pregnancy.

"Please?" I keep holding it up, and finally, he takes it. I sneak a glance when he puts it on and draw in a breath, wondering how in the world *that's* going to fit where it's supposed to go.

At first, it hurts so much that I cry out, and he stops and asks if I'm sure I want to do this.

"Don't stop," I say. That chill is still there inside me, and Nick's warm body against mine is the only thing I can imagine melting that block of ice.

The ground's hard against my back, and the pressure between my legs is still sharp and intense. The pendant Nick wears digs into my chest. His hair smells faintly of soap and smoke as it falls into my face, and his breaths get faster and sharper as I clutch his back.

Nothing lasts, I tell myself as our bodies move together. The pain fades a little and a wonderful, amazing heat spreads through my body at last as our pace quickens. *Nothing. But let me have this one thing for just a little while. Please.*

MOM'S SITTING glassy eyed in the living room when I come home late that afternoon. A faint scent of exhaled alcohol hangs in the air and she stares at the Scene as if she's still reliving what happened there. Gram sits in Geoff's armchair, looking at something on her iPad. Thunder rumbles outside. I beat the rain home by seconds.

"Hi," I say. They both stare at me, and I wonder if they can somehow tell what I've been doing. My face turns pink.

"Hi, hon," Gram says at last. "How was town?"

"Okay. Kind of boring." I avoid their eyes as I move to the kitchen to get a glass of water.

"Must be nice," Mom mutters when I come back.

"What's that?"

"To get away. I can't." There's an edge in Mom's voice.

"Tara, I'd be happy to take you out anywhere you want to go." Gram scowls over her reading glasses. "I've said before, I don't think staying in this house all the time and drinking yourself insensible every day is doing you a bit of good. I know how much you're hurting, but you're going to have to get out there and start living your life again sooner or later."

"Can't take me away from my own mind, Mother," she slurs back.

"I know that. But focusing on something else could help. Even if it's just for a little while."

"Gram's right, Mom."

Mom glares at me, her shining, bloodshot eyes narrowed. "Easy for you to say. You didn't give a damn about him."

My mouth drops open. The words are a slap to the face. "Jesus, Mom. I didn't want *that* to happen to him. Or you."

"Wouldn't even give him a chance," Mom says, her voice fuzzy. "Not *ever*. Nothing he tried ever worked with you."

"Tara?" Gram says. "Enough."

My pulse pounds in my temples. I know Mom's been drinking. I know I should turn away, go up to my room, let it go. But Mom's words, which sound a lot like the things I've been telling myself, sting. And the anger I've been sitting on since we moved out here reaches a boil.

"Like it would have mattered? You didn't care if I liked him or not. You didn't care about my feelings at all. You just dragged me out here and expected me to go along with everything because it was what you wanted."

Mom flushes bright pink. "Go along with *what?* With me trying to give us both a happy family again?"

"Okay, you two. This is so not the right time for this." Gram stands, holding her hands up.

"Butt out, Mother." Mom waves a dismissive hand. "I want to hear this. I need to know why I'm such a *terrible* parent."

Gram's right. This discussion is going nowhere good, and it's going there fast, but this has been simmering inside me for too long. Fierce rage, keen and sharp, rushes through me. The beast inside wants out again.

"You seriously thought you could replace Dad with *him,* and I just wouldn't care? That I'd just turn into a nice little Geoff clone going golfing with him and grilling steaks or whatever other stupid shit he was always bugging me about?"

Mom's mouth is a round O-shape, and her face goes bright red, and I wonder if I've said too much. But I decide I don't care. If Mom wants to pick a fight now, she's going to get one.

"I'm sorry about what happened to him. Nobody deserves that. But he was never, ever Dad. You just shoved him down my throat and acted like I should be happy you came up with some kind of Dad replacement. You say you wanted to give us both a happy family, but you never cared what that meant for me. Marrying Geoff wasn't for me, Mom, it was for you. And besides, you were all ready to—"

"*Rachel.*" Gram's voice is cold and sharp. I know that tone too well. But I can't stop.

"What? She said she wanted to hear it. And now she knows."

Tears roll down Mom's cheeks, and just like when I told Mom about Geoff's secret first wife, I wish for a moment I could stuff all the words back in my mouth. My heart pounds. I feel sick with guilt, but what good were all those ugly feelings doing stuck inside me with nowhere to go?

Finally, Mom pulls herself up in her chair.

"You're right, Rachel. Geoff was nothing like your dad. And I do mean *nothing*. There was something I never told you about your father." Her eyes glitter.

"Tara, no. I really don't think this is the time." Gram steps forward as if she's thinking about running across the room and slapping a hand over Mom's mouth.

"She's sixteen, Mother, and it's way *past* time she knew the truth."

"What the hell are you two talking about?" My head throbs.

"You remember Aunt Maddie?" Mom never takes her glassy eyes off mine.

"Of course I do."

Gram sits back down with a sigh, holding a hand to her head.

Aunt Maddie wasn't actually my aunt. She was Mom's friend from college, and she'd come down from New York City to visit every so often. Maddie was fairy-princess beautiful. She had long, blonde curly hair and enormous green eyes, and she smelled like vanilla and lemons. She always talked to me as if I was another adult instead of a little kid. I adored her.

"Didn't you ever wonder why she stopped coming to visit?" Mom says.

"I...I never thought about it." All the warmth from the afternoon with Nick vanishes as my body goes cold and numb again.

Mom lets out a humorless chuckle. "Well. Turns out your *wonderful* father was getting ready to leave me for your sweet, delightful Aunt Maddie." Those words—*wonderful, sweet, delightful*—are etched in acid.

I feel like someone's punched me in the stomach. "No. He wouldn't."

"Oh, but he *would*," Mom says. "But after he died, I thought there was no point in telling you about any of this because I *do* actually care about your feelings, and you were hurting enough."

With that, Mom slumps back in her chair, as if delivering this bit of horrible information has taken everything out of her. Maybe it has. She's been carrying this for so long, and she's had to hear me talk so much about how perfect my father was.

But this just can't be true, I think. My dad would never do that to us—to me.

And yet, the last time I saw Aunt Maddie was at Dad's memorial service, and I assumed Mom had called her.

Red-eyed Maddie fussed over me and asked how Mom was holding up, and I pointed Mom out and said, "Well, she's right there. Haven't you talked to her?"

Maddie bit a crimson lip, shook her head, and said, "Maybe later." And that was it, the last time I remember seeing her or hearing from her.

Maybe I should have thought about how strange that was, given how close they always were, but what happened to Dad was an enormous black cloud hanging over my world, blocking out any light that might have shone on something else.

Dad. No. He wouldn't do that.

"Gram? Is this true?"

Gram sighs.

"I'm sorry, Rachel." Her voice is low and soft. "For whatever it's worth, I think you have every right to be angry about what's been happening here. I don't think Geoff was ever cut out to be a stepfather, to put it mildly. And I told your mother I didn't think rushing into all this the way she did was a great idea for any of you."

Mom continues her quiet weeping over in her armchair. Tears form in my eyes, but I blink them back.

"But people are complicated, hon," Gram continues. "Adults don't always make good decisions. Not even your father, I'm afraid."

I have no idea what to say to any of this, and I'm afraid if I say anything, I'll burst into sobs. My throat is painfully tight from impending tears. So, I turn away from them and run upstairs.

I go to the bathroom and take a long bath in the clawfoot bathtub as if I can wash away everything I've just heard, but the water does nothing to make everything inside stop hurting. I expect a knock on the door, but none comes. Voices ring out downstairs, sharp and argumentative.

Back in my room, I pull on an old The Cure T-shirt and faded purple shorts. The family photograph I loved so much sits on the dresser. Dad looks so happy with me and Mom. We're a beautiful, smiling, perfect family.

And it was all a lie. Was he messing around with Maddie even then?

"You promised you'd never leave me. You *promised*. You fucking liar," I tell the picture.

I snatch it up, hurl it into a wall, and choke back a sob as the frame falls apart and the glass shatters all over the floor.

Chapter Twenty

AFTERMATH

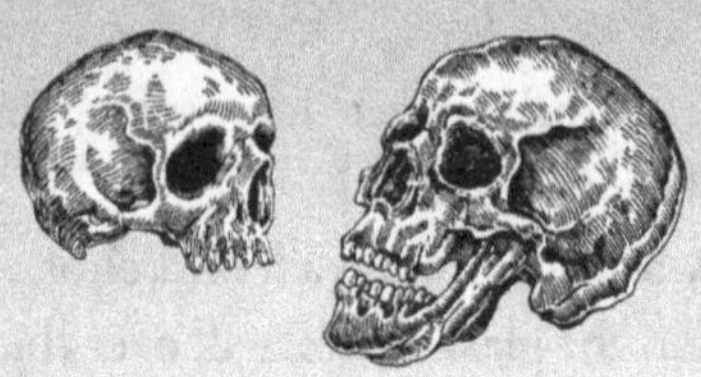

I EXPECT someone to come up to see me, but they don't. The arguing downstairs finally subsides. Footsteps make the staircase creak, followed by the sounds of Mom and Gram going to their respective rooms. The lights under my door fade.

Good. I can't face either one of them right now. I throw an extra sheet over the broken glass on the floor, figuring I'll take care of it tomorrow.

With that, I lie on my back on the bed, hot tears leaking from my eyes and streaming down the sides of my face. Everything inside me has gone cold again. If it weren't for the soreness between my legs, I'd have completely forgotten about my time with Nick this very afternoon. It already seems like something that happened to another person in a completely different time.

I doze off but wake up soon enough at the sound of someone crying. That dry, intense heat is back.

"Shut up," I tell whatever's in my room. "I'm not in the mood for you tonight."

It doesn't listen. The sobs get louder and more ragged.

"God *damn* it."

Instead of letting the things in this house—whoever or whatever they are—take me down to the basement, I'm going down there myself. I toss my purple blanket aside and ease out of bed. The floor is clear as I leave the bedroom.

I try not to make the stairs creak as I head down. I don't want Mom or Gram to hear me and come out to talk.

I rummage in the kitchen junk drawer until I find the key. The basement door opens onto the unlit steps, and I grope around the wall until I find the light switch. I shield my stinging eyes against the sudden brightness.

"Okay," I whisper to whatever might be listening. "I'm here. Do your worst. I don't even care anymore."

One of the steps creaks as I head down, and I freeze, positive the whole house must have heard the sudden squeal. Nobody stirs, and I reach the bottom of the stairs without making any more noise.

Again, I examine the walls and shelves, trying to figure out what it is down here that Geoff never wanted me to see. His unfinished woodworking projects are gone now. Mom and Gram must have cleaned them out. But plenty of things remain. A rack of yard tools hangs to my left. A dusty red can of gasoline sits on the floor. Another shelf holds a random assortment of items: flashlights, golf balls, a box of wooden fireplace matches, several containers of nails.

Why was he always so intent on keeping me out? Did he know what was lurking down here? Did he at least sense it, even if he pretended he didn't?

My heart thumps as I stare at the blank section of the wall where I keep seeing that door. I move closer and run my fingers over it. It's smooth and cold against my fingertips. There's a faint crack in the concrete, but I still can't find any sign there's ever been any kind of entrance here, much less a hidden room behind it.

I draw a hand back and hit the concrete wall. "*Show* me," I hiss. "What's wrong? You afraid?" Maybe they weren't expecting me to bring the fight to them. Good.

But then the basement goes black, and fingers of bone wrap

around my ankle and pull. I put my arms out just in time to keep from hitting my head on the floor as I topple over.

A shady figure moans, dragging itself across the floor towards me with that low *shh-shh* sound. An ice-cold wave floods my insides. I can see only an outline of its body, but I'm sure it's another woman. She's hauling herself on her forearms as though her legs don't work anymore. Her hair drags over the floor, snagging on shards of bone as she gets closer to me.

The shadow man, the same one I've been seeing over and over, slams the door open and storms in behind the woman. He raises a cleaver over her, his long, lean body silhouetted in the dark, and I can't see his face.

He speaks to her in a language I've never heard. I don't know what he's saying, but those harsh-sounding, guttural words make my scalp prickle. That's the voice I've been hearing down here this whole time. Smells of smoke and iron and rot fill my nostrils, and I don't want to open my mouth—don't want to take any of this fouled air into my body as he strikes downward with the cleaver and continues to chant. The woman writhes and screams before making a long, low rattling sound. Then, she goes still as the shadow man drops the cleaver and crouches low over her with a moan of ecstasy. A wave of dizziness sweeps over me.

Why did I think it was such a great idea to come down here? I have to get out. The basement door shines, but it moves away from me at the same pace I crawl towards it, and my heart speeds up. Why can't I reach it?

Just as I'm finally drawing close, fingers knot themselves in my hair and yank my head back. That strange and furious language sounds in my ear as something sharp presses into my neck.

I wake up on the basement floor, gasping for air. Nobody's leaning over me this time. No one's down here at all. Cold, frightened, and alone, I haul myself to my feet and make my way up the basement stairs.

This time, I don't bother locking the basement door behind

me. What difference has the lock ever made? Whenever those things in there want me, they can get me.

Bright sunlight streams through the kitchen window onto a very chilly scene when I come downstairs the next morning. Mom and Gram sit at the kitchen table, staring at their coffee, saying nothing. Gram glances up and gives me a small smile.

"Did you get any rest, honey?"

"I guess. A little." I help myself to coffee in the biggest mug left in the cabinet.

Mom studies us and then the wooden table for a moment before speaking.

"I'm sorry, Rachel. I shouldn't have just blurted all that out last night."

What is she expecting me to say? *That's okay?* Well, it's not. The knowledge of Dad's betrayal gnaws hot in my chest, like I've lost him all over again.

I shrug, staring at the plate of sesame bagels in front of me. Mom and I still can't meet each other's eyes. Gram changes the subject and talks about how it might do all of us some good to get out of this house and go somewhere today. Mom makes a few noises that might or might not be agreement. And I definitely think Gram's right. I'm so ready to get out of this house again.

But I'm not going anywhere with them. After breakfast, I go back to my room, lift the sheet on the floor, and wrap a paper towel around my hand to pick up the broken frame and the shattered glass. The picture itself isn't scratched or torn, much to my relief. After sweeping up the remaining glass shards, I throw the broken parts away and hide the photograph in a drawer. I'm not ready to look at it every day, but I don't want it gone either.

Once the floor is clean, I wash up, put on black shorts and a sleeveless purple T-shirt, and ride my bike to Milledge's Book Company. I'm still sore from yesterday, and I blush as I think about my time with Nick in the woods. Do I feel different? Isn't your first time supposed to be a life-changing event? Movies and books always make it seem that way—like your life will change from black-and-white Kansas to technicolor Oz after you've "done it."

Maybe I've already had too many life-changing events happen recently, but I still feel like the same person, virgin or not.

Toby click-clacks over to greet me when I walk in the store, and I kneel and hug him, delighting in the sensation of his soft ears against my cheek. The skylight lets in the sun, and for just a moment, I feel safe from all the darkness of the last several months.

Mrs. Milledge walks over, carrying a book I'd ordered.

"I heard about your stepfather, Rachel. I'm so sorry." She hands me the novel.

"Thanks. You can leave it up here. I'll pay for it when I figure out if I'm getting anything else."

Mrs. Milledge gives me a huge, warm smile. "From the sound of things, you could definitely use an escape right now. How's your mother holding up?"

"I don't know. I think my grandmother's the only thing keeping us both from falling to pieces."

Mrs. Milledge shakes her head. "Again, you and your mom have my sympathy. If there's anything I can do..."

"Just keep being here with this store."

She smiles. "I fully intend to."

I go to the little coffee bar in the back of the store and sit there with a latte. A few minutes later, a warm hand grasps my shoulder. Nick slides in on the stool next to mine and kisses my cheek.

"Hey. Thought you might be here," he says.

"Good guess." I smile at him.

"You didn't answer my texts last night."

I'd heard the phone chime, but I hadn't been ready to talk to Nick. Or anyone. "I know. I'm sorry. Huge, enormous drama bomb when I got home."

"Uh-oh. Everything all right?"

I don't know how to explain all the things that happened last night. I'm not even sure if I want to tell him about Dad. That knowledge still feels like a raw, throbbing wound.

"My mom was drunk and started in on me about not caring about Geoff. And then...ah, I don't know. It was a mess. I think things are going to be messy there for a long time."

"Shit," he says.

"Yeah. Welcome to my life."

He runs a finger over my arm, and I remember his touch on my body yesterday. "Anything you want to do today? We could go hang out somewhere." Something inside me tingles at that thought.

"Like where?" I ask.

"I dunno. Are your mom and grandmother going to be home?" The touch becomes a little more sensual as he runs his fingertip up my bare skin.

"I guess so. They didn't say anything about going out."

"That's too bad." He takes his hand away. My pulse speeds up.

"Could we go to your place? Is your uncle really that bad?"

He shakes his head. "You have no idea. I don't want to put you through a visit with him. You've already had enough going on."

I can't help but wonder why Nick believes his uncle is more terrifying than anything that's happened to me in Morgan House. "What's wrong with him? What does he do that's so awful?"

Nick looks down at the counter. "He's just always got different things going on. He says I get in the way. And like I told you before, he doesn't like it at all when I bring girls over. Not that I've done it much," he adds when he sees the look on my face.

"Why don't you just get your own place?"

He frowns. "Well, sure—if I were made of money, that would be easy. But it's not exactly cheap to live around here. I work part-time jobs when I can to help support my uncle, but it's not enough for me to live by myself."

"What about college?"

Nick shakes his head. "What about it? That costs money, too. And I didn't have the grades to get into a good school, to be honest." He glances down at his hands. "I want to save up enough money to get out someday, but it's not happening any time soon."

We sit in disappointed silence for a minute before I have an idea.

"Gram's been making a lot of noise about getting Mom out of the house, and I think Mom might be coming around to the idea. If they go out somewhere, I'll text you. Maybe we can get some time alone then." A warm flush starts at my collarbone as I consider what *time alone* with Nick likely means now.

He smiles. "Sounds nice. If it's what you want." His hand is on my thigh now.

"It is." Maybe he doesn't notice how much I'm blushing.

I pay for my book, and we leave Milledge's hand-in-hand. He buys me another giant lollipop at Rocket Pop, even though I haven't opened the first one yet. For just a little while, things feel normal again.

I kiss him goodbye longer and harder than usual when he walks me back to my bike, like I can draw extra strength from him before facing everyone at home again.

"Don't forget to text me if you're alone in the house and you get scared." He winks, and I turn red again.

"You bet."

I'm positive I can still sense his gaze on me as I pedal off.

WHEN I GET HOME, the house is empty. A note on the kitchen table in Mom's loopy handwriting tells me she and Gram went out to the nearby town center. They hoped I don't mind that they went without me, but they figured I was busy with Nick.

I consider texting him and telling him to come over right now, but the thought of having a little space to process everything going on in my head without a well-meaning person buzzing around me sounds too good to waste. Even if it does mean I'm alone here.

I settle on the black leather sofa and open my iPad, checking my email and the texts from last night. A notification pops up telling me I have a direct message from someone named AmbrosiaGurl. For a few seconds I can't remember who that is—but then the connection slams into my head.

Amber.

Amber Whittaker wrote back.

Chapter Twenty-One

REVELATIONS

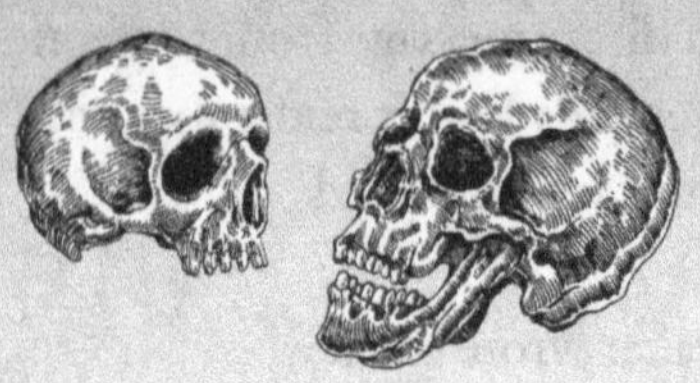

My skin prickles as I stare down at the messages.

> Hey Rachel. Sorry, but I don't use this account much anymore. Just saw your message.

> Yeah, my mom was married to Geoff Barber. It didn't last long. He was kind of a dick to me, I had a lot of problems, and she got us both out of there before I could really get hurt. I hated that house.

I take a breath before continuing.

> Hated him, too, to be honest. No offense if you like him. Don't know how any of this is going to help you with your mom, though. Good luck. - Amber.

Clutching the iPad with shaking hands, I think hard about what I want to say. I have a million questions, and I know this near-complete stranger doesn't owe me an answer to any of them. She might write me off as a freak for even asking, but I have to at least try.

Thanks for writing me back.

I chew my lip before writing the next words.

Just so you know, Geoff is dead. Someone broke into the house, and they killed him when he confronted them.

That sounds a little cold when I read it over. Amber's message didn't exactly make me think she'd be broken up by the news. Even so, I eye the black box holding Geoff's ashes on the fireplace mantel with more than a little guilt.

My mom inherited Morgan House and we're kind of stuck here for now.

I rock myself in place, wondering if it's a good idea to ask Amber the next thing I want to know. Will she even answer?

Screw it. I figure it's worth a shot.

Did you ever end up in the basement of Morgan House and not know how you got there? Are you and your mom OK now? I know you don't know me, and all this is weird. You don't have to answer if you don't want to. But I'd like to know.

I send the message before I can change my mind. As I'm about to close the iPad, a gray text bubble pops up on my screen. It's Nick.

Hi. How's it going?

Crazy. I just heard from Amber.

Nick's reply takes a few moments to come in, and I curse the signal in here.

Amber?

Guess I didn't mention her before. She's Geoff's stepdaughter from that marriage he never told my mom about. I DMed her on Twitter to see what happened with him and her mom.

Another minute passes before his next text pops up.

And what did she say?

Not much. She thought she was having emotional problems and her mom got her out of there and divorced Geoff. But I think maybe she was seeing the same stuff here that I am.

Another long pause.

Does any of this matter now? She's out of there.

Is that a serious question? I stare at the screen, clucking my tongue. After everything that's happened, does he still not get why this is so important to me?

Yes, Nick, it matters. I'm still stuck here. If she heard all that stuff too, I want to know why. I want to know what the hell happened here and then convince Mom to get us out. It's getting worse.

You sure doing all that is a good idea?

Annoyance flares inside me.

What do you mean?

Don't forget—the last time you went poking around in Geoff's past, all you did was get people upset at you, and it didn't make any difference anyhow. Your mom still married the guy.

That beast in my chest, the one I thought only Mom and Geoff could stir, claws at my insides, threatening to break out.

What are you getting at?

Look. You dig up this stuff and throw it around without thinking about what it might do to other people. What if this Amber doesn't want to talk about any of this?

Then she can block me.

Like I'm just about to do to Nick. Why is he being so weird about this? I expected him to be on my side. He's *been to* the house. He's seen it in action. He knows what I've been dealing with for months now.

Well, at least take some time before you write her back. If she doesn't answer you, don't push her.

Like I can make her do something she doesn't want to do. Anyway, have to go. Mom wants something.

Why is he so concerned about Amber? What about me and what I want?

Just before I flip the iPad's cover down, I see one last message from Nick:

Don't be mad. I love you.

When Mom and Gram get home an hour later, I haven't moved from the sofa. My mind is still reeling from Nick's last words. He *loves* me? Really?

And do I love him? I thought I did, even if I'd never said so. I wouldn't have slept with just anyone, and I honestly thought he understood me—that he was on my side.

But with that patronizing lecture just now, he sounded a lot like Geoff. That isn't a good look on anyone, no matter what Nick thought he was doing.

"Hi, honey," Gram calls. "Come help us with some of these bags."

When I see everything they're carrying, I burst out laughing. "Geez, Gram. What did you two do, buy the whole state out?"

Gram's lugging in what looks like dozens of grocery bags from Wegmans. Mom has packages from Ulta and Lush.

"Just helping the economy," Gram says, her face flushed. "We're givers like that. Might be a few things for you in there, too."

"You okay, Rachel? What's with the glum look?" Mom asks, brushing hair out of her face.

I shrug. "I dunno. Just some Nick stuff." Mom seems like she's in a halfway decent mood for the first time since Geoff's death, and there's no way I'm bringing up Amber Whittaker now.

"You should invite him over sometime," Mom says. "I'd like to get to know him a little better. I bet he'd be pretty impressed if you cooked for him."

She's acting completely normal, as if we didn't just have a huge fight, and it's weirding me out. "Maybe. I'm kind of pissed at him right now." I'm still kind of pissed at her too.

Mom and Gram exchange looks that might or might not be amused. "Oh dear," Mom says. "Well, if you make up with him, I'd love to have him over some time."

Love. There's that word again.

That afternoon, I check my iPad a ridiculous number of times. There's no response from Amber.

Nick's *I love you* is still hanging there. After thinking about it and gnawing my lip, I reply:

> I love you too. But don't talk to me like you're my dad. Or my stepdad.

Mom opens a bottle of white wine shortly before dinner, and I see the exact moment when her improved mood gives way to the darkness that's been shrouding her since Geoff died. Morgan House and what's happened here haunts her just as it does me. Her shoulders and eyebrows slump at the same time as her eyes grow glassy. Tendrils of hair fall out of her messy ponytail, and she doesn't bother tucking them back in. Still, she doesn't try to pick a fight with me, and Gram hustles her upstairs around nine, persuading her to lie down.

"Oh well. At least she didn't start that at noon today. It's progress," Gram says when she returns.

"I guess."

Gram sits down next to me on the sofa and folds her arms. "Okay. Spill."

I frown. "Spill what?"

"You've been in a mood about something since we got home, Rachel. I know that look. So, are you upset with Nick, your mom, me, or is something else going on?"

I study the fringe of gray roots at her hairline for a moment, trying to figure out what to say. "Does it have to be just one thing? I can multitask."

Gram chuckles. "Well, sure. You've had a lot going on lately, God knows."

I sigh.

"Nick was trying to talk me out of something today and I don't like him trying to boss me around. I mean, just because we—"

I break off. I almost blurted out something I might not be ready for Gram to hear yet.

Gram cocks her head, looking at me with narrowed eyes. "You two getting pretty...serious?" There's a tone to the word *serious*.

I feel my face turning scarlet. "Yeah."

"Rachel, I told you. That's nothing to be ashamed of. You're being careful though, right?"

I roll my eyes. "Didn't Mom tell you Geoff found the condoms?"

"She might have mentioned that, yes. But remember, when I say *be careful*, I'm not only talking about sex. What else do you know about him?"

I strongly suspect *not that much* is entirely the wrong answer.

"Nothing that makes me worry about him. He grew up here. He hates his uncle, but he can't afford to live on his own yet. Besides, we've spent a lot of time talking about what happened with Geoff. He's been so great at helping me to get through that." I remember what we were doing in the woods yesterday and blush again.

"That's nice. But still. Be careful not to rush into things."

"I'm not thinking about getting *married* to him, Gram. Jeez."

"I know that. But I stand by what I said."

I study my fingers for a moment. I wonder why she seems so mistrustful, and then I wonder if it has anything to do with what I learned last night about my father. Maybe that shook her trust in husbands and boyfriends in general.

"Gram? Did you hate Dad?"

Gram's mouth drops open for a second before she recovers. "Hell yes, I did. He broke my daughter's heart. How else was I supposed to feel? I don't like hating people, but he hurt Tara horribly and with one of her good friends, no less." Her voice gets louder and harder as she speaks.

"Do you hate him now?" I ask.

"To tell you the truth, I don't know. And honestly, where you're concerned, it doesn't matter. Whatever might have happened with Tara, he would have kept being a good father to you. That, I'm sure about." Gram shakes her head before continuing. "People are complicated, Rachel. Like I said before, they aren't all one thing or the other."

I'm still trying to square the image of my loving, caring dad with a man who'd walk away from his wife and child just to pursue another woman.

"I wish I could have stopped Tara from telling you last night, though. This is already a hard enough time for everyone without that coming up." She sighs.

"I would have had to know about it sooner or later, right?"

"I suppose. But maybe with everything that's been happening, later would have been the kinder option." She reaches over and squeezes my shoulder, and I put a hand over hers.

I think of Nick's words again. *You throw this information around without thinking about what it will do to other people.* Maybe I should tell him it's genetic.

"Well, it's been a busy day." She gets up and yawns. "I'm going to go upstairs to read and probably conk out before too long."

She pecks me on the forehead and heads upstairs. My body tenses as her bedroom door closes. I'm essentially alone in Morgan House now, and my pulse speeds up as I wonder what it might do to me tonight.

My iPad buzzes, and I pick it up. Nick's messaged me again.

You still mad?

I roll my eyes.

I better not be, I guess. Mom is all excited to have you over here for dinner sometime.

Oh really?

Yes, really.

I'd rather come over sometime when she's not there.

That makes me giggle.

Yeah. I know. She's getting around to feeling like leaving the house again. But not quite yet.

He doesn't need to know she's already been out and about.

> We could go out to that place by the cemetery tomorrow. I think we'd have it to ourselves again.

I bite my lip as a warm, tingly flush spreads through me. Maybe tomorrow, I'll be ready for him again. Maybe I'm ready for him now. He'd probably jump in the car and drive here right away if I asked. If we're careful and quiet, we could—

A notification pops up on the iPad screen.

A direct message from AmbrosiaGurl.

My hand trembles as I tap on the message.

It's short.

> Jesus. Did Geoff tell you about me ending up in the basement?

Chapter Twenty-Two

THE MISSING PIECE

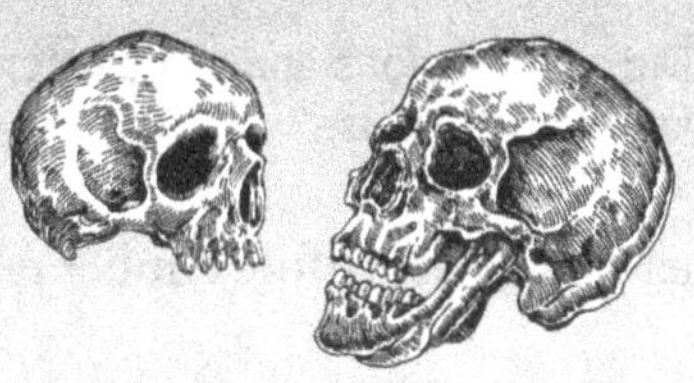

My stomach flips. The room around me lurches.

> He didn't have to tell me. I keep ending up down there and not knowing how I got there. And seeing awful things. Did you, too?

I know what the answer is going to be, and I'm not surprised when Amber messages back one word:

> Yes.

And then a little more:

> God. I thought something was seriously wrong with me. So did everyone else.

My hands tremble so much it's hard for me to tap out a response.

> No. NOT you. This house. Something awful happened here. I don't know what, but I think something's trying to make it happen again.

Her next message is slower in coming.

So, you see those dead women?

Yes.

Seriously crying right now. My mom got me out of there and divorced Geoff because she thought I was so messed up, and he wasn't helping.

Did all the visions and voices stop when you left Morgan House?

There's another long pause before Amber replies:

Yeah. I thought the doctors I had to see helped me get over all that.

Doctors? This is all a bit beyond me now.
She sends another message quickly.

Geoff was always such a dick about it. He thought I was making it up to drive him and my mom apart.

I shake my head like she can see it.

He accused me of the same thing, only he thought you put me up to it.

The hell? Like everything is my fault even after I'm gone?

Something molten and uncomfortable spreads in my midsection. Guilt. Whatever I thought about him before, I feel bad about trash-talking Geoff. He'd died trying to protect me and my mom from an intruder. I avoid looking at the black box on the mantel. It's as if he knows that even now, I won't give him a break. I tap out another message to Amber.

Well, anyway, I'm glad you got out. I hate this house. I don't like St. Mary, either. A couple places here are pretty okay, but the rest of it sucks.

Motion outside the window catches my eye. A shadowy form moves through the woods, coming straight towards the house. Twigs snap as the shape moves closer.

My head tingles and I hold my breath. *Shit, shit, shit. What if it's the person who killed Geoff, and they're coming back to ransack the house or something? Oh, shit—*

The person comes out from the trees and approaches the window. In the light from the house, I can see that it's just Nick. I nearly sob with relief as I toss my iPad aside. After fumbling with the locks, I wrench the window open.

"What the hell are you doing out there? You scared the crap out of me." I laugh, hoping Nick won't notice that I'm shaking.

Nick pushes his black hair out of his face and smiles, looking a little baffled at my greeting. "Sorry. But I really wanted to see you. Just wanted to see if you were still up. Is that okay?"

"Of course. Of *course*."

He climbs over the windowsill, catches a foot on the frame, and nearly stumbles into the living room. I engage in some exaggerated shushing, holding a finger over my lips and then jabbing it upwards.

"Sorry," he mouths. He straightens himself up and kisses me, and I tangle my fingers in his hair as I return his kiss. Even if I was pissed at him earlier, I'm so relieved to see him. Especially now that I know someone else heard all the same stuff I've been hearing in this place. Between that and the knowledge that Geoff's killer is still out there, Morgan House feels more unsafe than ever.

"Nick," I say quietly, "Amber wrote me back. She was hearing those voices here too. She even ended up in the basement."

His dark eyes widen. "No way."

"There's something really bad in this house. I wasn't just imagining things."

Nick looks around as though he'll be able to spot whatever's going wrong in here. His glance stops on the chunks of obsidian Mom's placed around the living room.

"Are those yours?" he asks.

I shake my head. "Mom put them out. She says they help absorb—"

"Negative energy, right?" He raises an eyebrow.

"How did you know?"

He gives me a half-smile. "I've read about some of this stuff. Crystals. The Tarot. Didn't know your mom was into that."

"She seriously thinks those will help dispel all the things happening here. But they aren't working—at all." I start trembling as I remember my last encounter with the shadow man in the basement.

He narrows his eyes. "No. You'd need something much stronger than those."

"What do you mean?" Something in that answer puzzles me.

"No offense to your mom, but do you really think this mass-marketed new age-y stuff does anything at all?"

I shrug. "It makes her feel better. But what did you mean about something stronger?"

He's quiet for a minute, and then he pulls me close against his warm body.

"I meant me. I'm here now. I won't let anything take you away." He turns my face up to his and kisses me, calming my thoughts and filling my mind with something else as I kiss him back and feel the heat rising between our bodies.

I know this is a terrible idea. Gram's a light sleeper, and ever since Geoff's death, Mom sometimes comes down to the kitchen for a glass of brandy when she can't sleep. And yet. He's here, right in front of me, and he's warm and smells like soap and wood smoke. It makes me think of yesterday in the woods again.

Keeping my arms wrapped around him, I move backward, bringing him along, easing us toward the black leather sectional.

"Where is everyone?" he murmurs.

"Upstairs. Asleep. Can you be quiet?"

"I can if you can."

He sits on the sofa and pulls me down with him. His skin tastes like salt, and I cling to him as if only he can save me from all the horrible truths floating around Morgan House.

"Jesus, it's hot in here," he whispers. He's right. "Why is it always so damn hot in this place?"

I run my hands under his t-shirt and savor the sensation of his skin against my fingers. "Hurry up and make me hotter."

We pull our clothes up and down and out of the way. He lifts his black T-shirt, revealing the pendant he wears around his neck, which I've never actually seen. It's a large antique key, weathered and ornate. It looks like it's a couple hundred years old.

"Wow. That's gorgeous." I reach for it, and Nick pulls back a little.

"That's been in my dad's family for a long time," he says. "I try to be careful with it. I'd feel awful if something happened to it."

"It's really cool." It is. Maybe someday, he'll let me wear it. He wraps his arms around me, and we kiss. The key presses into my chest, but after a few minutes, I stop thinking about it. I swipe a hand around for my purse to unearth one of the condoms I stashed there.

The blue art glass vase Mom put on the fireplace mantel falls to the floor with an enormous crash.

We both jump, and I press my face into Nick's shoulder to keep from shrieking.

"Christ," Nick breathes. "What the hell was that?"

We're pressed so tightly against each other, I can feel his heart beating as his key digs into my chest. I expect to hear footsteps running down the stairs at any second.

We hold completely still. I only exhale when it gets too painful to keep holding my breath. Nothing else happens.

"That was really weird," Nick murmurs.

"Mom says old places settle."

He looks down at me, his eyebrows knotting. "Settle? What does that even mean?"

"Don't know. It makes stuff break and scares the hell out of us, I guess. They think that was why the window broke." I never did figure out what Geoff meant by houses settling, but I don't want to dwell on that right now. We fall back into the sofa cushions, and I work a hand under the waistband of his black jeans.

Something drips on my other arm, which is wrapped around Nick's back. The liquid *plinks* are so faint at first that I'm not even sure they're happening. The dripping gets heavier, more regular as it strikes my arm.

I can't stand it anymore. "Ugh. Do you feel that?"

"What?"

"I think the ceiling's leaking or something. Hold on a minute."

I pull away from Nick and sit up. Red fluid rolls down my bare skin, warm and viscous.

Blood red fluid.

A spot at the back of my neck goes ice cold. "Nick. What the hell is that?"

More red liquid falls from the ceiling, splattering Nick's back.

"What *is* that?" He reaches around behind himself, and I lurch off the sofa. The red liquid spatters all over the couch. I can't take it anymore. Terror and disgust well up inside me, and I scream.

"Rachel! Quiet!" Nick's reaching for me when we hear it—footsteps on the staircase. We barely manage to yank all our clothes back into place before Gram and Mom reach the living room. Both of them hurry through the arched entrance and freeze when they see us.

Mom's mouth drops open. "What on earth is going on in here?"

"Really, Nick. We've simply *got* to stop meeting like this." The corner of Gram's mouth turns up as Nick shrinks into the sectional.

I can barely talk. "Mom. The sofa. The *ceiling*."

Mom looks around, her eyes huge. "What about them?"

"They're leaking." I look again. The red liquid is gone. My arm and the sofa are completely clean.

"But..." I say, just as Nick catches my eye. He narrows his eyes and shakes his head. *Don't*, he's saying.

"My vase!" Mom says. "What happened to my vase?"

"I don't know." I feel ridiculous. "It just *fell*."

Gram walks over and examines the couch, the ceiling, and the floor. "I don't see anything leaking now."

Mom blinks her bleary eyes and breaks off from staring around the room to look at Nick. "So, you're Nick?"

He can't even meet her eye. "That's right."

"Well. It's nice to finally meet you. Even if I wasn't expecting it to be like this."

"Um, yeah. I just stopped by. You were already in bed. Sorry." He reaches around and rubs the back of his neck.

Mom's lips are trembling. I can't tell if she's mad or if she's trying not to laugh. "I was just telling Rachel I'd like to have you over for dinner sometime."

"Yeah. She told me."

"But not right now." Mom shrugs.

He actually blushes at that. "I guess not. Anyway, I should be going."

I glance up at the ceiling. It's clean, or as clean as it ever is, but I know what we both saw and felt.

"Ugh. So hot in here again." Gram fans herself with a hand.

"Sorry to scare you guys," I mumble. "Nick, I'll walk you to the door."

Nick and I head to the foyer and slip outside into the humid evening.

"This house, I swear. This *house*," I moan. "What the hell is this place?"

"Shh." Nick squeezes my shoulders. "Rachel, I know the stuff it shows you is messed up. But I don't think it can actually hurt you, or it would have by now. Right?"

"I guess." I'm not sure I'd call being scared out of my wits and hauled into the basement by unseen beings a lack of actual harm.

He stares down at me in the moonlight.

"Your mom's nice. And nice-looking."

Those words distract me from the evening's shocks just enough to for me to smack him on the arm.

"What?" He pretends to look hurt. "I was going to say I see where you get it from."

"Very funny."

"I wasn't trying to be funny." He steps closer to me. "So... want to meet up somewhere tomorrow?" I suspect he's thinking about the woods by the cemetery. That seems to be the only place we have anything like privacy. And the cemetery is much less creepy than this house.

Yes, I want to finish what we started, but I'm also horribly distracted after what's happened. Plus, I suspect Mom and Gram might be spying on us from the front window.

"Okay. Text me when you're up," I tell him.

We cling to each other for a while and share a long goodbye kiss. When I pull away from him at last, he says "I love you" again.

"I love you, too. It's nice to say so in person." I touch his face before he turns away and walks back into the woods.

He didn't even drive down here? He must have really wanted to see me. I listen until I can't hear his feet crunching the leaves and twigs anymore.

BACK IN THE LIVING ROOM, Mom sits on the sofa, clutching a glass of amber liquid as Gram finishes sweeping up the remains of the vase.

"Well, he's cute," Mom says. My ears grow hotter than the air in the house.

"Sorry. I didn't mean to scare everyone."

Gram dumps the vase shards in the kitchen trash, then returns to the living room with her own glass of brandy.

"What was that you said about something leaking?" she asks.

"I...nothing. I thought I felt something dripping from the ceiling, but maybe I didn't." I shake my head, trying to act casual, like my mistake is a totally easy, natural one to make.

Both of them stare at me. Mom just looks confused, but Gram's look is more narrow-eyed. She peeks at me over the top of her glasses.

"I heard you scream, Rachel. Did he maybe try to do something you didn't want him to?"

Mom gasps, and my mouth almost drops open. "No, Gram. He's not like that. He wouldn't. I don't know what happened, but that wasn't it."

"Hm." Gram frowns down into her glass, and something inside me sinks. She still doesn't trust him.

"Oh, well. Probably going to head up to bed soon," I say. I grab my iPad, leaving Mom and Gram to their nightcaps.

Upstairs, I lift the iPad cover and see that I missed a reply from Amber.

> Yeah, St. Mary is pretty boring. The only thing I miss is this guy I was seeing while I was in town. Nick. But he totally ghosted me. Never heard from him again after we left. :(

I blink. I read her message again, not trusting my own eyes. The name *Nick* pulsates in my field of vision, and no matter how long I stare, it refuses to change itself into another one. My mouth goes dry, and my ears ring as blood rushes to my head.

This guy I was seeing while I was in town.

Nick.

It can't be.

He didn't know who Amber was. It can't be.

Nick.

He didn't want me talking to her.

Nick.

No. It's a weird coincidence. That's all it is. Surely there's more than one Nick in St. Mary.

I yank my iPad's green cover down over the screen and toss it on my nightstand. The breeze outside picks up as I pull my purple blanket down and climb into bed, still seeing the text *Nick* in my mind.

Chapter Twenty-Three

SPINNING A TANGLED WEB

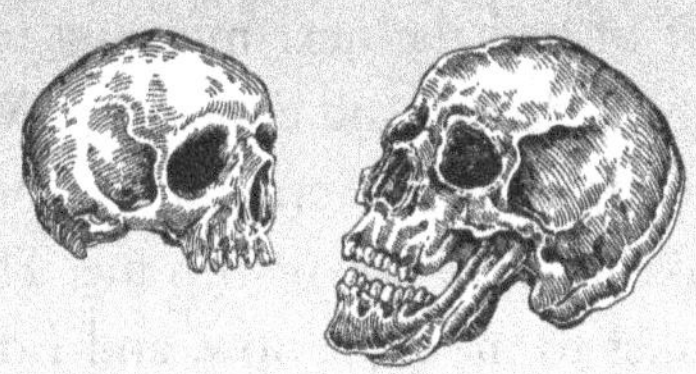

I TRY TO SLEEP, but my brain won't let up. The sticky, humid air hanging in my room makes me restless as I shift positions, trying to find one that'll let me doze off without getting too hot. Nothing can stop all the thoughts running through my head.

Nick isn't exactly an unusual name, so maybe I'm jumping to conclusions.

He would have told me. Wouldn't he? He didn't recognize her name when I mentioned it.

Or did he? Was he just pretending not to know her?

But she's older than me. He couldn't have been dating her back then.

But Nick's older than me, too. And I don't even know by how much.

Does anyone in this shitty place ever tell the truth about anything?

My tears roll down my face and wet my pillow.

It's not like I thought he'd never been with a girl before me. He obviously knew what he was doing when we were together in the cemetery the other day.

He might have lied to me about Amber, and if he was dating

Amber, he had to have some idea of what was going on with her while she lived in Morgan House. That's a very big deal indeed.

Maybe there's another explanation for all this.

"There better be," I tell the darkness.

I DON'T GET out of bed the next morning until the smell of coffee wafts into the bedroom and entices me. My chest feels like someone filled it with cement overnight as I head down to the kitchen. I don't take my iPad down with me. That thing is like a nest of hissing snakes to me right now, and I don't want to see what new messages there might be or what new betrayals they might bring.

"Hi, sweetie," Mom says around a mouthful of wheat toast.

"Morning, sunshine," Gram says. She takes a closer look at me. "Bad night?"

"Something like that." I fill a coffee cup and down most of it in one swallow. The chime of an incoming text message sounds from the living room. Crap. My phone is still down here.

I'm not ready for this yet. The coffee burns like acid in my empty stomach, and my head throbs.

I take a deep breath, head to the living room, and pick up my phone. A blue text bubble comes up on the screen. It's from Nick.

> Hey. You up yet?

I sigh before coming up with something to say.

> I am, but I don't feel too good today. I don't think I'm going to be up for going anywhere.

This isn't even a lie.

Oh no. Do you want me to come over? I could bring you something if you need it.

No. I just need to rest.

Well, rest up. Maybe if you feel better later, we can get together. ;)

I toss the phone on the sofa, knowing that I can't avoid him forever. And there is a possibility that this has all been a weird coincidence.

But I know in my bones that it's not.

He doesn't try contacting me again until the afternoon. I'm up in my bedroom trying to nap when I hear the text chime.

How you feeling now?

Still not great.

It's still the truth.

Want some company?

No.

Is something else wrong?

This is going to go on forever if I don't say something. I take a deep breath, and my chest flutters as I type the next sentence.

You used to go out with Amber, didn't you?

There's a long pause.

Why?

And there it is. A simple yes or no question, and he can't give me a straight answer.

> She told me she dated someone called Nick while she lived here. That was you, wasn't it?

After just a few seconds, my phone lights up and starts buzzing. I let it go for three rings before answering.

"Rachel. Listen."

"I'm listening." I study the bedroom ceiling. There's a spider web high up in one corner because this is still a creepy old house, and of course, there's a web.

"Yeah. We went out. It wasn't that big of a deal."

"She seemed to think it was. She said you were the only thing about St. Mary she misses. Maybe you should call her. Ghosting people is a shitty thing to do, you know."

"Seriously, we weren't even together that long."

"That's not what I care about, Nick. I figured you'd had girlfriends before me. But you pretended like you didn't even know who she was. Why would you keep that from me?"

His frantic words tumble out in a rush. "If she'd ever told me anything that might have helped you figure out what's going on now, I'd have mentioned it. Really. But she never said a word about anything bad going on in that house."

He can't see it, but I shake my head. "I find that very hard to believe. She still sounds pretty upset about it all, even now."

"I swear. Believe me. She never talked about anything like that."

If I ask her about it, will she say the same thing? Somehow, I bet Amber would have a different take on this. "Didn't you wonder why she and her mom left town so quickly?"

"She said she was having problems, and her mom and her stepdad were fighting. I didn't realize that was the same guy your mom married. I didn't put it all together. I guess if I'd thought about it...but I didn't." His voice is louder now, panicked.

"So, you never came out to where she lived? You honestly didn't know she was in Morgan House, too? Is that how you knew how to get here without me telling you? Or did *she* get to meet your mysterious uncle?" I press.

"Rachel, I had no idea. Swear to God. Honest. I met her in town, and we just hung out there most of the time."

I want to believe all this. I want to go back to loving him—to planning the next time we can sneak off together. But try as I might, I just can't buy it.

"Is there something about this place that makes men lie their asses off about what's happened here? What the hell, Nick? First, I find out Geoff never told Mom about his first wife, and now I find out you were dating his last stepdaughter and didn't think it was worth talking about."

"But it's the truth. I didn't see any reason to tell you. I knew you'd just get upset."

I grit my teeth. "Aren't you listening to me, Nick? I'm not upset you dated girls before me. I'm upset you tried to act like you've never even heard of her. I'm upset that you kept lying even when it would've been easier to come clean."

"The thing I had with her was never that serious. You're overreacting." His voice takes on a sharp edge.

I would give anything, anything at all, to be the kind of person who doesn't cry when I'm upset. But my throat tenses up, and heat builds behind my eyes as tears, stupid tears, blur my vision. Dammit.

"I'm so tired, Nick. I'm tired of being kept in the dark. So, is there anything else I should know about? Were you going out with anyone else who lived here? Any other weird connections to my dead stepfather?"

"No. Honestly. I swear."

I sigh, feeling drained. I don't know if I can believe what he's saying. I need some time to figure it out.

"Can I come see you?" he almost whispers.

"No. I'm not sleeping well, and I need rest."

"Rachel, please."

"I said *no*, Nick." I end the call before he can get out another *I love you.*

I sprawl on the bed, willing the annoying tears to stop. But I'm taunted by visions of Nick and Amber in that same clearing by the cemetery. Did he take her there, too? Did they have sex there? Did he tell Amber he loved *her*?

It doesn't matter what he did with her, I remind myself.

After lying around the house for most of the day, I'm restless. Mom's in her studio working on her latest mood board, and I have no idea where Gram is. I head down to the kitchen and fish around in the cupboards until I find my box of Lemon Zinger tea.

"There you are." Footsteps sound behind me, and when I look, Mom's leaning against the kitchen doorway, wiping her hands against her paint-stained smock. "Everything okay? I heard you on the phone. I wasn't trying to snoop, but you sounded a little angry."

I want to duck the question and tell her everything's fine, but when I open my mouth, an entirely different answer spills out.

"Why do guys have to lie about absolutely everything?"

Mom looks startled for a second and then bursts out laughing. "What on earth brought *that* on?"

When she realizes I'm completely serious, she clears her throat and pulls herself together.

"I don't think it's a boy thing, Rachel. It's a *human* thing. People tell lies to get themselves out of trouble, and then they have to tell more lies to cover up for the first lie. And by the time the truth finally comes out, it feels bigger and twenty times more awful than it would have been if only they'd been honest about things in the first place."

Mom's face darkens, and I remember that she's had plenty of experience with dishonest people. Not only that, but she's harbored her own secrets, and they weren't easy ones to keep. It makes me hurt for her, more than a little.

"So." Mom breaks the silence. "These aren't idle questions. What's going on? Are you and Nick fighting?"

I still don't want her to know I've been talking to Geoff's other stepdaughter. "I don't even know, really. It's like you said: if he'd just been honest about something to begin with, it wouldn't be that big a deal. But he lied to me, and now I'm wondering what else he might have lied about."

Mom nods. "That's the problem with the little white lie approach. And I'm sorry. I hope things work out for the best. Whatever 'the best' is."

I don't know what "the best" is, either. Do I love Nick? I thought I did, but the knowledge that he's been hiding something so important burns like a coal inside me.

Mom hangs around the kitchen doorway twirling a strand of hair around her finger, and after a minute, she speaks up again.

"Rachel? I'm sorry about the other day. The things I said. I'm still hurting a lot, but that's no excuse."

Remembering what I'd learned about Dad, I swallow hard.

"I'm sorry too, Mom," I manage. "I didn't know all that was going on."

"You couldn't have known."

"I feel like I should have."

"How?" she asks, but the teakettle whistles before I can come up with an answer.

"You want a cup?" I ask.

"No thanks. I already have coffee."

I drop a teabag in a mug and pour hot water over it before telling her the other thing I want her to know.

"And I never wanted Geoff to die. I know we didn't really get along, but I didn't want any of this to happen."

Mom's eyes well up. "I know. I'm sorry for acting like I thought differently."

"I feel like I should have tried harder to get along with him." My throat aches again.

Mom shakes her head. "He didn't make that easy, sweetie. I just wanted things to work out so badly. I kept hoping you'd get used to each other and things would calm down. And by the time

I finally accepted that wasn't going to happen...well. It doesn't matter now anyway."

We have a very quiet dinner. I make spaghetti; something about the smells of oregano and simmering garlic have always been comforting to me. I'm not up for anything fancier, and Mom and Gram are more interested in trying some of the wine they picked up yesterday. I consider asking if they'd let me have a glass, too, but I think better of it.

Mom and Gram turn in early, and I head upstairs soon after they do. I'm not tired, but I don't want Nick showing up outside the living room window again. I can't very well ignore him if he's right there looking in at me. The thought of him lurking outside and watching the house gives me a chill as I go to my room.

I collapse on my bed and open my iPad. Amber's last message hangs there unanswered. So does Nick's last text. At least he didn't try to sneak in one more "I love you."

I look at social media sites, hoping for a distraction. Elena and her family are visiting relatives in San Miguel de Allende, Mexico, and she's posted tons of photos of herself with Laura and David, doing things like standing by brightly-painted walls covered with rows of handmade masks. Elena's relatives look as happy and bright as the Garcia clan always does. I feel a deep, stabbing sense of longing again. What would it be like to be part of that family? All those relatives? Two living parents? Siblings? Happy, sun-drenched vacations?

If I keep thinking about this, I'm going to get weepy again. I grab the novel Mrs. Milledge gave me. An escape, and boy, do I need it.

A noise like fingernails scraping against my bedroom door lances through me, and I almost drop my book. I hop out of bed and prop my desk chair under the doorknob again. I know that won't help, but I can't stop doing things that give me the illusion of safety.

"Go away," I tell whatever the hell is out there. "You didn't get Amber. You can't have me either."

But something outside taps at the door, tentatively at first and then louder as if it's gaining strength. The hair stands up on my arms.

"What do you want with me?" I say out loud. "Who are you? What is this?"

The room falls still. There's no sound other than trees rustling outside and the hum of my window fan.

My body relaxes, and my eyes are fighting their way shut when a rush of air hisses over me, and cold, clammy fingers wrap around my ankle. Everything around me goes black, and I turn and tumble. I can't tell which way's up or where I am. When the rush of motion stops, piles of jagged bone fragments are under my back, poking into my skin.

I'm in the hidden room again. Faint light streams inside from that shining door, and the throbbing heat and stink of decay surround me. I stay still until my breath slows.

"Yeah, you've done this before. Is this all you got?" Maybe they'll leave me alone if I sound unimpressed. Maybe they can't hear how fast my pulse throbs as I struggle to my feet.

But a person stands between me and that elaborate door, too short to be the shadow man. When I get a better look at him, my breath catches in my throat.

It's Geoff.

He's whiter than skim milk, so pale it's like he glows in the dark. A gaping wound in his forehead trickles a continuous stream of blood that flows down his nose and onto the front of his striped polo shirt. The shirt's already bloody from the wounds in his chest.

And oh, his eyes. They're worse than those cold gray ice chips he'd fix on me whenever I made him angry. They're white and blank. His face is turned in my direction, but I can't tell where he's looking with those dead marble eyes, and I don't want to know.

"You can't be here," I tell him. "You're dead. I *saw* you."

When he parts his lips to speak, blood streams from both sides of his mouth. It looks like he's trying to say *Rach*, but his hand claps over his mouth before he can get anything out.

Being faced with Geoff again, even if it's not actually him, makes pulsating guilt fight with terror in my chest. Until now, all the tears I cried over his death weren't for him. They were for Mom and her grief. But the scalding tears I shed now really are for Geoff and for what happened to him.

"Geoff, I'm so sorry. About everything. I never gave you a chance because you weren't my dad, and it turns out my dad did a really shitty thing to my mom anyhow. And you probably knew it."

Geoff shakes his head hard like he's trying to dislodge his own hand from his mouth.

"Are you trying to tell me something? What is it?"

He raises his other hand and points toward the outline of the door or maybe at something I can't see.

I don't want to look at Geoff's bleeding, blank face anymore. I run for the door, but that man, the shadow man, shoves it open with a bang and storms inside, bringing those odors of smoke and iron and rage with him. He points.

And Geoff begins to burn. His shirt catches fire, followed by his hair.

"Geoff!" I scream.

The shadow man disappears behind billows of smoke as gray ash pours out of Geoff's mouth and nostrils. I can't bear to see any more of this, but no matter how hard I try to get to the door, my feet refuse to cooperate. Fingers tangle in my hair and pull my head back, and I scream as Geoff is reduced to blackened bones and ashes in front of me. Something sharp and hot presses into my throat. A low voice sounds in my ear.

Soon, my love. Very soon, we'll be together. Always.

Then, he begins to speak in that unfamiliar language, repeating the same pattern of guttural sounds as if chanting a spell. The terrifying rhyme repeats again and again and again until I think it's going to drive me out of my mind.

But now someone's calling me from far away.

Rachel.

I want to shout back, but something presses harder into my throat. It's excruciating, and I can't breathe, and—

"Rachel. *Rachel!*"

"Good *God.*" Gram's voice. The basement light is on, the glare like blades to my eyes. The floor, now bare, is cold under my back.

"It's okay, sweetie. I'm here." Mom squeezes my shoulders hard. I can't shake the image of a burning and bleeding Geoff. The sight of him is still tangled up in the webs of guilt I have about him and his death, and I can't scream my way free of the hurt as Mom holds my arms.

"Dear God, Tara. Is that what she's been doing this whole time?" Gram holds a trembling hand to her head.

"Yes, Mother," Mom says in an abrupt tone. "Rachel? You're okay. We're here now. You just had another nightmare."

"No!" How is she still not getting this? "Not a nightmare. Something wants me. Some*one*. And he almost got me this time."

"Sweetie. It's okay now." She smooths my hair.

"It's not." I shake my head, grabbing for Mom's hand. "We have to get out of here."

"Sounds like a plan to *me*," Gram mutters. She and Mom flank me and help me stagger to my feet and climb the creaking stairs. I can't calm down. My breath is coming in quick, *hah-hah-hah* pants, and my heart thunders away under my ribcage. I hold a hand to the spot on my throat where I felt a blade pressing to it. There's no blood.

Not this time.

We reach the living room, and Gram clicks on the light. Mom guides me over to the black leather sectional.

"She's burning up," Gram says. "Are you getting sick, Rachel?"

"I'm not sick, Gram. It's this house. It's always been this house. Whatever's in here is getting stronger, and it wants me dead. I'm afraid I'm going to get pulled down there and never come up again."

Soon, my love.

Mom grabs a glass of water from the kitchen, and Gram suggests giving me a much stronger drink in a tone that makes me think she's not entirely kidding.

"It's okay now, sweetie," Mom says. Again.

"Would you please stop saying that? It's not okay. It's never been okay. This place. This place..." And I dissolve into tears, wrecked by the memory of Geoff's dead marble eyes fixed on me —or on something behind me. I can't—just can't—tell Mom about that.

Mom hugs me until I cry it out. I finally drop off there on the living room sofa, her arms still around me.

THE WARM, bright morning sun on my face wakes me up. It takes me a moment to remember I'm on the sofa. The living room is empty, but Mom and Gram are in the kitchen, talking in low voices. A spoon clinks inside someone's mug as they stir their coffee.

My head is clouded and foggy from a lack of sleep, and my eyes are still red and raw from crying. But the smell of coffee is enough to get me moving, and I ease myself off the sectional.

Mom and Gram glance up at me as I approach the kitchen table.

"Did you get any rest, honey?" Gram asks.

"I guess so." I shrug as I reach for the olive-green mug.

Nobody says much, but Mom has her MacBook in front of her, something she usually doesn't do at the table. She's always been big on people putting away devices and other distractions while they're eating.

But today, Mom's looking at something very intently while she chews on her pumpernickel bagel.

"You know, it's funny. I keep thinking I can't afford these places, Mother. But I guess now I can."

"I'd certainly hope so."

"What are you talking about?" I ask.

Mom looks up at me and smiles softly.

"I guess it's time to tell you the truth, Rachel. I never did like this house very much. I mean, sure, it's big and elaborate and historic and whatever, but it's also ancient and creaky. It's going to be an absolute pain to keep warm in the winter and gets so drafty when it's colder outside." She looks around the room with narrowed eyes. "And I always thought something about the energy in here didn't feel right."

I raise an eyebrow. "You and Geoff made it seem like you loved the place back when we were moving in."

Mom frowns. "Well, when Geoff was still here, it was different. It was his, and it made him happy. Now that he's gone and we've been giving away his things, it just feels...wrong." She glances in the direction of the Scene. "I can't stop reliving what happened to him here. And it's clearly not doing you any good at all."

There's not much arguing that. I take another long drink of coffee, but I don't really need it now. My head's clearing fast because I'm pretty sure I know what Mom's about to say, and my rising excitement banishes all the horror from last night.

"I have a lot of money that we didn't have before because of... well, because of what happened to Geoff." Mom breaks off and frowns down at the table for a moment before continuing.

"So, I was thinking maybe we could get a nice place back in Rockville. Doesn't have to be too big—nothing like *this*—but I've been looking at the listings. We could afford something pretty decent now. We'd be close to where we were before, and you could go back to your old school. Would you like that?"

My heart races. "Are you serious, Mom? Can we leave right now?"

Gram laughs. "What about your boyfriend?"

What about him? nearly flies out of my mouth. "He has a car. And Rockville's not *that* far from here. Just one state over. He could come visit."

Maybe he just won't contact me again—the same way he ghosted Amber when she left St. Mary.

But right now, getting the hell out of Morgan House for good is more important. If Nick and I are meant to be together, it'll work itself out.

And if we aren't? I'll live.

Chapter Twenty-Four

ALMOST FREE

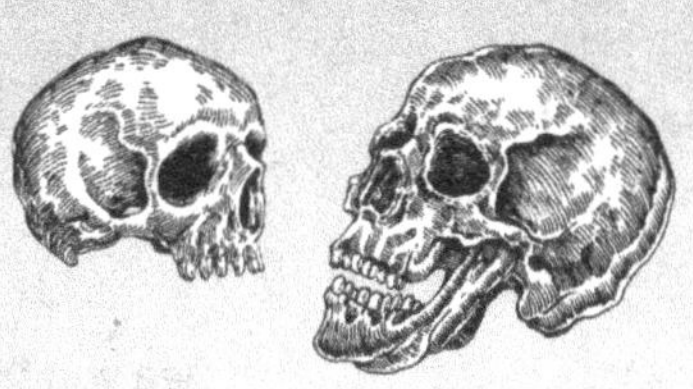

As I HEAD to my room, I practically float up the stairs. I've never been any good at singing or dancing, but I seriously want to do both things with the idea that we're going to escape this place and everything in it.

I snatch up my iPad and send a quick text to Elena: WE ARE MOVING BACK TO ROCKVILLE!!!!! Multiple exclamation points usually annoy me, but they fit my mood today.

Nick. I'm going to have to tell Nick. It's only fair.

And then he'll probably stop talking to me.

My elation fades as I wonder what to say to him. The least I could do, I figure, is break the news in person. Sending a text would be pretty cold, even if I'm still pissed at him.

And part of me still cares for him, maybe even loves him. Maybe I was too hard on him. Maybe he truly didn't know what to say to me when he realized I was talking to the same Amber he'd dated.

I think again of Geoff in the basement with those terrifying marble eyes. Mom was right that I'd never really given Geoff a chance. I shouldn't make the same mistake with Nick.

After staring at the iPad screen for a few minutes, I type *You around?* and send it to him before I can reconsider.

He writes back only a few seconds later.

Yeah. What's up?

I tug at a piece of hair.

Want to meet up somewhere? Milledge's?

A longer pause this time.

What time?

See you there at noon?

Sure.

I stare at the ceiling for several minutes after I close the iPad. Too many emotions are rocketing around inside of me. I'm still mad at him. I still care about him. I want to sleep with him again.

I don't know what I want from him anymore. But I can't figure any of it out if I don't at least talk to him.

I'M RESTLESS, fidgety, and full of energy at the thought of getting out of Morgan House and St. Mary, so I hop on my bike and ride up to Milledge's a little early. I chain up outside of the store and mop my damp forehead. When Mrs. Milledge greets me as I walk in the door, I have an idea.

"You know Nick? That guy I meet here sometimes?"

She nods. "Mister Tall, Dark, and Quiet?"

"Right. Him. Do you..." I take a breath, trying to think of what to say. Toby ambles over to say hello, and I pet his soft ears for a moment. "I'm sorry. This sounds weird. But what do you know about him?"

She shakes her head, her eyes narrowing. "Not much,

honestly. I opened here about three years ago, and he's been stopping by on and off ever since. Pleasant enough, but he sure keeps to himself."

"Does he ever come in here with anyone else?"

"I've never seen him with another girl if that's what you're wondering." She raises an eyebrow. "I've asked him about himself, but he's not a big talker. As you might have noticed."

That's for sure. "Have you ever met his uncle?"

She shakes her head, looking confused. "He has an uncle? What's his name?"

"I don't know." And it suddenly feels strange that I don't know. "He said that's who he lives with."

"Hm. Well, like I said, he's never been in here with anyone else until you. Maybe I've met his uncle, but I didn't know the relationship."

Nick wanders in just as she finishes that sentence. His hair is back in a ponytail, and he's even paler than usual. He sees us talking and looks at me through lowered eyelids, shyly, like he's afraid I might start yelling at him right there.

"I wasn't sure you'd talk to me again," he says in a low, sad voice when I approach him.

I stand on tiptoe and give him a quick kiss in response.

"I'm still a little upset. But I thought I should give you another chance. And there are some things we need to talk about."

He bites his lip and looks around the store. "I don't think we should talk here. Not very private."

"I guess not. What did you have in mind?"

"We could go to the clearing by the cemetery again."

That makes me swallow hard as a flush of heat spreads through my body. "Sure. We could." Is that a good idea? I don't know anymore. "But there's something you need to know first, Nick."

He raises an eyebrow. "That sounds serious. What's going on?"

"Mom and I are moving."

His eyes widen, and his face gets even more pale. "What? When?"

I stare down at the polished wooden floor. As elated as I've been at the thought of getting out of Morgan House and St. Mary, this is hard to say to him. "Mom wants to go back to Rockville. As soon as possible. She doesn't like being in that house anymore after what happened to Geoff. And...and last night was bad, Nick. Worse than it's ever been." Geoff's gray, dead-eyed, bloodied face floats into my mind again. "If we stay there much longer, I might never get out."

Nick's mouth is a thin, pressed line when I look at him, and there are two red spots in the center of his otherwise pale cheeks. "So that's it, then? You're gone? Just like that?"

I fiddle with the silver chain bracelet around my left wrist. "We've talked about this before. Rockville's not that far away, you know. You could come visit any time you wanted. And I should be driving before much longer, so I can always come out here and see you too."

His dark brows meet over his nose as he stares down at me.

"How can you do this to me?" he says in a cracking voice.

I almost laugh. But then I realize he isn't kidding. He hasn't said a word about what the house has been doing to me. His response is all about him.

"I'm not doing anything to you, Nick. I mean, it's not like it's even my choice. If my mom goes, I kind of have to go with her." And it *is* my choice anyhow, even if I don't say that.

"This is serious, Rachel. You can't leave me." His voice rises in volume enough that other customers glance over their shoulders as they walk through the stacks.

"Nick. It doesn't have to be that big of a deal." My knees start shaking. I wasn't expecting him to take things this badly. Or weirdly. I start backing away from him.

"How can you say that? I thought I meant something to you." His voice is even louder.

"You do, okay? You know you mean a lot to me." Why is he making this about how much I care about him? Doesn't he care that I'm not safe in Morgan House?

He grabs my upper arm and holds on. Tight. Too tight. Pain sears through my arm to the point I can practically feel bruises forming under his steely fingers.

"I love you." He moves his face close to mine. His voice is low and cold. And angry. "You can't walk away from me like this. Why would you do this?"

My heart pounds, my mouth dry as I try to make sense of his words. It's like he's losing his grip on himself and clinging to me instead. "Nick, let me go. That hurts."

"Tell me you'll stay." His face is starting to remind me of the angry way he looked at Geoff on the night the window broke, and my pulse races.

"I can't stay here all by myself. Like my mom would even let me." I try to yank my arm free, but his grip on my upper arm is like a too-tight iron cuff. My heartbeat thrashes in my ears as he pulls me close.

"Stay with me," he says, his voice shaking. He sounds furious, but his eyes are wide and watery as if he's afraid. Where is this all coming from? What happened to the Nick I've been dating? Tears sting my eyes.

"Let me go. Please."

"I can't. Not again."

"What the hell do you mean, 'not again'? Get off me." I try harder to wrench my arm from his grip.

Fast footsteps sound behind me on the wooden floor, and Mrs. Milledge walks right up to Nick.

"What's going on here?" Mrs. Milledge isn't warm or friendly or beaming anymore. She's glaring a hole through him.

I finally wrench my arm loose as Nick stares at Mrs. Milledge.

"Everything's fine. I was just leaving," I say. "Sorry about that."

"Rachel, do you need me to call someone?" Mrs. Milledge doesn't take her eyes off a glowering Nick.

"No. Thanks, though." I nearly knock over a display of travel books as I hurry through the stacks and out the door, but not before I hear Nick say something. Something that sounds a lot like *You can't leave me.*

Somehow, I get on my bike despite my shaking legs. I change my usual path and ride over sidewalks and through clusters of trees, places where Nick can't follow me in his car. My chest aches, and my eyes blur with tears to the point I worry I'll run the bike straight into a ditch.

My arm still throbs where he grabbed it. What happened to the kind, understanding guy I've been dating all summer? I never in a million years thought he might take my news quite that badly, and now I have no idea what to do. Thoughts of his anger and his bizarre words make me pedal even faster as if I can outrun my own thoughts.

AFTER I SLAM the front door of Morgan House behind me and lock it with a shaking hand, I lean against the door to catch my breath. Sweat beads on my forehead, and my legs wobble.

Mom is in the kitchen, packing our remaining dishes and silverware in large blue Rubbermaid containers strewn all over the tiled floor. She takes one look at me when I walk in and freezes, still holding a plastic pitcher.

"My goodness, Rachel. What's the matter?"

"I told Nick we were moving. He...didn't take it well." My arm throbs where he grabbed me. I think I can feel each of his fingertips where they dug into my skin.

She notices me rubbing my arm, and her eyes widen. "Sweetie? Are you okay?"

"No, I'm not. He got angry. Really angry. He scared me."

Mom sucks in her breath at those words. "All the more reason to get the hell away from here as soon as possible, wouldn't you say?"

"Definitely. You haven't found a place for us yet, have you?"

She smiles. "Actually, don't worry about that. I had something to tell you anyhow. Mother offered to let us stay with her while I'm getting this place ready to sell so the two of us aren't stuck here. I've got the bad memories of Geoff, and you've got... whatever it is this house does to you." She sweeps strands of hair off her damp forehead. "And after what you just told me, I think getting out of here as soon as we can is a really good idea."

Getting out of Morgan House and away from Nick never sounded more appealing. "I agree. But who's going to pack up this place?"

Mom rolls her eyes. "We will, Rachel. We'll all work on it during the day, of course. But we'll spend nights at her condo until everything's finished. And I'd like to get things wrapped up as soon as possible. Trust me, I'm ready to be done here. I don't even have to ask if you are."

"Okay." I exhale. "I like that plan. A lot."

As if she knows we're talking about her, Gram comes downstairs at that moment.

"So. Did I miss anything?" she says. "What's wrong, hon? You look all wound up again."

"Mom told me about staying with you at night."

"Don't sound so happy about it." The corner of Gram's mouth turns up as she studies my face.

"I'm not unhappy about staying with you. It's...Nick."

"He didn't take the news about the move too well," Mom says.

Gram shakes her head, sighing. "Why am I not surprised? This place isn't going to let us go that easily, is it?"

"Doesn't look like it," I say.

"Well, I'm going to head back to the condo tonight and get the place ready for you two. Tomorrow, we'll get as much packing and cleaning done as we can, and then the two of you will come back with me. It can be like a big slumber party every night until St. Mary is in the rear-view mirror and you've got a new home. Sound like a plan?"

Relief spreads through my chest, and I smile. "It does."

Gram claps her hands. "Super! How about we get some work done now, and then you can put together a quick dinner before I head out?"

I spend the afternoon packing up the Funko Pops and most of the books on my bookshelf, and I feel a little lighter every time I place something else in a box. It's like I'm buying my freedom from Morgan House, one personal item at a time. I save a few heavy books and prop them up in a stack against my bedroom door. The last thing I want is for the house to try trapping me in here again. Not when I'm so close to getting out of this place at last.

For dinner that night, I put together a pan of sesame tofu stir fry. The aromas of sesame, ginger, and garlic fill the kitchen, and my stomach growls from hunger for the first time in days. Mom and Gram sound happier than they have since Geoff's death. I try to share in the excitement, but my head is still spinning as I remember what happened with Nick. Or maybe it's from the heat in the house. Even with fans and the window AC units going, it's incredibly warm in here.

Gram hugs us goodbye and heads home after we finish washing the dishes, promising again to take us with her the next night. Mom and I pack up a few more cookware items we're unlikely to need right away. When we're done, I head to my room.

I'm half expecting to see a barrage of angry texts from Nick when I open my iPad, but the screen is blank, just my usual wallpaper of an Aubrey Beardsley print. I bite my lip.

Is this how it ended with Amber, too? Is this why she never heard from him again? I'm tempted to message her and ask, but then again, Amber has no idea that I was involved with Nick, too. Who knows what she'd think? Given how good I've been at upsetting people without trying to lately, it might be best to leave that one alone.

Exhausted from all the day's events, I stretch out on my bed, resting my head on an arm. But then the door creaks. When I turn to look, it's pushing the stack of books. The books slow it down, but they aren't stopping it. My stomach lurches as the door begins to slide shut.

I leap out of bed and hurry out of the room just as the stack of books topples. But the door stops moving once I'm in the hallway.

A thud sounds downstairs, like something heavy hitting the ground hard enough to shake the floor. Mom probably dropped a box. But still, something about the noise makes the skin on my arms prickle.

"Mom? You okay?" I call.

No answer.

And it's baking hot up here.

Footsteps sound downstairs. Heavy ones. Nothing at all like Mom's light tread. They remind me of the footsteps downstairs on the night Geoff was killed. My heart speeds up, and my face gets warm.

"Mom?" I move to the landing and call down the stairs. Still no answer. But a shadow crosses the floor in the foyer.

My legs shake, but I place one foot in front of the other as lightly as possible as I move down the staircase, trying to keep it from creaking. I peer over the railing.

Nick passes by the entrance to the living room. My breath catches in my throat as I jerk back, hoping he hasn't seen me.

How did he get in here? I made damn sure to lock the door behind Gram. Did Mom let him in? No. She wouldn't. Not after I told her what he did.

Mom. Where is she? Why didn't she answer me? The back of my neck turns icy.

I sense another wave coming, knocking me over, rolling me around until I'm disoriented. What do I do now? Should I creep back up to my room and call the police? Find something I could use to fend Nick off if need be?

"I know you're there, Rachel." Ice-cold fear slams into my chest at the sound of his voice. "Why don't you come down? We have a lot to talk about."

That's the absolute last thing I want to do. But it's scaring the hell out of me that Mom won't answer me. What has he done to her?

I take a deep breath, square my shoulders, and trudge down the stairs and into the living room. But I make damn sure I have a clear path to the front door as he comes into view again.

Nick's standing by Geoff's bookshelf, holding my purple glass skull. There are leaves stuck to his black clothing as if he's been hiding in the woods, and his hair sticks to his sweaty forehead. That antique key he wears sits on top of his shirt.

"Nick? What are you doing here? How did you get in?"

Nick studies me for a moment. Then he smiles.

"This is *my* house, Rachel. It always lets me in."

Chapter Twenty-Five

THE FORBIDDEN PATH

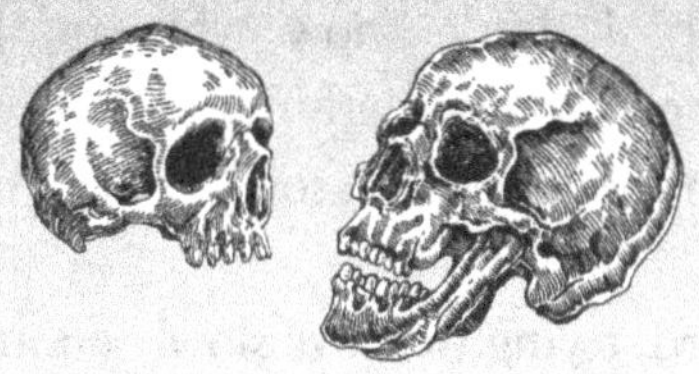

"What are you talking about?" I glance around the living room. The Rubbermaid containers are still scattered all over the floor, but I don't see Mom. Or hear her. My body trembles.

He raises his chin and smiles. "I'm Nicolas Morgan. This is my family's house. My father built it. And it always lets me in."

He told me his last name was Alexander. I don't understand.

"Your father? But this house is more than a hundred years old."

"There are a lot of things I haven't told you." As he moves towards me, I take a step backward.

Nothing he's saying makes any sense, and I wonder what the hell happened to him, why he's changing into a completely different person. I've heard about guys turning into obsessive stalkers before, but until today, I never dreamed Nick could be one of them.

Scanning the room, I spot my phone sitting on the coffee table. I could try to grab it, but Nick's looming like a giant between me and that table. The phone might as well be a million miles away. If I'm going to call for help, it's not going to happen that way.

"Nick," I say, holding my hands up. "I'm sorry. I should have told you we were leaving town earlier. The way I did that wasn't fair." I don't mean any of that, but I'm hoping it'll calm him down.

Nick shakes his head and gives me a soft smile. "It doesn't matter. You don't have to leave. We can always be together."

Oh God.

"Nick, I can't stay here. But you can always visit me. We don't have to break up. I don't know why you keep acting like Rockville's on the moon or something."

His dark eyebrows meet in a scowl. "Don't be glib, Rachel. It isn't cute."

I step backward, trying to move slowly enough that he won't catch on to what I'm doing. Just a few steps to the left, and I can make a break for the front door. Can I outrun him? He's much taller than me and has longer legs, but still, I'm going to have to try.

But I still haven't seen Mom. A slick, tight fist clenches my insides.

"Did you do something to my mother?"

Nick shakes his head. "She's fine. Only sleeping right now." He puts my purple glass skull on a side table. As he does, I take a small, careful step to my left, not daring to breathe. What does he mean, she's only sleeping?

"Nick? What did you do?"

When I edge a little more to the left, the kitchen comes into view. My heart lurches in my chest.

Mom's red hair is fanned over the black and white checkered floor.

Oh, God. Oh, no. Oh, please no—not her too. Instead of running for the door, I rush towards Mom's still form in the kitchen. That's the opportunity Nick needs. He steps in front of me and grabs my shoulders, pinning me in place. His palms are damp against my skin.

"Rachel, I love you, and you love me. You don't have to go. You never have to leave me."

Oh, God, what do I even say to that? What *can* I say or do? "I do love you, but I have to get to Mom. I need to be sure she's all right." I try to keep my voice from breaking. I need him to believe I'm not going to call the police the second I get the chance.

His fingers tighten until they're biting into my shoulders. "I told you. She's fine."

"She's *not* fine. She's unconscious, Nick."

"I didn't hit her that hard."

Tears spring to my eyes. "You knocked her out!"

"I promise you. When we're finished, I'll make sure she's okay."

"What do you mean, 'when we're finished?'" I try to twist myself out of his grip, but he digs his thumbs hard into my collarbones. Intense pain shoots through my upper body and almost drops me to my knees.

"What are you going to do? Rape me? Kill me?"

His eyes widen. "Jesus, no. I'd never do something like that to you. How could you think that?"

I bark out a frigid laugh. "Are you serious, Nick? You assaulted me at the bookstore, and then you broke into our house and attacked my mother. That's why I think that. Can you blame me?"

"She'll be fine. And you'll see. When we're finished, you'll be a part of me. Always." He looks around the half-packed living room cluttered with boxes and containers.

"Morgan House isn't just *mine,* Rachel. It's *me.* It's my beating heart. And the people I've loved are here too. We're all together. Forever."

The windows start rattling as if there's a windstorm outside.

My vision wavers. Is it from the shock of what's happening or from the surging heat in this room? Maybe this is all just another bizarre, terrible scene Morgan House is showing me. *Please let this not be real.*

Nick tilts his head towards my face like he wants to kiss me. His familiar scent of wood smoke fills my nostrils. As I think of how I trusted him, how I loved him, burning anger uncoils inside my chest. It's that beast, the one that took up residence inside me when we moved to St. Mary. It claws at my insides. My head and my heart pound.

I always fight this part of me. I'm always afraid of what my anger might do if I let it out and tell people what I really think. I always feel ashamed afterward, as if I don't have a right to speak out, as if my anger is something that needs to be buried.

But now it's time to let the beast free. Even if it hurts someone.

"Nick? I have no idea what the hell you're talking about, but this? Whatever you're thinking about doing, this is *not* happening. If you leave here right now, I won't mention you to the cops when I dial 911 for an ambulance. I'll tell them she fell off a stool or something," I lie.

He looks down at me and shakes his head, his eyes sad. "There's nothing to be afraid of. Don't you want to be with me?"

"*No*. Not even a little bit."

His eyes widen, and his head jerks back as if I've slapped him.

Rage makes my voice harsher. "I thought I did, but now I know I don't. First, you lied to me, and that was bad enough, but now you're breaking into the house and attacking my mom and me."

"Rachel..."

"Now let me go." My voice rings off the walls as another idea occurs to me. "Gram's coming back with some packing boxes, and she'll call the police the second she sees what you did to her daughter. You can't go after her without letting me go. This is your last chance. Leave."

He rolls his eyes and chuckles, and I swallow hard.

"I was already here when your grandmother left. I heard her. I know full well she's coming back tomorrow to take you away from me. Don't lie to me. I don't like liars."

"*You're* the liar. Get *off* of me." I jerk my upper body backward. His sweaty hands slip against my skin, but he digs his fingers in harder.

"Calm down. This is a beautiful thing. It always is."

"What do you mean, *it always is*?"

He smiles like he's about to offer me a wonderful gift. "The two of us bonding together forever. It's like when we make love, only it never has to end. I tried to tell you in the cemetery that death isn't the end, but you didn't believe me. Now, you'll see. You'll be with all the others. With my Miranda."

My breath catches. "Miranda?"

His expression goes wistful. "Don't you remember? I told you about her." Right. He talked about the girl he'd lost at the river. Back when I still thought he was amazing. "We'd been together for years. And I loved her, Rachel. So much. Almost as much as I love you. She was so gentle. So kind. We were going to be married.

"But she got sick. She couldn't eat, and she didn't have the strength to leave her bed. All she did was sleep and wither away, and I thought there was nothing I could do but watch her die. Then, I heard a neighbor of mine had a chest full of books all about the Forbidden Path."

My skin prickles. What the hell is he talking about? "The Forbidden Path?"

"Yes. Old rituals you could perform to bring yourself fortune or power or love. With enough learning, you could even cheat death itself. You could get in terrible trouble if someone caught you. It was subverting God's will, they said, but for the right price, there'd always be someone willing to teach you. I had money after my parents died—and time. And if God was so determined to take Miranda away from me, I didn't give a damn about Him or His will anymore."

His smile grows wider. "And I learned how to keep her with me. She was so, so weak when I took her downstairs. And as I said the words over her and released her and allowed her blood to flow onto the floors of Morgan House, she became a part of me forever."

I want to believe this story is nothing more than delusions from a very sick mind, but all the horrible things I've seen in this house looked a lot like the scene he just described, minus the romantic spin he's putting on it.

"What are you talking about?"

"It was so beautiful, Rachel. She might have looked dead to anyone else, but I could feel her soul filling me as the life left her. Her love made me so strong. Strong enough that even time itself could no longer take me."

"I don't understand," I say. But I'm pretty sure I do.

Stars practically light up his dark eyes as he talks. "That's the real magic of the ritual. All the other people around me grew older and stooped and sick, and eventually, they died. But I stay the same. I don't get sick. I'll always look the way I do now, and I'll always carry you and the others I love with me. How could anyone not want this? How could something so beautiful ever be wrong?"

Oh God. Oh my God. My body shakes violently in his steel grip.

"I never thought I'd meet other women I'd love as much as Miranda, but as time passed, I did. Sometimes, they already lived here, and sometimes, I had to bring them here, but I kept them with me, too."

He starts moving backward towards the basement door, pulling me along with him. "I had to leave this place because sometimes the people in St. Mary came looking for the ones I loved, and I didn't want them to find me and stop me. But this house always welcomes me back. My loves are always here. Their blood has bound me to this place. So much so that I can't stray far from here. Nobody can leave their heart behind."

I want to believe Nick's making all this up because something inside him is so broken after all the loss he's suffered. He can't be hundreds of years old. He can't have done what he's talking about doing. Nobody can just take someone else's life force and become immortal, right?

I've seen and experienced too much in this house, though, and at long last, when it might be too late to matter, I understand what's been happening since the first night Geoff and Mom brought me here. And why.

Morgan House hasn't been trying to hurt me.

It's been trying to *warn* me.

"I wanted to do this with you earlier, Rachel," he says, almost whispering now. His eyes are shining, and his face is close enough to mine that we're almost touching foreheads as he pulls me forward another step. "Especially that last time you talked about leaving. But your stepfather heard me in the house, and he got in the way."

Geoff got in the way? Nick's meaning hits me like a kick in the stomach, and my eyes blur as terrible images flash through my mind: Geoff dead on the floor, and Geoff covering his mouth in the basement—as if someone was puppeteering him—so he couldn't warn me about Nick. All the dead women I'd seen doing the same thing. They were trying to tell me the truth, and each time, some dark, otherworldly force gagged them.

"Oh my God. It was you, Nick. You killed him."

He raises an eyebrow, looking puzzled by my reaction. "He drove Amber away, and he was driving you away too. And you never even liked him. I thought you'd be pleased when he was gone."

"I didn't want him to be *killed*, for God's sake. I just wanted to be away from here." How could I be with someone who could do these things? How did I never see any of this before? How did he hide this part of himself so well?

"I couldn't have that. Amber left me, and the pain almost destroyed me. I couldn't let you go, too."

He's still moving us towards the basement. I dig my heels in and try to stand still, but he just pulls that much harder. My arms are nearly numb from how tightly he's gripping me. "Nick, please. Please stop this."

"We don't have much time left. Your mother will wake up

soon. I don't want to have to do anything else to silence her, but I'll have no choice if she gets in the way like your stepfather did. Now let's go to the basement."

At the threat to my mother, anger flares up inside me like a raging fire, and I act without thinking. I lunge forward and stomp on his foot. His body jerks, and he screams. I yank an arm loose from his sweating hand and rake my fingernails over his eyes. He shouts, and his hands fly to his face.

Finally free, I run for the kitchen, towards my mother's still form on the floor, but Nick grabs my hair, whipping my head back. I slam an elbow behind me and hit his chest, but he pulls me around and shoves me towards the basement door. And oh, god, he wasn't wrong. He's strong. Incredibly strong. I'm like a ragdoll as he wraps arms like steel cuffs around me and half-carries, half-drags me across the living room.

I can't let him put me in the basement. If he does, there's almost no chance of getting out unless I can get past him.

He keeps one long arm wrapped around me as we reach the basement door, and he throws it open.

"Get down there." The earlier tenderness in his voice is gone, and he's all cold fury as he pushes me.

I stumble in the darkness at the top of the stairs, and I make a desperate grab at him to stop my fall. I claw at his shirt front and manage to grasp his key, but the chain breaks, and I fall backward into the basement, the antique key in my hand.

The door slams shut as I slide down the wooden stairs. Pain rockets through my knees, hips, and elbows as I hold my arms close to my head for protection. Nick's key digs into my palm. He shouts something from upstairs as I tumble.

I hit the cold floor of the basement on my side, nearly jarring the breath out of my body. As I lay still for a moment, waiting for the pain and the dizziness from my fall to subside, an unfamiliar light fills the basement with an eerie glow. I look up.

The door.

The elaborate metal door I've only seen in my hellish night-time visions is in front of me as if it's always been there. Tarnished silver scrollwork covers its front in vinelike patterns, and it glows as if lit from within.

Something about it looks familiar, and not just from my visions. I raise Nick's antique silver key to my eyes. The door shines so brightly and clearly in the darkness that, for the first time, I see the vinelike pattern scrolling around the face of Nick's key.

It looks like it was made for that door.

Chapter Twenty-Six

THE KEEPER OF THE KEY

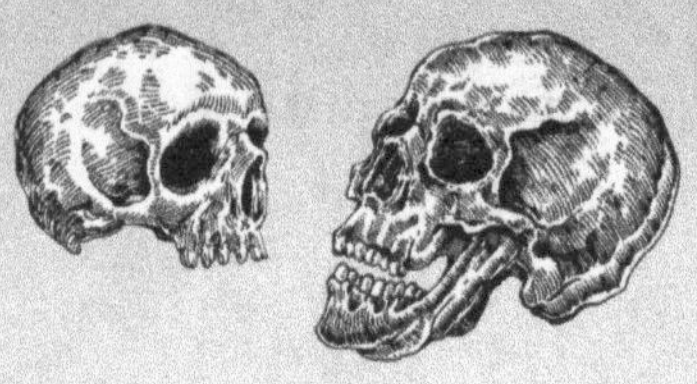

UPSTAIRS, Nick roars and slams his body against the door to the stairwell. The crash startles me so much, I drop the key. It hits the ground with a clank. The door vanishes, and the basement goes black.

"What? *No*. Come back. Please!" I'm not sure how, but I know that door's presence is a good thing, and I have to bring it back and fast because Nick's getting more forceful upstairs.

"Open. This. Door." Every one of Nick's words is punctuated with a slam.

I can barely see the basement floor, and I squint and scan the area until a glint of light reveals the key. The minute I grab it, the door reappears.

As long as I'm holding the key, I can see that door.

For the first time, I hear the voices of those who are trapped here, where they died. They are all around me, their words floating toward me and surrounding me in the dark, damp air.

Don't let him get the key.

Set us free.

Set us free.

SET US FREE.

"Rachel!" Nick shouts from upstairs. The shadows of his feet move in the strip of light under the door to the living room. "Your mother's up here. Open this door, or I'll punish her. I really don't want to do that, but you're not giving me much choice."

Fear shoots through my midsection. *Mom.* I can't let him hurt Mom.

"I'm not doing anything to the door, Nick," I yell. "I guess nobody else wants you down here either."

That's when I remember the other times a door in Morgan House became mysteriously stuck.

When Nick came over while I was alone during Mom and Geoff's honeymoon.

When Geoff was shot dead.

My bedroom door only got stuck when Nick was here.

And then there was the mysteriously shattered window. The broken vase. The blood dripping from the ceiling.

Something—no, some*one*... maybe *lots* of someones—tried everything they could to keep Nick away from me.

I run to the secret door and am about to unlock it when I hear a crash from upstairs. The wooden door breaks into splinters and planks. Faint light from the living room streams in as Nick hurtles down the steps so fast that he almost falls—*please, let him fall and knock himself out.* He seizes me before I even have time to run, his arms wrapping around me until I can barely breathe. Odors of smoke and iron are rolling off him now, smells I remember all too well from the times I've been down here before. He always had that pleasant smell of wood smoke around him, but now he smells metallic and acrid like blood and fire. Like death.

"Where is it?" His voice is jagged.

"Where's what?" I struggle against him, but he tightens his grip.

"My key."

"I don't know. I dropped it when I fell down the stairs."

"Liar. You have it." My arms press into my ribs. He'll break my bones or suffocate me if I can't get away from him.

"What would I want with your stupid key? It fell under the steps. I can see it."

He hauls me towards the steps and past a rack of Geoff's old tools. Light glints off the tips of the sharp implements. That gives me an idea.

"Where is it?" His mouth is against my hair, his breath hot against my scalp. "Show me."

This has to work. *Please.*

"You want your fucking key?" I snarl. "Go get it." I toss it across the basement floor as far as I can manage. It clanks and clatters as it skitters across the concrete. The door vanishes again, plunging the basement into darkness, and I sense a flash of loss that isn't just coming from me.

It'll just be for a few seconds, I think, hoping whatever else is down here can hear me.

Nick lets me go and runs for the key. I spin around, grope at the wall, and grab a pair of large shears from Geoff's tool rack.

Nick crawls across the floor, patting the concrete. His hand closes around the key, and he jumps to his feet. As he turns towards me, I rush forward with the shears held out, too fast to stop and think about what I'm about to do.

I jam the shears up under his ribcage. He howls, staggering backward, his eyes huge in the dim light. Sinking the shears into his chest feels like I'm stabbing a knife into a slab of steak, and a sick, dizzy sensation spreads through me. He was my first lover, and at some point, I truly cared about him.

Now I've wounded him, maybe fatally, and even though he was going to kill me like he has so many others, the idea that I'm committing murder makes me ill. I draw in shaky breaths, trying not to listen to the spluttering, choking sounds he makes, willing myself not to faint. If I lose consciousness down here and he's not dead, it's all over.

He stares at me and groans before coughing up a gout of blood. As his hands go for the shears buried in his chest, he drops the key.

The key. I reach a shaking hand out for it, but he kicks it away before falling to his knees.

Oh, no. No, no, no. It's too dark down here for me to make out what's on the floor. I'll never find it.

"Please," I whisper to whoever might hear me as I rush away from Nick. "Please. I promise I'll let you all out, but you have to help me find that key again."

Nick lets out a shout of pain behind me. I turn to look just as he pulls the shears out of his chest with one last bellow. He tosses them to the floor with a clank.

"Rachel, I told you before that injury won't stop me. My loved ones keep me strong. I wish you wouldn't keep fighting this." He pauses to draw a rattling breath. "I promise you. It's a beautiful thing."

Rage slices through my fear. "It's a beautiful thing for *you*," I snap. "I don't think all the women you murdered agree."

A faint ray of moonlight from the high window glints off something on the floor. It's only for a split second, but it's enough.

The key. I race over and snatch it off the floor. The basement brightens at once. The door emerges as if from behind cloud cover and glows like a full moon in the basement.

Set us free.

"Yes," I tell the voices.

"Rachel! No!" Nick lurches to his feet as I hurry past him. His fingers brush my arm, grabbing at my shirt.

"Don't touch me!" I whirl around and smash a fist into his still-bleeding chest wound, and he screams again, letting me go.

I run right for that hidden door, jamming the key into the doorknob at last. My hands are so sweaty and slick with Nick's blood that, at first, I don't think the knob is going to turn. What if I can't even open it? What if he's the only one who can make it work?

Please! Oh, shit. Oh, no. Come on, please.

Nick's pounding footsteps close in on me just as I turn the

knob and shove the door open at last. Damp air, sodden with the smell of rot, washes over me, and I gag.

"You—" Nick grabs my hair and hurls me away from the door. I land on the concrete in a heap, still clutching the key. My teeth click down on my tongue from the impact. The metallic taste of blood floods my mouth.

The door opens on an empty chamber. The only sounds in the basement are Nick's jagged breaths and my own pulse as it thuds in my head.

There's nothing behind that hidden door after all.

Nothing's coming to help me.

All the rage and pain and frustration I've bottled up for the last few weeks, months, and years come pouring out. My sobs feel more like screams, sharp and serrated, as if they're going to tear me apart as they leave my body.

Nick's jeering laughter echoes off the basement walls. "Did you seriously think they were on *your* side? They're *my* loved ones. They're all a part of me." He walks over and stares down at me. "Rachel, we've wasted enough time down here. Come now. I promise, it'll be just a minute or two of pain. It's so much easier if you don't fight it."

If you don't fight it.

Those words repeat in my head until only one stands out: *Fight.*

My fingernails dig into my palms, and energy surges through me with their bite. As Nick's looming shape grows sharper and clearer, I see him for who he is—the Shadow Man. It was always him. He was the man in my nightmares, slamming through the door, stealing the life from those women. His victims haunt Morgan House, and he created the ghosts. I won't let him have me too.

My arms shake from the adrenaline coursing through my body. I take a deep breath and glare at him.

"Go to hell." I swing a foot at him in the darkness, hoping to knock him down. If I can topple him and get Geoff's shears from where Nick tossed them, I can slow him down long enough to get upstairs and get Mom and myself out of here.

My foot connects with his calf, which feels like concrete. The kick isn't enough to knock him down. He looms over me, looking ten feet tall in the gloom of the basement.

"If you want to be childish, that's your call." His tone is high-pitched like he's talking to a baby.

He bends over, his long fingers snagging in my hair, and yanks hard. Searing pain shoots through my scalp, making my vision go starry. The key is still wedged in my fist, and I strike out at his arm. He only jerks my hair, dragging me towards the now exposed room. I thrash and kick out at him, at the wall, at anything that might make it harder for him to get me in there. But there's nothing I can grab to slow us down.

And then a wispy, pale stream of light floats out of the room towards us.

Nick pauses, releasing my hair. My head thumps against the floor.

Another stream floats out, and then another one, and yet another one. The wisps get larger and brighter and faster as they move towards Nick and me. They take on familiar shapes as they emerge—eyes, mouths, heads, limbs.

The basement is bright enough that I see Nick's eyes widen as he looks around at them.

"No," he murmurs. "You can't. You're supposed to stay here. With me." His shoulders sag.

I hear what the wraiths say to me even through my harsh, ragged breathing as they drift through the air, pale and bright:

Shhh.

Shhh.

Quiet now.

They're skeletal and ghastly, but right now, they're the most beautiful things I've ever seen.

Something wonderful and comforting spreads through me. A warm sensation rises in my chest as the forms become distinctly female—trailing skirts, long hair, slender fingers. So many of them swirl around me, speaking soothing words.

How many women did he kill down here?

They swarm towards Nick, and their movements become fast. Harsh. Angry. One of them stretches out an arm and reaches right into the wound in Nick's chest, making him cry out.

"But you can't do this. I loved you." He staggers backward. A wraith leaps into his chest, and he gasps as it disappears inside of him. Another one soars into his open mouth, making him retch.

I pull myself to my feet and back away on legs that feel watery and weak. Nick screams again, but it sounds like he's got a mouthful of something. He chokes as the wraiths whirl around him and into him, invading his body. A miasma, foul-smelling like rotten meat and black as smoke—dark as the women are light—pours out of his mouth and hovers over him.

He drops to his knees, and his skin shrivels like fast-decaying fruit as I watch, unable to turn away. His gorgeous, long black hair turns gray, then white. And then it all falls to the floor as he jerks and flails, trying to free himself from his victims.

No matter how much he deserves this, I don't want to watch anymore...yet I can't look away.

Nick has withered like an old man, his dry white skin wrinkled, spotted, and practically translucent. He stretches his arms toward me, and his mouth opens and closes soundlessly like he no longer has the strength to scream. Then, he collapses on the basement floor and lies still as the wraiths swarm around him, over him. *Through* him.

I think of his beautiful, deep brown eyes the first time I saw him at the bookstore. I can't reconcile that with the ancient, lifeless husk on the basement floor. The sight makes me ache. I wonder if maybe once, a long time ago, he might really have been the kind boy he'd pretended to be with me.

It doesn't matter now.

The ghostly forms move away at last from what little is left of

Nicolas Morgan. There's a pile of bones and white hair tangled up in his shredded black clothing on the concrete floor.

"Thank you," I manage to whisper.

The forms swarm around me again, blurred ghostly faces peering at mine, their eyes wide, their mouths unsmiling. And my body tenses. What if they aren't done? What if they want to take me too?

Burn it down, they whisper, a host of female voices in unison.

"What?"

The words come at me fast as if several women are murmuring them at random: *He can still come back. He will. The house is his heart. Burn the house and end him. End this. Set us free. Please. Set us free, please. Setusfreesetusfree.*

My heart pounds harder. Burn a house down? I'm not an arsonist. I don't know if I can do this. I'm not even sure how I *could* do it.

Please, they whisper to me. *Please*.

A long, raspy breath sounds from the pile of bones, hair, and clothes.

He will come back. Soon. Please.

The low gasping breath sounds again. The skin at the back of my neck goes cold. When I look at Nick's remains, a faint light that wasn't there before shimmers over them. And in that light, the pile already looks more human-shaped. Fuller.

Nick told me himself, after all. Morgan House is his heart. I think of the pulsating walls in that secret room.

Please hurry. Please.

Another rasping breath sounds. That's enough to make me move. I ease my way around the basement walls, trailing my fingers over all of Geoff's cold, dusty metal shelving, trying to avoid Nick's body.

My right foot bumps the gasoline can. Several feet away, my fingers close around a long, skinny cardboard box, and I pick up Geoff's fireplace matches.

I twist the lid off the gasoline can, intending to pour it before realizing that setting a fire on a cold concrete floor might not do much.

Upstairs, the floor creaks. Faint footsteps sound near the basement door. My breath catches.

"Rachel?" Mom's voice is shaky. "Where are you? What's happening?"

Oh yes, oh, God. Oh, thank you, God.

I make my way to the staircase, avoiding passing too close to Nick's remains, and move upstairs. As I walk up to the main floor, I pour gasoline down the wooden basement steps. The wraiths swarm around the pile of rags and bone on the floor, and the raspy breathing sounds ever louder. The acrid chemical stink of the gas burns my eyes.

"Mom?" I call. "You need to get out of the house. Don't wait for me."

"Are...are you okay?" Mom's voice is spacy and confused. And it sounds like she's coming closer.

"Don't come down here. Get out. Now."

"But what's happening?"

I reach the landing. Mom stands near the basement door, her lips slightly parted, running a hand over her hair. A thin trickle of blood runs down her forehead and smears when her palm drags over it. I think of the time Elena suffered a concussion when she fell and hit her head while we were ice skating. Mom's glassy, puzzled eyes look just like Elena's did, and the sight makes me want to run back downstairs and kill Nick all over again.

"This place is about to burn to the ground." I drench the floor by the curtains, knowing that those will catch easily. To think I wanted to do this from the second I first walked in here, and look at me now. I'm losing it. I actually have to suppress a giggle.

Mom touches a hand to her head again, swaying on her feet.

"Rachel. What on earth are you doing?"

"Setting everyone free. Including you. Get out of the house, Mom. *Now.*"

But she doesn't move. She shakes her head and blinks as if she's just woken up from a deep sleep. Of course. Nothing about this is going to be easy if it can be ridiculously hard.

"For fuck's sake, Mom, *move*!" She stares at me with those vacant eyes but doesn't react to that F-word at all. And that really scares me.

I hurl the empty can down the basement stairs, light a long match, and toss it down after the can. The trail of gasoline catches almost at once with a hiss that builds into a roar.

There's barely enough time for me to get my phone off the living room table and grab Mom. Smoke billows from the basement. The hissing and crackling fire already sounds too close.

There's one more sound, something a lot like a low, anguished scream from below. My scalp prickles.

"We have to get out, Mom. There's a fire." I snatch Mom's car keys off the table in the foyer and guide us both out the front door into the humid summer night. The air is damp and warm and far from refreshing, but I take a deep breath anyhow.

Mom wobbles, horribly unsteady on her feet as I hurry us along the path leading from the house. There's no way in hell she's going to be able to drive. She'll smash us both into a tree.

"Rachel, what's going on? I was washing the dishes, and then I woke up on the kitchen floor. And now there's a fire? What about our things?"

I try not to sound scared. "Don't worry about that. We can always get more things. It's going to be okay now." Is it? I glance over my shoulder. A hellish red glow emanates from Morgan House's front windows. Smoke pours from the open front door. Several crashes sound from somewhere inside.

"Mom. Wait." I fumble with my phone and dial 911.

"I'm calling from Morgan House. We were attacked, and there's a fire, and my mom has a head injury," I blurt. I don't know how fast fire can move, and I don't want the woods going up along with the house. Something inside me still feels guilty about Geoff, Mom, all of it, and I have enough on my conscience without knowing I started a forest fire, too.

I continue to half-drag, half-walk Mom up the long and twisting drive. The woods grow darker the further we move from the house. The gravel is lumpy and uneven under our feet, and it makes us stumble a little like we're drunk. I sweat from the effort of keeping both of us upright and moving. Very little moonlight gets through the thick canopy of leaves over us. I can't hear any sounds other than my own panting and the gravel crunching under our feet.

"Rachel? Where are we going?"

"I don't know. But it's going to be okay." Why am I saying such a stupid thing? Mom and I are about as far away from okay as we've ever been right now.

In the distance, sirens sound, and flashing red lights pierce the night.

My muscles relax, and I exhale. I stop walking and wrap my arms tightly around Mom. She rests her head against my shoulder.

"Mom? How's your head?"

She moans. "It hurts. I need to rest."

"Soon. Help is almost here." I'm still holding her upright when the ambulance reaches us.

When I look back in the direction of Morgan House one last time, all I see are billows of black smoke rising above the trees, blotting out the reddening night sky.

Chapter Twenty-Seven

AFTERMATH

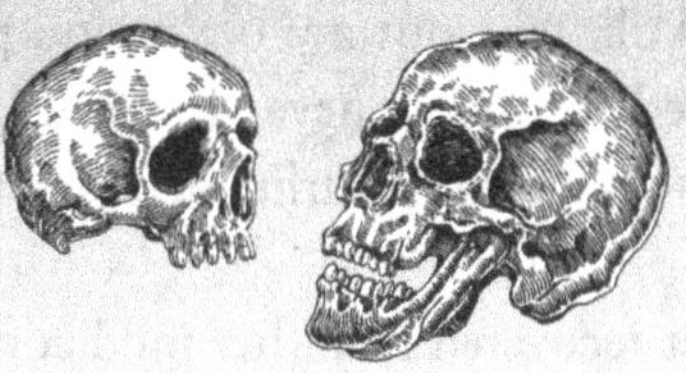

Dear Amber:

There was nothing wrong with you or with me. It was that house. But the house wasn't evil. It was trying to warn us—to protect us.

From Nick.

If your mom hadn't taken you both away from there, you'd be dead now.

I STUDY the message for a moment and then trash it, just like every one before it. I've been trying to figure out how to tell Amber that she's okay, that she's always been okay. But every text sounds more bizarre and unbelievable than the last one, and now I'm wondering if there's any point in what I'm trying to do.

It's over. There's no more Morgan House and no more Nick. Amber sounded like she was in a pretty good place, and if I tell her the truth about Morgan House—and about Nick—what would it do to her? Maybe it's time to leave her and everything else connected to St. Mary alone. I put my phone down.

Even though it's the middle of August, there's a slight chill in the air as I sit out on Gram's deck and gaze at the lake. Her wind chimes ring in the breeze. The smell of mown grass makes my nose itch. The sun glints off a spear of smoky quartz Mom's placed on the wicker coffee table, and the air is warm and slightly humid. Autumn's coming.

It can't come fast enough, even if it means the start of school and the end of freedom for nine months. I would do anything to blot this entire summer out of my mind. I sometimes wish I could open my skull, take out my brain, and put in a new one. Or do what I used to do whenever I screwed up a video game and simply revert myself to an earlier save. A pre-Morgan House save.

Mom's almost recovered from her mild concussion, but even so, she moves around slowly, tentatively, as if she's expecting another blow from someone. And I worry about her, fearing that so much horrible stuff happening so close together might break her.

But we're living with Gram for now. After the fire, she scooped us up and took us to her place, two wounded birds she was trying to get ready to release from her nest again. Whatever we're both dealing with, I don't doubt for a second that Gram's strong and stubborn enough to hold us together until we mend.

I sleep on Gram's foldout sofa in her living room at night. Mom wanted us to share the guest room bed, but I know we'd just lay awake at night listening to each other toss and turn.

Besides, in the living room, I'm close to the screen door that leads to the deck. Whenever I wake up confused or terrified in the middle of the night, the noise the lake water makes as it laps against the grass lets me know I'm no longer in Morgan House or anywhere near it.

Mom and Gram are in St. Mary today, taking care of some of the last details connecting us to that place. They invited me along, but I refused. Going near St. Mary makes me think of Geoff, and the subject of Geoff catches in my throat like a pill that won't go down all the way. He was a pain in the ass and a control freak, and I don't think we'd ever have gotten along. But he died trying to protect us. Maybe if I'd just met him halfway, we could've worked something out...but no.

Instead, I'd brought Geoff's killer into our lives. St. Mary reminds me of Nick, too.

My fist tightens around the item in my right hand until its sharp edges bite into my skin, and I uncurl my fingers.

Nick's tarnished silver key sits in my palm.

Nobody knows I have this, and they don't need to know where it came from. I can imagine what they'd say. *Why in the world would you want to remember that horrible person? That horrible time? What's* wrong *with you, Rachel?*

They wouldn't understand.

The key isn't about Nick. It's my reminder that you can't hide the truth forever. It will always come crashing through whatever barriers you've set up to keep it away, no matter how many you build. Someday, you'll find out your father wasn't the model of perfection you'd always believed he was. Sometimes, the boy you love is hiding a monster inside. The truth of things will always come out in the end, and I don't want to forget what I've learned.

Voices carry from inside the condo. Mom and Gram are back. I slip Nick's key—mine now—into my shorts pocket and stand to greet them.

They've asked me again and again what happened on the night of the fire, and every time, I give them the faintest outline of the truth but no more. I know I can't keep it from them forever, and I have no doubt Gram could handle the entire story.

But Mom? I'm not sure about her. She walks towards me now with the slow, small steps she developed after her concussion. The corners of her mouth tremble a little when she smiles at me, as if she's nervous about expressing any kind of happiness.

Mom says she doesn't remember anything about that night, and I don't think she's ready to hear the truth about Morgan House. Not yet. For her, I'll keep it quiet.

But just for now. Not forever.

She steps out onto the deck and wraps her long, freckled arms around me, and I relax into her embrace. Behind her, Gram raises a bulging white bag from Milledge's Book Company and grins. Warmth spreads inside me, banishing all thoughts of Nick and Morgan House. The most important people in my life are right here.

We're not okay yet. But we will be.

Acknowledgments

The Keeper of the Key has been a long time in the making, and I hope I remember to thank everyone who's had a hand in shaping it. Even the person who told me I'd never sell this book. *Especially* him. I love proving people wrong.

Thanks as always to my family, especially my incredibly supportive mother, Barbara Willson, and mother-in-law, Donna Murphy.

I took this manuscript to many a workshop. Thanks so much to my classmates in the Borderlands Writers Boot Camp and the Futurescapes Writing Workshop for their feedback and their support.

Malorie Nilson at Parliament House Press gave Rachel and her story a home at last, and my editor Alexandria Buchanan worked diligently and patiently with me until the story on the page matched the one in my head. Thanks also to Cho-hyun Kim for the stunning cover.

Ever since the start of the quarantine in 2020, Eric San, otherwise known as Kid Koala, has livestreamed Music To Draw To, two hours of curated tunes, almost every Monday night. These have become Music To Write And Edit To sessions for me, and I'm so grateful he's still doing them.

I came to rely on my Pitch Wars Class of 2017 group and my 2021 Debuts group for business advice and emotional support well beyond my debut year. Thanks for always being there.

Thanks also to every person who's told me something nice about *Tidepool*, *The Shadow Dancers of Brixton Hill*, and any of my other work. A simple compliment can keep me going on days when I'm wondering why I still do this.

And special thanks to my husband Bill Murphy for listening to my endless talk about all facets of writing, being a trusted first reader, bringing online classes and workshops to my attention, and surprising me with book cover cakes. I couldn't have done any of this without your support.

No thanks to my cats Leo and Lotus, though. I got all this stuff done in spite of you guys. But you're adorable anyhow.

About the Author

Nicole Willson lives with her husband in Northern Virginia. She's spent time in haunted houses but has never been lucky enough to actually live in one.

Nicole is an active member of the Horror Writers Association. Her first novel *Tidepool* debuted in August 2021 and was a finalist for a Bram Stoker Award® and the Ladies of Horror Fiction Award for Best Debut. A Spanish translation of *Tidepool* is available from Dilatando Mentes Editorial.

Her novella *The Shadow Dancers of Brixton Hill* (Cemetery Gates Media) was published in June 2023. Her short fiction has appeared in Cemetery Gates Media, Death Knell Press, and in Hinged on Medium. She is also a recipient of a 2022 Ladies of Horror Fiction Writers Grant.

www.Nicolewillson.com

Also by Nicole Willson

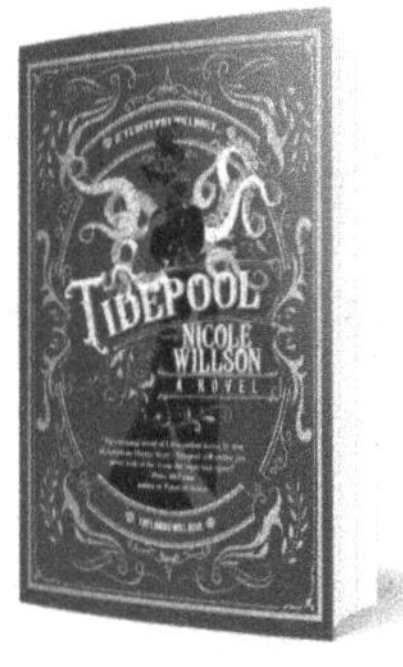

Tidepool

Printed in the USA
CPSIA information can be obtained
at www.ICGtesting.com
LVHW032057081124
796158LV00008B/31
9781956136852